Ann Barker was born and educated in Bedfordshire. She is currently studying in Cambridge, and enjoys reading, cooking and taking breaks in the family home in Norfolk, where she lives with her husband, the local vicar.

# DERBYSHIRE DECEPTION

When Freya Pascoe accompanies Claudia Bryce to Derbyshire for a bet, the objectionable Miss Bryce is unaware that her paid companion is immensely wealthy, for Freya has promised not to reveal her circumstances to anyone. She is also attracted to Claudia's brother Piers, the handsome mill owner, who seems to reciprocate her feelings. Once in Derbyshire, she meets Lord Ravendale, Claudia's fiancé, a man of unsavoury reputation, whose reasons for marrying are wholly mercenary. Almost against her will, Freya finds herself drawn to him. Gradually, she discovers that both Piers Bryce and Lord Ravendale differ from her expectations . . .

*Books by Ann Barker*
*Published by The House of Ulverscroft:*

HIS LORDSHIP'S GARDENER
THE GRAND TOUR

ANN BARKER

# DERBYSHIRE DECEPTION

Complete and Unabridged

# ULVERSCROFT
*Leicester*

First published in Great Britain in 2003 by
Robert Hale Limited
London

First Large Print Edition
published 2004
by arrangement with
Robert Hale Limited
London

British Library CIP Data

Barker, Ann
    Derbyshire deception.—Large print ed.—
Ulverscroft large print series: romance
1. Derbyshire (England)—Social life and customs—
19th century—Fiction
2. Love stories 3. Large type books
I. Title
823.9′14 [F]

ISBN 1–84395–438–9

Published by
F. A. Thorpe (Publishing)
Anstey, Leicestershire

Set by Words & Graphics Ltd.
Anstey, Leicestershire
Printed and bound in Great Britain by
T. J. International Ltd., Padstow, Cornwall

This book is printed on acid-free paper

For Ann, my cousin, my namesake
and my friend,
and for all the 'Bradwell regulars'

# 1

'Coming? Of course you're coming,' declared the Countess of Terrington forthrightly. 'How could I possibly hold my final party of the season without my best friend being present?'

'Quite easily, I should think,' replied Freya Pascoe. 'I cannot imagine that the success of your party stands or falls by my presence. Have you seen this picture, Eunice?' Her ladyship glanced at the striking landscape at which her friend was pointing. The two ladies were visiting Somerset House in search of a gift for Lord Terrington from his lady to mark his 35th birthday.

'Mmm. Who is the artist?' Freya looked down at the paper in her neatly gloved hand.

'Turner.'

'It's not really Thomas's style. And don't change the subject,' she went on severely. 'I am not concerned about the success of my party. That is, of course, understood! I am referring to my own wishes, and it is my desire to have you there.'

'I can't imagine why,' said Freya frankly. 'After all, I'm scarcely party material.' Although most of Freya's friends would have loyally disputed this pronouncement, there was no doubt that if being party material consisted of being what was regarded as attractive by many members of the polite world, then Freya did not easily fit this definition. Unfashionably dark, she was 5′10″ in her stockinged feet, and built generously to go with her height. It was true that she had a clear complexion and fine hazel eyes which sparkled when she laughed; but the number of gentlemen who cared to admire such attractive features whilst looking up at them was comparatively small.

It also has to be said that polite social gatherings did not tend to bring out the best in Miss Pascoe. She did not suffer fools gladly and sadly enough, she often felt that it seemed to be her lot to suffer quite a few of them. The folly that she saw around her tended to arouse her sense of humour, and not many people understood what amused her. Worse still, some of those same people were inclined to look down upon her because she was not set in a fashionable mould.

'You judge yourself too harshly,' said Lady Terrington. 'There is a number of people in London whom I could name who find you very stimulating company.'

'Or possibly they find my money even more stimulating,' remarked Freya cynically, as they wandered on to look at more pictures.

'Freya!' exclaimed the countess. 'You cannot possibly mean that!'

'Can I not?' replied Freya. 'I'm afraid, my dear Eunice, that unlike myself, you have not had the experience of seeing people suddenly become much more friendly, when they realize that I am not just plain, oversized Miss Pascoe, but Miss Pascoe of Pascoe's bank. It's a most salutary experience, I can assure you.'

Lady Terrington allowed a small sigh to escape her lips. 'You know, Freya, sometimes I fear that you have so put yourself on guard that you would not know sincerity if it went down upon one knee and offered you hand and heart. How you are ever to find a husband . . . '

'I don't want a husband,' replied Freya calmly. 'I shall retire to the country and breed dogs and refuse to see anyone, and gradually become more and more eccentric.' Lady Terrington opened her mouth to reply, then saw something that gave her thoughts another direction.

'Oh good heavens, it's Claudia Bryce,' she exclaimed in horrified accents. 'Pray she doesn't see us!' She turned towards the nearest picture — which happened to be of dead animals and fruit — and began to examine it intently.

'Who is Claudia Bryce?' asked Freya, looking round curiously.

'The most tiresome female! A beauty, undoubtedly; but she puts on such languid, die-away airs; and she patronizes me, Freya!'

Freya could not help spluttering with laughter. 'Patronize? You? Now this I *must* see,' she declared. Lady Terrington was certainly not normally the kind of person that would expect to be patronized. Although quite young — she was only twenty-eight — she had become known as a leader of fashion, and invitations to her parties were much sought-after.

'*You* may wish to see it, but *I* certainly don't wish to endure it,' answered the countess. 'Mind you, her brother is very handsome,' she added, looking speculatively at her friend.

'If you are thinking of him for me, then he had better be tall as well as handsome, and hopefully less tiresome than his sister,' responded Freya.

'I am told that he is very charming,' murmured the countess. 'In fact, it could almost be worth enduring Miss Bryce's conversation in order to procure you an introduction to her brother.'

'Pray do not trouble on my account,' said Freya hastily. 'Let us leave immediately!' As they turned to leave, a fashionably dressed lady floated elegantly towards them.

'Too late!' breathed Lady Terrington. 'Here she comes!' Then she was upon them and there was no escape.

'My dear Lady Terrington,' exclaimed the newcomer in a rather tired voice. 'How agreeable to meet you here, of all places!' She was small, but with a perfect figure, golden blonde hair, a peaches and cream complexion and light blue eyes.

'Miss Bryce,' murmured her ladyship, almost outdoing the other in languor. 'We hardly are here; in fact, my companion and I were just leaving.' She turned to introduce Freya.

'Oh, a companion, how useful,' drawled Miss Bryce. 'I wish I had one; but it is so hard to find good servants these days. Tell me, Lady Terrington, do you go to the Grandfields' ball on Wednesday?'

Lady Terrington's bosom swelled with indignation at the slight to her friend; but before she could give voice to this, Freya said quickly, 'I believe you told me that you would go, did you not, ma'am?'

Miss Bryce looked up at her, the expression on her face much the same as if a very large insect had spoken.

'Good heavens, aren't you tall?' she said.

'Why, you might be a man! Don't you find it vastly inconvenient?' Without waiting for a reply, she turned back to Lady Terrington. 'Then I shall hope to see you there. At least we shall each of us be sure of some good conversation!'

After she had floated away, Freya whispered to her friend, 'Come, let's get you out of here before you explode!' They made their way to the entrance, where they waited until her ladyship's carriage arrived.

'Why did you not allow me to correct her mistake?' demanded Lady Terrington, all indignation. 'How dared she assume that you were a paid companion? How dared she?'

'Well, I suppose it's understandable in a way,' answered Freya in a reasonable tone. 'Look at me.' The countess looked. Freya was dressed in a plain grey gown, made high at the neck with a pelisse of a slightly darker shade. Lady Terrington examined her critically.

'You are dressed plainly, it's true,' she conceded. 'But that gown is cut in the latest fashion, as anyone but an idiot would recognize.'

'Well then you have your answer,' retorted Freya flippantly. 'How can I possibly want to be introduced to an idiot, or even the brother of an idiot?'

'Freya, you know perfectly well that it's the slight to you that I resent,' said the countess as they climbed into the carriage which had by now arrived outside Somerset House.

'I know,' replied her friend. 'Dearest Eunice, you have been combating slights against me ever since I overtook everyone by at least a foot when we were at school, and stood head and shoulders above them all.'

'Yes, and I shall continue to do so! Why people must be ruled by the dictates of fashion, I shall never understand.' Freya took one look at the countess, petite, fashionably blonde, and stylishly dressed in a pale blue high-waisted gown with a bonnet with matching ribbons, and burst out laughing. 'I don't see why you should laugh! I am only trying to take your side, after all.'

'Yes I know, and don't think I'm not grateful. But please believe me when I tell you that I don't desire to be acquainted with the Miss Bryces of this world, or to have their good opinion. Remember that I have resolved that this shall be my last season. Never again will I be inflicted with the torture that other women seem to like to put themselves through!'

'But what will you do with yourself? And don't give me that story about breeding dogs, for I won't believe you.'

7

'Immediately? Well, John and I are to travel on the continent as soon as his business is concluded. After that, who knows? Thankfully, father left me well enough to pass that I don't need to worry about how to make ends meet.'

The countess sighed. 'How I wish you could find someone like Thomas,' she murmured.

'No, really? *Exactly* like him?' asked Freya quizzically. The countess had to laugh then, for Thomas was modest in stature, and although taller than his lady, was obliged to look up at her friend.

'You know what I mean,' she said insistently, when they had both stopped laughing.

'Yes I do. But pray do not be concerned for me. I'm very well content with my life, I assure you.' By this time, they had arrived in Brook Street, where Lady Terrington set her friend down outside the house which she and her brother occupied. Freya invited the countess to step inside, but she declined.

'I have a hundred and one things to do in preparation for my ball,' she explained.

'To which you will now have to add another,' said Freya. Her ladyship wrinkled her brow. 'You forgot to buy Thomas's picture.'

Eunice waved her hand dismissively. 'I dare say it would not have done,' she replied carelessly. 'He only likes pictures of horses. In fact, I believe it might be better if I bought him a horse instead!'

Freya laughed, and after waving to her friend, entered her house by the front door, which was being held open by the butler.

'Is my brother at home, Fry?' she asked him.

'No, miss.'

'Then bring tea to the saloon if you please. I'll be down shortly.' She went upstairs to take off her bonnet and pelisse. Before she did so, she looked for a few moments at her reflection in the mirror. Did she really look like a companion or a poor relation? She had never considered the matter before, but now that the idea had been suggested to her, she had to admit that she found it unwelcome.

Knowing that she was not a fashionable shape or size, she had schooled herself into believing that her appearance was a matter of indifference to her. Her godmother, Mrs Edith Cox, who had kindly brought her out eight years ago, had been determined that Freya's stature should not deny her any fashionable frills or furbelows. Freya had therefore been attired in the same pastel pinks and blues as Mrs Cox's two daughters,

9

and she had felt over-dressed, over-trimmed and clumsy.

Eventually, she had decided that the only way to survive was to make herself as insignificant as possible. Something told her that strong colours would suit her better than pale ones, but a dread of drawing attention to herself prevented her from experimenting. She had heard too many derogatory remarks about her height and her build to risk attracting more. If she closed her eyes, she could still feel the pitying glances and hear the sniggers . . .

Abruptly, she shrugged and hurried downstairs. What did the remarks of one more silly woman signify, anyway?

★  ★  ★

The following morning, as it was fine, Freya set out to go for a walk in the park. It was only a short step from where they lived, through Grosvenor Square to Hyde Park, and Freya often walked there, sometimes accompanied, but often alone. When friends, among them Lady Terrington, had protested about this, Freya had declared that a woman of twenty-six and of her stature should surely be able to walk in the park without molestation, and her friends, knowing how stubborn she could be, had held their peace.

As soon as she reached Hyde Park, it seemed as if she could breathe more freely. When she troubled to think about the matter, it sometimes seemed strange to her that she should feel so much more at home in the country than in the town, for she had been born and brought up in London, only going into the country from time to time, and less frequently than some. Yet so it was. She was much to her regret an indifferent rider, being to her secret shame somewhat afraid of horses, but she loved walking. Several years ago she had had a holiday in Derbyshire, and had enjoyed tackling the more challenging terrain there. She would very much have liked to go back, but her brother John had his heart set on continental travel, and although Freya rebelled so much as to walk unaccompanied, even she shrank at the gossip that would inevitably result if she went travelling alone.

Hiring a companion was a possibility, but where would she find someone congenial who shared her interests? Besides, something within her shrank from the necessity of paying anyone to be her friend. All of her school friends were married, and most of them had set up their nurseries by now, so none of them would be in a position to go with her.

11

She pondered over these ideas, not for the first time, as she entered Hyde Park, and began to set a brisk pace. The day was fine, and there was a refreshing breeze, but Freya looked at the flat landscape and neat grass with some dissatisfaction. Something a little more rugged would have pleased her more.

A number of people were about, mostly on horseback, and in twos and threes. She had walked some distance from the entrance, when she saw an open carriage coming towards her. Driving it was a handsome young man with a fine head of dark brown hair, and seated next to him was Miss Bryce, whom Freya had met at Somerset House the previous day. If Freya had hoped that Miss Bryce would not recognize her, then she was doomed to disappointment. The languid beauty was one of those who take in keenly the appearance of other members of their own sex, if only to compare them unfavourably with themselves.

'Miss . . . Pascoe, isn't it?' she drawled, having indicated to her companion to draw up.

'Yes, that's right,' replied Freya pleasantly. 'How are you, Miss Bryce?'

Miss Bryce looked as surprised as if the parlour maid had enquired after her health.

'I am well, thank you,' she replied after a slight pause.

There was an awkward silence, which was broken by the gentleman in the carriage, who said, in a well-modulated voice, 'I believe I haven't met this lady. Pray, introduce me, Claudia.'

'Oh, this is Miss Pascoe, Lady Terrington's companion,' she said carelessly, giving Freya's name first, and thereby leaving her in no doubt as to which of the two she considered to be of superior rank. Then, turning to Freya, she said, 'This is my brother, Piers.'

'I'm delighted to meet you, Miss Pascoe,' said Bryce, his eyes twinkling.

Freya acknowledged his greeting, and she felt her heart skip a beat. Handsome men did not often look at her in that kind of way. Clearly, though, Miss Bryce had no intention for there to be further conversation between them, for she said to Freya, 'Kindly help me down, Miss Pascoe. I would like to speak with you on an important matter. My brother will drive around for a while.'

Freya could not help being curious at this request, but she did as she was bid. She glanced up again at Mr Bryce, who was still smiling warmly down at her. Telling herself severely that his expression would not be nearly so warm when he discovered — as was more likely than not — that she was taller than he, she gave her full attention to Miss Bryce, not even looking as the carriage moved away.

The two ladies walked a little way in silence, then Miss Bryce said, 'We will sit on the bench for a little while. Walking is so fatiguing, is it not?'

'I don't find it so,' Freya responded.

'No, I don't suppose you do,' sighed Miss Bryce. 'You are built as robustly as a farm labourer! But those of us who are made on more ladylike lines have far less energy, I'm afraid.'

Freya glanced surreptitiously at the other woman's face, but could detect no malice there at all. She took a deep breath in order to answer, but before she could say anything, Miss Bryce went on.

'Tell me, for how long are you engaged to Lady Terrington?'

'Engaged?' repeated Freya, put off her stride, and unable to imagine what Miss Bryce might mean.

'How soon may you cease your employment with her?'

'My employment?'

'Yes, your employment,' said Miss Bryce impatiently. 'My brother and I are to leave London in a few days and I shall want a companion to go with me to Derbyshire.'

'To Derbyshire?'

'Really, Miss Pascoe, you are going to make very tedious company if all you can do is echo everything I say! Yes, we are going to Derbyshire. My brother will probably ride for most of the way, and I shall want company on the journey. Once there, I shall need you to help stave off the boredom of everyday life among all those wretched streams and hills.

'I am engaged to Lord Ravendale, whose estate lies next to ours, and his aunt is to give a costume ball for us, at which the betrothal will be officially announced. I dare say she will want help with the preparations, and you can make yourself useful to her. In addition, I expect some friends to come and stay in time for the ball, and I shall need you to help prepare for them. Once they arrive, I shall have no need of you, and you can come straight back to London, or if I find you agreeable, then I might decide to keep you. What do you say?' Freya was silent. 'If it's money that concerns you, I can pay you twice as much as Lady Terrington.'

Freya opened her mouth to say no, not at any price, when two thoughts came into her mind. One was that a woman so presumptuous and mannerless as this one deserved to be led down the garden path a little. The

15

other thought, which was a far more fleeting one, was that here might be an opportunity to revisit the Derbyshire scene that she remembered so fondly. So instead of saying 'no' immediately, she said thoughtfully, 'I . . . let me speak to her and see if she will release me.'

Miss Bryce looked at her for a moment, then nodded. She took a card out of her reticule and handed it to Freya. 'Let me know what you decide. I shall be at this address. And now I see my brother approaching. Help me up, Pascoe, will you?'

Freya gave the assistance requested, but said quietly but firmly, 'Let this be understood, Miss Bryce. If I come with you, it will be on the understanding that I am addressed by my proper title. Nothing else will be acceptable to me.'

Miss Bryce accepted her help without a word, but once she was seated, said, 'Goodbye, Miss Pascoe.'

'Goodbye, Miss Bryce,' replied Freya. She looked up at the occupants of the curricle, and in so doing, caught Mr Bryce's eye. There was in his expression something that might have been respect.

As she watched the curricle drive away from her, Freya thought about the scene that had just taken place and she suddenly found the laughter welling up inside her. For a few minutes she stood there in the park, almost shaking with mirth. *Pascoe!* she said to herself. *Just wait till I tell Eunice!* Suddenly, Freya had no further wish to continue her walk, and turning round, she headed for home, intending to go and call on her friend immediately. As luck would have it, however, she arrived at the front door at the same time as Lady Terrington's barouche drew up.

'Eunice! The very person I wanted to see!' exclaimed Freya, as her friend was handed down by her footman. 'The most amusing thing has just happened! Do come inside and I'll tell you all about it!'

'Very well, but don't think that you can distract me from the fact that you have been walking alone again!' They met John Pascoe in the hall. Like his sister, he was tall, dark and generously built, and he greeted them in cheerful style.

'Are you going out?' asked Freya. 'Do come and join us for a moment. I have something very diverting to tell.'

'Yes, she hopes to divert us from the fact that she has been walking alone again, John,' said her ladyship.

'I hope you don't expect me to do anything about it,' he said calmly. 'She's quite beyond my authority now, thank God.'

'If I was ever under it,' retorted Freya. 'Thank you, Fry,' she added, as the butler took their bonnets. 'Bring us some wine into the drawing room, please.'

'Fry,' said Lady Terrington, detaining him. '*You* do not approve of Miss Pascoe's walking alone in the park, do you?'

'I have ventured to say as much, my lady,' said Fry austerely. 'But Miss Pascoe is a lady with very strong ideas.'

'I shall take that as a compliment, Fry,' said Freya. She led the way into the drawing room, and when they were seated, she went on, 'Now let me tell you about the very amusing thing that happened to me in the park.' She then proceeded to give them a spirited account of her meeting with the Bryces, only withholding how handsome she had thought Mr Bryce.

'Good heavens! The insolence of the woman! 'Pascoe', indeed!' exclaimed John.

'Say rather, the ignorance of the woman,' snorted Lady Terrington. 'Why, the merest fool could see that you are a woman of quality.'

'I think she only sees what she wants to see,' mused Freya. John poured himself another glass of the wine that Fry had brought when Freya was part way through her story.

'The only thing I would like to know is, why did you not put the wretched woman in her place?' asked the countess.

'I fully intend to,' replied Freya with a twinkle. 'But I thought that I would wait just a *little* while before doing so.'

John grinned. 'You want to teach her a lesson, I suppose.'

'Exactly so. Never judge by appearances, or some such thing. And besides . . . ' She fell silent.

'Well?' prompted Lady Terrington.

'I have to admit that I did feel a little tempted,' admitted Freya sheepishly.

Lady Terrington, who had been taking a sip of wine at this point, almost choked. 'Tempted! To take the post of a companion, and to such a woman! Freya, you must be out of your senses!'

'I agree,' put in John. 'But I think that I can tell you why.'

'I thought you might,' said Freya, smiling at him.

'Then perhaps one of you will have the goodness to tell *me*,' demanded Lady Terrington in exasperated tones.

'In a word, Derbyshire,' John answered. 'Am I right, Freya?'

'Derbyshire,' agreed his sister. At that moment, as they sat grinning at each other, they looked very much alike.

'And what is that supposed to mean?' asked the countess.

'Well, Eunice, it's a fair sized county in the north of England,' John began, his eyes twinkling.

'I didn't mean that, and you know it,' she declared forthrightly. 'Now someone give me a straight answer before I knock your heads together!'

'Freya is forever pestering me to take her there,' John explained. 'But this year, I very much want to visit the continent. After all, with Boney defeated it's about the first opportunity that there's been to go there safely for a very long time.'

'Surely you will enjoy going to France, Freya?' asked Lady Terrington.

'Oh yes,' agreed Freya. 'It's just that I have such happy memories of the holiday we spent in Derbyshire. You remember, John, when mama was alive.' He nodded.

'I can understand how you feel,' said Eunice. 'I have always been attached to Lyme Regis for that very reason. But I cannot imagine that going anywhere with Miss Bryce would add to the happiness of your memories. In fact, it might even spoil them. Come, my dear, confess! You weren't seriously thinking of going at all.'

Freya threw up her hands. 'I admit it,' she said, laughing.

'Just as well,' put in her brother. 'You'd never endure it, my dear. I'll wager we'd see you back in London on the very next mail coach!'

'Perhaps I have greater powers of endurance than you think,' his sister retorted. Then the conversation turned to other subjects. Soon after this, Lady Terrington left to keep another appointment, and John went to the bank, while Freya occupied the rest of her day with a few housekeeping tasks and making some calls.

That evening, John came in looking rather grave.

'A problem?' Freya asked.

'I'm afraid so. Some dishonesty in one of the senior employees has resulted in a lack of confidence among some of our investors.'

'Nothing major, I hope,' said Freya concernedly. 'Is my fortune safe, or do I need to take the position with Miss Bryce in good and earnest?'

He smiled slightly, but Freya was quick to notice signs of strain behind his eyes. 'It's serious, but not beyond mending,' he assured her. 'Your thousands are tied up independently, as you know, little sister. But there can be no continental holiday for the present.

This is quite the wrong time for me to be absenting myself from London. I must remain on the spot until things are more stable.'

'Yes, of course,' agreed Freya, hiding her disappointment. 'The question remains, however, what to do with myself in the meantime?'

'Why not go to Norfolk with Eunice?' he suggested. 'I think she intends to pay a visit there in a few weeks.'

She nodded thoughtfully; but she had been to Eunice's house before, and she could not help contrasting her memories of the flat landscape around Terrington St Clement with the hills of Derbyshire. Almost without realizing it, she was beginning to think more seriously about Miss Bryce's suggestion.

The following evening was the night of Lady Terrington's ball, the event which for many marked the end of the season. In the end, Freya had agreed to go but only, she had stressed, as a favour to her friend. Once attired in a lace-trimmed gown of pale blue made high at the neck, she looked at herself in the mirror and sighed.

'What is wrong with me, Pringle?' she asked her maid.

'Why, nothing's wrong, ma'am,' the worthy declared loyally. Originally hired by Mrs Cox, and unalterably committed to Mrs Cox's ideas of suitability, she had served her mistress for ten years. 'You look just as a lady should.'

'I dare say,' replied Freya, sighing. The whole effect, though certainly ladylike and fashionable, was somehow dull and unattractive; but she could not think what to do to put it right.

John was waiting for her in the hall, looking very distinguished in his black evening coat, with snowy shirt-front and black pantaloons.

'Oh John, I sometimes think I should have been a man,' she declared as she came down the stairs. 'You look so smart, whilst I . . . '

'Nonsense! You look perfectly ladylike,' he declared, unconsciously echoing Pringle's words. 'Now, let's go.'

'Are you sure you want to?' she asked him. 'You're looking tired.'

'Yes,' he said positively. 'My appearance at an occasion like this will give confidence in the bank.'

The ball at Berkeley Square was certainly a glittering occasion, with the street crowded with carriages, setting down their magnificently dressed occupants then drawing away again.

'Why, the world and his wife must be here,' declared Freya to her brother as they waited for their own carriage to set them down outside the Terrington mansion.

'Probably Miss Bryce too, then; and thus your little deception will have to come to an end,' teased her brother.

Freya was pleased to see him in good spirits. Perhaps the problem at the bank was not so great as he had imagined at first. As if reading her thoughts, he said, 'Matters at the bank are not quite so grave as I feared; but I still feel that I should remain in London.'

Not long after this, it was their turn to be set down, and they were soon entering the crowded hallway, handing their cloaks to a servant and mingling with friends and acquaintances as they climbed the stairs.

'This will be the last time, John,' said Freya under her breath as they made slow progress up to where Lord and Lady Terrington were receiving their guests. 'I cannot endure another season.' John laughed.

A lady whom Freya knew slightly said to her, 'We all say the same, my dear; but after a few weeks' boredom in the country or by the sea, back we all come!'

'Yes, we all say the same; but the difference is that I mean it!' replied Freya sincerely. When they reached the top of the staircase, Eunice was genuinely delighted to see them, especially Freya.

'We will enjoy a comfortable coze later, when I have finished my duties here,' she promised.

Freya and John wandered into the ballroom and soon separated in order to talk to various acquaintances. Although they were by no means the last arrivals, the rooms were very full; but however Freya might examine the faces that she saw, she could see no sign of Miss Bryce, or, more disappointingly, her handsome brother. She was conscious of having very mixed feelings.

'The Bryces?' said her hostess when they had a moment to talk. 'No, they are not here, thank goodness. I felt obliged to invite them, but most fortunately they had another engagement. Don't tell me you are disappointed at missing her!'

'By no means,' answered Freya truthfully.

'Perhaps, of course, you are missing her handsome brother,' teased the countess.

'Certainly not,' said Freya, a little too quickly.

'Confess that you are tempted to go to Derbyshire for the sake of his wavy dark hair and twinkling eyes!'

'Eunice, you are being ridiculous,' protested Freya, but with a blush, because undoubtedly Mr Bryce *was* handsome.

'Perhaps it's as well that you aren't going

after all, though,' remarked Eunice in matter-of-fact tones. 'You would never have got away with the deception even for a week, you know.'

'Why should I not?' asked Freya defensively.

'My dear, you would give yourself away before ever you got halfway to Derbyshire. You are too much accustomed to command, to take orders from that little madam. And in any case, I don't think you'd be able to tolerate the woman.'

'She is dreadful,' agreed Freya. 'But I would certainly be able to sustain my role for that long — and more. In fact, I'm more than half inclined to take the position, just to prove it to you!'

'Easy to say,' replied the countess scornfully. 'You know, of course that you will never make good your words!'

'And why is that?' demanded Freya.

'Why, you're afraid of course.'

'Afraid of what?'

'Afraid that the handsome Mr Bryce will overturn your plans for a quiet, retired spinsterhood,' answered the countess triumphantly. 'No, you'll never go, for fear I'm right!'

'Very well then, let's settle the matter with a wager,' challenged Freya.'

'A wager! Are you serious?' asked the countess incredulously.

'Yes. Yes, I am,' Freya said decisively.

'But what about your holiday with John?' asked Eunice curiously.

'That is what makes it so convenient,' answered Freya. 'John finds that he cannot get away just now, so it will give me something to do.'

'Very well, then. Let us agree terms. I suggest a fortnight.'

'A fortnight!' exclaimed Freya.

'Certainly. Why not? Or do you doubt your ability to tolerate her for so long?'

'No, of course not. Very well, then, let it be a fortnight. But that is to include the journey there.'

'Of course. What stakes do you propose?'

'It's simple,' replied Freya. 'If you win, I'll come back for the season next year and you can find me a husband.'

The countess gave a crow of triumph, but Freya held up her hand.

'But, if I win, then you accompany me to Derbyshire for a proper holiday, which must take place immediately, because I shall need it. Agreed?'

'Agreed,' declared the countess. 'I must say, I'm looking forward to taking you about next year. Although it will all be spoiled, of course, if you are already engaged to the handsome Mr Bryce.'

Ignoring the last part of this speech, Freya said merely, 'For my part, I'm very much looking forward to my Derbyshire holiday!'

'How very satisfactory,' said her ladyship. 'Such intriguing stakes! How the gentlemen can bear to gamble just for money eludes me.' She glanced at the entrance to the card room. A tall, fair-haired man with his back to them was just going inside. 'Take Ravendale for example,' she went on, indicating him with her fan.

Freya looked at him with interest. 'Ravendale? I believe that Miss Bryce said that she was betrothed to someone of that name,' she said.

'I heard a rumour to that effect,' agreed Lady Terrington. 'No doubt he hopes to go through her fortune now that his own is gone.'

'I am tempted to say that they deserve one another, but I don't think that any woman deserves that,' murmured Freya.

The countess nodded. 'His whole family has been beggared by a ruinous addiction, and he is clearly no better. Why can some men never learn?'

'I suppose it is a kind of sickness,' replied Freya. 'Thank God John does not have it.

What right do people have to gamble away their substance and leave their dependants without any means of support?'

The countess nodded again.

'Like Maria Wakelin,' she said. They were both thinking of a girl who had been at school with them for a time, but who had been taken away from the seminary after her father had lost everything at the gaming tables.

'Well, our wager is not of that nature,' said Freya.

'What wager is this?' asked John. They had not heard him approach.

'Why, a wager about Miss Bryce,' said the countess confidentially, after she had glanced round to make sure that no one else was listening. 'If Freya can last for a fortnight as her companion, then I go with her immediately on a holiday to Derbyshire. If not, then she allows me to sponsor her in London next year for the season!'

John smiled at her words, but later after they had returned home, he said, 'Freya, I could wish that you hadn't made this bet at such a time.'

'Why, John?' she asked him, wrinkling her brow.

'There have been some doubts expressed about the bank,' he said. 'Nothing I cannot deal with, but it might cause unrest if anyone were to suspect that you really do need to seek employment.'

Freya's expression became conscience-stricken. 'Oh John, I'm sorry. I didn't think. Do you want me to call off the bet? I needn't say why. I could just pretend that I'd lost courage.'

'No, by no means,' he answered emphatically. 'Far be it from me to be the means of subjecting you to another London season, which I know you hate! We'll put it about that you're travelling on holiday with friends. But you must promise me that you will not disclose your connection with the bank to anyone until I give you leave — and I do mean anyone, Freya.'

'Of course, I promise,' she declared. 'I won't even say anything to the Bryces at the end of my time there. I'll just make my farewells and leave.'

'I'm hoping that the trouble with the bank will have blown over by then,' he said. 'If so, then I'll give myself the pleasure of fetching you in person. That'll give the Bryces something to think about!'

# 2

'How tedious this all is! Do you not find it so?' complained Miss Bryce, and she sighed for what seemed to Freya to be the millionth time.

'Why no, I confess I do not,' Freya owned. 'The change of scenery, the — '

'Oh, *that*!' said Miss Bryce contemptuously. 'If you find *that* kind of thing interesting . . . '

They had been travelling for three days, and it had rapidly been borne in upon Freya that Miss Bryce did not care for it. She found fault with every inn. The roads were too rough; the carriage was not well-sprung enough; the weather was too warm; it was too cold; it was too sunny; it was too dull; and Freya herself came in for some criticism. 'Miss Pascoe, you are too quiet! Say something to entertain me!' or 'Miss Pascoe, I have had enough of your chatter! You weary me.' Such behaviour as this made Freya reflect on more than one occasion that paid companions who served such as Miss Bryce earned every penny of their wages.

Were it not for the breaks at the inns on the

way, Freya might have given the whole thing up and returned to London, despite the bet. But at least every evening brought some respite. Miss Bryce usually rested as soon as they arrived anywhere, giving Freya time to walk about the towns or villages where they stopped.

Not for the first time, Freya decided that to push Miss Bryce out of the carriage would be inappropriate behaviour. Briefly, she imagined herself appearing before the magistrate, charged with the offence. The verdict, she decided would depend very much on whether the magistrate had ever met the lady. Had he done so, she was persuaded that acquittal would be inevitable.

'You smile, Miss Pascoe,' drawled Miss Bryce, interrupting her thoughts. 'What amuses you, pray?'

'Oh . . . only someone falling off his horse,' she improvised rapidly.

'What can you expect in the country?' asked Miss Bryce wearily.

At this point, Freya finally asked the question that had been on her mind for some time. 'Miss Bryce, if you hate the country so much, why do you come?'

'Why? Well, because I am obliged to, of course,' replied Miss Bryce in the tones of one stating the obvious. Then she went on,

'My brother owns a mill in Derbyshire. He is not responsible for its creation, you understand. He inherited it from his uncle. But the property is most foolishly left. He cannot sell it, or benefit from any of the proceeds unless he spends a certain period of time there every year.' Freya said nothing, and in a moment or two, her patience was rewarded. 'I have no share in the mill; but I am dependent upon him until I marry, then I gain control of my fortune. And that day, thank heaven, should not be far distant.'

Freya murmured something intended to express polite gratification.

'I don't know whether you met Lord Ravendale while you were in London?'

'I believe that someone may have pointed him out to me,' Freya replied.

'Of course, his owning land near our property makes everything very convenient. Of all the stupid things, though; he seems to like the countryside! I cannot understand it. Do you suppose it might have something to do with having been in the army?'

Freya struggled to find a connection, failed to do so, and contented herself with looking very struck by the idea.

'In any case,' Miss Bryce went on, 'his days of living in the countryside will be over when we are married. I intend to live in town all the time, apart from the summer months when I shall perhaps go to Brighton. I might let him go to Ravendale then.'

'And will Lord Ravendale agree to that?' asked Freya curiously.

'He will have to, seeing that I will hold the purse strings,' replied Claudia complacently. 'In any case, he will find plenty in town to divert his mind.'

Thinking of his love of gambling, Freya decided that Miss Bryce was probably right in that belief, but she wondered whether the new bride might not do better to keep the earl away from the very amusements which were so ruinous to him.

Not long after this, Miss Bryce closed her eyes for a nap and Freya was free to enjoy the passing scenery without interruption. As Miss Bryce had predicted, her brother had chosen to ride, and from time to time, Freya caught a glimpse of Mr Bryce as he rode beside the carriage. There was no denying that he cut a fine figure on a horse. In conversation with her, he never showed any presumption or impropriety, but she was often conscious of a glow in his eyes, which seemed to tell her that he found her attractive. She told herself severely that he was probably only spending time with her because there was no one else to flirt with and nothing else to do. Still, it was very pleasant to have a handsome man making himself agreeable to her, whatever his motives. At least, she told herself, he could not possibly be paying attention to her because of her money.

Miss Bryce continued to sleep, so Freya amused herself by trying to imagine Lord Ravendale's appearance. She had seen that he was tall, and fair. In her mind, she gave him a rather weak chin and mouth, and slightly bloodshot eyes from late nights at the tables. Her imagination was checked somewhat when she recalled that he had served his country as a soldier. Had he been the kind of officer who had bought his commission for lack of anything else to do, and had then kept as far away from the action as possible; or had the terrible things that he had witnessed given rise to his degeneracy?

Did Miss Bryce know about Lord Ravendale's ruinous habits, or was she unaware of their extent? If they had been neighbours for years, she could hardly be unaware of his weakness. After all, they had been in London at the same time. She hoped that Miss Bryce's fortune was a substantial one, and that she would know how to preserve it from the depredations of her husband-to-be.

On the fourth day of their journey, they arrived at Castleton, which was only a short distance from the Bryces' home. The intention had been that they should only stay overnight at 'The Castle', which was the best inn in the town, and travel on in the morning, but that evening, Mr Bryce declared himself to have a slight chill.

'Nothing to worry about, but I shall keep to my bed for a day or two,' he declared.

'How tedious,' sighed Miss Bryce. 'Do not give it to me, I beg. I can do without any extra trouble, when I find myself in the midst of this benighted, Godforsaken country.'

Freya could not help feeling a little leap of excitement. It looked as if they might be in Castleton for a few days, and as Miss Bryce never rose before noon, there might be an opportunity for a walk or two. She had noticed that Castleton seemed to be sur-rounded by hills on every side, and the idea of climbing one of them appealed to her enormously. In fact, her opportunity was to be even better than she had hoped, for before she retired that night, after the excellent meal which 'The Castle' had provided, Miss Bryce said to her, 'If Piers has caught a chill, I might be in danger of having one too. I have decided to spend the whole of tomorrow in bed, so you may spend the day as you please.'

The following day dawned bright, but with a little cloud, and as she had the day to herself, she decided to climb the hill that was known as Mam Tor. If they stayed for another day, she might attempt to walk up to Peveril Castle, but that climb would be manageable in a morning. Mam Tor would definitely take the whole day. With this in mind, she asked the waiter if he would have some provisions packed for her to take on her expedition. When she explained what she was planning, he looked a little doubtful.

'You aren't going alone, ma'am, I hope,' he said, frowning.

'No indeed, I am meeting some friends at the foot of Winnats Pass,' she lied. Her heart was set on this outing, and she had no wish for anyone to try and persuade her not to go.

'Clouds look a little threatening,' he added. 'I reckon the mist might come down later.'

Freya looked out of the window. The day still looked bright and sunny, but the clouds were thickening a little. 'I can't help that,' she said. 'It might be my . . . I mean, our only chance.'

She went upstairs to put on her coat and bonnet, well aware that she might need warmer clothing on the hilltop than in the town. The waiter brought her a small package in a canvas bag, which he helped her to sling over her shoulder. He eyed her sturdy boots with approval.

'If the mist comes down, stay still where you are until it lifts,' he advised her. 'There's many a soul has got hopelessly lost up there through blundering about in the mist.'

Freya thanked him for his warning, and set off along the main street at a brisk step. It was a great relief to be walking without either of the Bryces. Even Mr Bryce, handsome though he was, tended to maintain a dawdling pace which she found rather tedious.

Some of the shops looked as if they might have interesting wares, but although she slowed down a little to glance in the windows, she did not linger. A gentle walk to look around the shops would be as much as Miss Bryce would want to do another day. There would certainly be another chance to visit them.

The climb, though almost imperceptible, was steady until she got to Winnats Pass, a road which wound up between two massive rock faces, and it then began to be much steeper. There were very few other people about. A man with a bundle on his back walked past her on his way to Castleton, and nodded courteously, and a shepherd over on a more distant pasture whistled to his dog; but apart from that, she saw no one. She bit her lip at the thought of how she had said she was not climbing alone. She certainly seemed to be doing so today!

Part way up Winnats Pass, she paused to get her breath back and turned to admire the view. There was quite a lot to be seen already, and it made her impatient to reach the top.

Having got her breath back, she turned again towards her objective. There were a few clouds gathering around the summit, but nothing to signify, and although there were other clouds to be seen, they were in the opposite direction, and quite small. After a brief pause, she started walking again, relishing the cool breeze on her face as she stepped out. The wind caught at her bonnet a little as she moved into a more exposed spot, and she became aware that the day which had begun so promisingly was starting to look rather overcast. The summit was not far ahead, but the clouds which had seemed so distant had drawn closer and now seemed to engulf it. She looked at it a little doubtfully, then looked back the way she had come. Her way back was very clear; but it seemed a pity to return when she was so close to her objective.

She was beginning to feel hungry, but she decided to eat after she had reached the summit. 'After all,' she told herself, 'I need only stay there for a few minutes, just to see the view, then come down.'

The last part of the climb was steep, and Freya found that she needed to keep her eyes on the ground, so as to avoid tripping. But when at last she reached the top, there was no view to be had. The clouds had come down to meet the land and there was nothing to be seen in any direction except swirling mist. She recalled the words of the waiter, when he urged her to remain absolutely still if she was caught in the mist whilst climbing on the hillside. 'But I am not on the hillside, I am on the top of it,' she said to herself. At once, this made everything seem far more hazardous. Although she might be convinced in her mind that the summit of Mam Tor was a perfectly roomy place to be, to know that she was on the top, surrounded by mist, made her feel as if she was balancing on a pinhead.

'Perhaps if I just take a few steps back down, I shall feel better,' she said, speaking out loud because she needed to hear a human voice, even if it was only her own. But looking around at the small area of ground that was now visible, she found herself unable to decide with any certainty which way she had come, and she felt a fluttering sensation in the pit of her stomach that was very much like panic. With the mist all around her, every direction looked the same, and there seemed to be no identifying landmarks. She was about to pick a direction at random, when her eyes lit upon a small rock over which she could remember stumbling as she reached the summit, and with an exclamation of relief, she made for it, and began the downward climb.

Going downwards seemed to be more treacherous than coming up, and once or twice she almost slipped; but regaining her footing, she continued a little further, until she reached a little gully which she could not avoid crossing, and which she had certainly not encountered on her way up.

'Bother!' she exclaimed, and in the dank air her voice seemed to come back to her as if to mock her mistake. Now, she could not decide whether to go on or to remain where she was. If she continued, there was no telling where she might end up; but she had no way of knowing how long it might be before the mist would lift. Then, as she stood in indecision, she heard something that sounded like footsteps.

Instantly, there came into her mind a story which, in the comfort of the inn parlour last night, had merely seemed intriguing and mysterious, but which now appeared ominous and threatening. It concerned a young couple who, some fifty years ago, had been eloping when they were brutally murdered in Winnats Pass. Their bodies were discovered ten years later, and those responsible, although never punished by the law, had all come to sticky ends. Nevertheless, Freya could not help wondering whether other similarly murderous characters might be found in the vicinity.

She had no weapons about her, so carefully she bent down and picked up a small rock with a pointed end. It was a pitiful enough weapon, but the hard feel of it in her hand comforted her a little. She was just beginning to wonder whether she had been mistaken in what she had heard, when a large figure began to loom out of the mist.

'Take care!' she cried, in a voice which, to her disgust, was not quite steady. 'I am armed!' The figure snorted in a way which, to Freya, in her nervous state of mind, sounded extremely threatening and, in order to gain an advantage, she threw herself forward, slashing out with all her strength.

She found herself grasped firmly by the shoulders, the two of them rocked and almost fell, and the stranger exclaimed, 'God in heaven, woman, are you mad, stupid or both?' The tones, angry though they were, were clearly those of a gentleman.

'Oh,' she said blankly, and dropped her stone.

'What the deuce do you think you were doing anyway?' he went on. 'You might have killed me.'

'Hardly,' replied Freya, finding her tongue. 'It was only a stone.' The man snorted in a way that Freya recalled hearing at his approach.

'A stone which you wielded with sufficient gusto to rip my coat!' he retorted, drawing attention to a tear high up on its sleeve.

'Oh no!' exclaimed Freya, her hand going to her mouth. 'Oh, I do beg your pardon!'

'A moment's forethought would have been more to the point,' he replied crisply. 'Why, the meanest intelligence . . . '

'Sir, I am very sorry for damaging your coat, and for that I apologize,' interrupted Freya, beginning to feel more annoyed than guilty. 'But when you came striding at me out of the mist like some evildoer — '

'Like some *what*?' he demanded incredulously.

'Like some evildoer,' she repeated, wishing that the phrase, which had sounded so effective the first time, did not sound so lame on repetition.

'Don't be absurd,' he said contemptuously.

'I'm not being absurd at all,' she retorted indignantly. 'How could I know what your intentions might be, wandering about the hills in the mist?' Even as she spoke, she could feel herself blushing, and she devoutly hoped that the change in her complexion was not noticeable in the poor visibility.

'I was not the one wandering about,' he replied reasonably. 'It was the height of foolhardiness to allow yourself to become separated from your party.'

Freya said nothing, but stared up at him, biting her lip. It was unusual for her to have to tilt her head to look at any gentleman, and this one must have been well over six feet tall. Eventually, he said in long-suffering tones, 'Never tell me that you have actually come up here alone!'

'Indeed, I will not tell you, for I cannot imagine what concern it might be of yours what I choose to do,' she declared defensively.

'It would have been very much my concern if I had found your dead body at the foot of some precipice!'

'Now *you* are being absurd,' she answered. 'In any case, I hate to point this out to you, but I am not the only one up here without a party.'

'My good woman, I have lived in this vicinity or thereabouts for a large part of my thirty-two years, whereas if you have ever been walking in these hills before, I should be much surprised. Furthermore, I was not

44

wandering about. When the mist came down, I remained in one place, like any intelligent person, and would indeed still be there, had I not heard you blundering about.'

'Well, having stated your opinion, you might as well hold your tongue, for I have no further desire to converse with you,' said Freya forthrightly.

'For once, I am of the same opinion as you,' replied the man infuriatingly. 'If you will but sit down on that stone, I will sit on this, and we will remain silent until this mist lifts. I will then direct you down Mam Tor.'

Freya would have loved to reject his offer of help out of hand and flounce off, but she knew that this would not be wise. For one thing, she *was* lost; and even if she managed to make a safe descent, she might finish up miles from Castleton. For another, she placed no dependence upon the infuriating gentleman not to keep her there by main force.

She had but one weapon at her disposal and she used it as effectively as she could. Deliberately turning to face the gentleman, she took from the canvas bag the bread and cheese which the waiter at 'The Castle' had given her, and making furious eye contact with him, ate her lunch with all the relish of which she was capable. After a few moments of this, the gentleman snorted again — really, thought Freya, he seemed very prone to making this particular noise — and turned away. Smiling a little at the success of her tactic, Freya finished her lunch, then drank a little lemonade from the bottle that had been placed in her lunch bag.

They sat in silence for perhaps half an hour before the mist began to lift. After Freya's fury had subsided, it occurred to her that the presence of the large gentleman, however infuriating he might be, was extremely comforting. No more did thoughts of the murdered couple in Winnats Pass disturb her. She found herself thinking instead of the forthcoming days, and how they would be spent. Of course, it depended on how quickly Mr Bryce recovered from his chill, and on whether or not his sister had caught it as well. Freya allowed her thoughts to dwell on the handsome mill owner. What a pity she had not been marooned with *him* on the top of Mam Tor!

'The mist's lifting; we'll soon be on our way,' said the irritating voice of the large gentleman, breaking in upon her thoughts. She glanced around and saw that indeed, the mist was looking less impenetrable by the minute. 'If you're ready, ma'am, I'll show you the way down.' Unable to think of a way to respond to this without losing her face or her temper, Freya got up and shook out her skirts without saying anything. 'Come this way,' he went on.

'But you don't know where I'm going,' she protested.

'To Castleton, I assume,' he answered. 'You'd hardly be staying anywhere else.' They began to climb.

'I thought you were going to take me *down* the hill,' said Freya.

'I am,' he replied. 'But you were going down the wrong side. Besides, there's something I want to show you.' He began to climb and, after hesitating for a moment, Freya followed him. It seemed as if the mist lifted with every step until at last, as they reached the top of Mam Tor, they had a clear view around them of the valley below and the hills about, their slopes covered with different hues of green, purple and brown.

'Oh, it's magnificent!' exclaimed Freya, catching her breath. 'Magnificent!'

'Yes, perhaps,' said her escort grimly, 'But that isn't why I brought you this way. Look down, madam; just look down.' He took her firmly by the shoulders and held her so that she had no choice. Freya did as she was bid, and saw opening up below her a huge hollow gouged into the hillside, as if dug out by a giant hand.

She had no fear that he would let her fall, but he would not let her move either. The sight of the precipitous drop just before her almost made her dizzy, but although she swallowed rather hastily, she said nothing. She would not give him the satisfaction.

'There, ma'am. That is why you should never wander around in the mist! Now, are you sufficiently warned?' He pulled her back away from the edge and let her go then, and as she turned round, she looked up at him, able for the first time to see him properly. He was not just tall, but broad as well, with a strong face. His chin was firm with a deep cleft in it, his nose was hawk-like, his eyes were hazel, and his broad forehead was surmounted by a plentiful head of hair of a rich golden colour. His mouth was shaped generously; but now it was drawn in a thin line.

'I am aware of my fault, sir,' she declared, pushing back with an impatient hand the dark curls which had blown in front of her face.

'Just as well, ma'am,' he answered her, 'for I have no desire to chase you around any more mountain tops.'

'There, indeed, we are in agreement,' she retorted, 'for I have absolutely no desire for you to chase me, whether round a mountain top, or anywhere else!' She had intended merely to be forthright, and had not meant to imply any kind of innuendo; but as soon as the words were out of her mouth, she saw his lips curve into a smile and his eyes begin to gleam. To her extreme annoyance, she could feel herself blushing, and before he could make any kind of response, she turned away from him and began her descent with as much speed as the terrain and her dignity would allow.

# 3

On her arrival back at 'The Castle', Freya lost no time in hurrying up the stairs. It was true that Miss Bryce had declared her intention of staying in bed all day, but she might have changed her mind, and Freya had no desire to encounter her employer whilst looking flushed and windswept from her climb.

She reached the sanctuary of her room without mishap. A brief glance in the mirror confirmed her dishevelled state, and she immediately set about remedying matters. Then, tidy again, she decided that perhaps she ought to go and see how Miss Bryce was feeling, and whether she intended to dine downstairs. She found her employer sitting up in bed and examining her flawless complexion by means of a hand mirror which her maid had just given to her.

'I came to see if you are feeling better,' said Freya.

'Oh, I suppose so,' replied Miss Bryce, laying down the mirror. 'I think I have escaped Piers's horrid chill, but travelling does tire me so dreadfully. I think I shall get up this evening. If I don't get up at all, I shall never sleep tonight, and then I shall feel worse in the morning.' She eyed Freya critically. 'You had better go and start changing for dinner straight away. You have plenty to do if you are to be ready in time. I'll send Briggs to you later if I can spare her.' *Which*, thought Freya, *does wonders for my self esteem!* She returned to her room, took from the cupboard one of the three evening gowns that she had brought with her, and laid it out on the bed. Then she took off the gown that she was wearing, threw it over the back of a chair, and poured some water from the ewer into the basin, so that she could wash her hands and face.

It did not take Freya very long to get ready. She had long since decided that the more time she spent fussing over her appearance, the worse she looked. She was glad that Briggs did not appear. Ladies' maids, she had discovered, often had very little patience with those who, like herself, did not conform to conventional standards of feminine beauty.

At last, satisfied that she could do no more, she looked in the mirror and involuntarily let out a long sigh. Her high-waisted gown was fashionably cut, and its shade of pale pink, chosen by Freya's aunt, was quite inoffensive. There was undoubtedly something wrong, as indeed there always was, but Freya could never work out exactly what that might be.

It was no use repining now. For one thing, in her experience, the only alternative which she had with her would not make her look any better. But she could not help thinking, as she descended the stairs, that with a man as handsome as Mr Bryce about, it was a pity that she couldn't cut a bit more of a dash.

Mr Bryce was sitting alone in the parlour, and he rose immediately when she entered the room. He was looking very handsome in a dark blue coat, and showed no signs of ill health at all.

'Miss Pascoe. How charming you look!' he said with perfect courtesy, if not, as Freya suspected, with perfect sincerity.

'I trust you are feeling better Mr Bryce,' said Freya.

'I believe so,' he replied. 'No doubt you thought it a little pitiful that I should retire to bed for the sake of a chill, but both our parents were carried off by such a complaint, so I believe that it is wise to take precautions.'

'I am sure you are right,' answered Freya. 'In fact, I wonder whether it would have been wiser not to get up this evening.'

'Ah, but then I should not have seen you, should I?' he answered audaciously, with a twinkle in his eye. Freya was not sure how to respond to this remark, so she contented herself with enquiring whether he intended to travel on the next day. 'I shan't stay in bed, but I believe I'll remain indoors for one more day,' he said.

'A little fresh air might be wise,' suggested Freya.

'Perhaps a short walk — but only if you go with me.' Gentlemen did not commonly converse with Freya in this bantering style, and it confused her a little. She was glad when moments later, Miss Bryce came in, dressed in much the same shade of pink as Freya was wearing, but looking absolutely ravishing. She looked at Freya for a long moment, then turned to her brother.

'Piers, is that the new coat which you had from Weston? It looks very fine.' *Which just about sums me up*, thought Freya.

'You're looking very grand yourself,' answered Mr Bryce. 'Why on earth have you dressed up like that? You look fine enough for a ball.' His sister shrugged.

'Ravendale might turn up. I should hate not to look my best.'

'Is he up here, then?' asked Bryce. 'Why didn't he travel with us?'

'Some matter of business that took him by a different route, I think,' said his sister indifferently.

The conversation at the dinner table was all

of London society, and Freya, remembering what her brother had said, kept quiet. She had no wish to reveal any knowledge which might seem to be too extensive for a paid companion. Furthermore, the conversation was not of the sort which she enjoyed, consisting as it did of society gossip, some of which was rather unkind.

She could not help noticing that the gossip which they exchanged often revealed a very incomplete knowledge of situations and people. Some of it was old news, whilst other stories were certainly either partially inaccurate or completely untrue. It seemed that the Bryces were not as au fait with society as they would like others to believe. She was glad when the meal was over and, after a hand or two of cards, Miss Bryce declared herself to be very fatigued, and went up to bed. Freya went up at the same time, leaving Mr Bryce to enjoy another glass of brandy before retiring himself.

The next day, as she had expected, Freya was the first downstairs. Clearly, they would be leaving Castleton in a day or two, so she decided that she would climb the hill behind the church and take a look at Peveril Castle. It would, she thought, be an expedition very easily accomplished in a morning. She glanced at the clock on the mantelshelf in the parlour. It was only 8.30 a.m. She had plenty of time to walk up to the castle and back before the Bryces even made an appearance. She finished her breakfast quickly and went upstairs to collect her bonnet and change into her stout shoes.

The day was fine and bright, so at least there would be no danger of being marooned in the mist with a total stranger, she reflected as she set out. She crossed the road, walked past the church and headed for the hill on which the castle stood and for which, she presumed, the town had been named.

Daniel Defoe — whose view of Derbyshire, it has to be said, Freya found rather jaundiced — had nothing at all to contribute with regard to the castle, so she was reliant on other sources of information. A small book which she had found in the parlour at the inn had informed her that the castle had been begun by a knight of William I, but that it had passed to the crown soon afterwards, and later became part of the property of the Duchy of Lancaster. The landlord, obviously accustomed to such queries, told her that it had fallen into disuse some four hundred years ago, and had been a ruin for three hundred of those, and he also warned her that the path would be somewhat overgrown. Freya soon realized the justice of his warning, but she enjoyed the challenge and climbed with a will. As she got closer to her object, she saw that the ruins were very substantial, and felt that this was a tribute to the Norman builders who had erected it.

It was a healthy climb, and by the time Freya reached the top she felt breathless, but triumphant. The day remained beautifully clear and from the castle she could look down to the town and across to Mam Tor, scene of the previous day's disagreeable encounter. Resolving not to spare any thought for the arrogant stranger, she decided to explore the ruins. There was no one there to ask if she might do so, and it seemed to her to be most unlikely that she could do them any harm.

The landlord had told her that it was a popular spot for walkers. So far she had met no one else, but as far as Freya was concerned, this was a gain, as it left her free to exercise her imagination to the full. She entered the walled section and strolled about inside, looking at the sturdy walls and imagining Norman soldiers firing arrows through the slit windows to repel invaders.

She went to examine the keep from the outside, and would have liked to explore it, but the wooden staircase that had once led to the entrance had gone, and there seemed to be no easy way in. She decided to take another look at the view of Castleton and the hills surrounding it, before going back down the hill; but as she turned away from the keep, she heard a scrabbling sound behind her. For a brief moment, her imagination played with the idea of a Norman spectre emerging from his former home, but as she turned back towards the keep, she saw a figure in modern dress spring lightly down on to the grass. Her admiration of his athleticism was cut abruptly short, however, when she realized that it was the unmannerly gentleman whom she had met the previous day.

'You!' she exclaimed incredulously, then blushed with vexation at the absurdly theatrical nature of her reaction.

It obviously struck him in the same way, because he said, 'What the deuce do you mean by saying 'you' like that? We're not characters in a bad melodrama. I'm just as entitled to be here as you are.'

'Yes, perhaps, but — '

'But what?' he demanded, interrupting her.

Taking the bull by the horns, she asked suspiciously, 'Are you following me sir?'

'Following you? Good God, no.'

As he said those words, for a moment the years were stripped away, and once again she was the same over-tall generously built young woman in a fussily trimmed gown, seated beside her godmother in some fashionable London ballroom, waiting in vain for someone, anyone to ask her to dance. Suddenly feeling all the same hurt that she had felt then, she was about to turn away when he went on.

'I met you on Mam Tor yesterday and allowed you to walk all the way down it by yourself, without making any effort to find out where you live or where you're staying. In any case, I've certainly not followed you today, because I was here first. If I was trying to follow you, I'd say that I was making a pretty poor fist of it.' He paused for a moment, but before she had time to think of a response, he went on slowly, and with a penetrating look, 'Come to think of it, I was on Mam Tor before you were, as well. It looks to be much more likely that you are following me.'

'Oh, don't be so absurd,' exclaimed Freya rather breathlessly, feeling strangely relieved that he had not meant what she had thought at first.

'Well it makes just as much sense,' he replied. His blond hair stirred in the breeze, and his hazel eyes gleamed with amusement. Freya looked up at him. She had forgotten how tall he was.

'I don't see that it does at all,' she retorted.

'Why upon earth should I want to follow you?'

'I could think of a reason,' he drawled, 'but I'm too much of a gentleman to mention it.' Freya made a sound that was very like a snort. He went on, 'But you put me in mind of another matter, which is that you are out walking on the hills alone again, as far as I can see.'

'And if I am, is it any business of yours?' asked Freya, more relieved than anything by the change of subject, for she had found the previous one a little disturbing.

'It would have been very much my business yesterday, had I allowed you to blunder about in the mist on Mam Tor, thereby risking falling over a precipice and killing yourself.'

'Oh pooh, I would never have wandered as far as that,' answered Freya airily. 'And in any case, yesterday is gone, today is fine and clear, and I repeat, my choice of walking companions or lack of the same is none of your concern!' She turned to walk away, but he moved swiftly and blocked her path.

'As a gentleman, I feel answerable to your relatives or your husband, if any harm should come to you,' he replied.

'I have no husband, and I have reached the age of majority long since,' she answered quickly. 'In any case, what possible harm could come to me here?' She looked up at his face, saw the gleam in his eye, and sensing danger, she took a step back. Quickly, he took a step forward and too late, she realized that he had her backed into a corner. Now, he held her captive with one hand on the wall either side of her, not touching her, but making it quite clear that there would be no escape without his permission.

'This was a Norman castle, did you know?' he said conversationally. 'Begun by one William Peveril. What was he like, do you suppose? A gallant knight? My opinion is that he was a dangerous marauder.'

So saying, he took his hands away from the stone wall, but only to pull her into his arms and kiss her long and hard on her mouth. At first she was too astonished to resist, but then she began to struggle with all her might and at last he released her. She stared at him for a long moment, too angry to speak. Then at last, she uttered, 'You . . . you . . . '

'That was what you said when we met a few minutes ago. Yes, it's still me; and I still maintain that you shouldn't walk alone.'

Furious, and unable to think of anything else to say, Freya turned on her heel to walk back down to Castleton.

'Mind the stones,' called her infuriating

assailant. 'Unless you want me to carry you down the hill.'

She turned then. 'Over my dead body,' she declared.

'That, my dear girl, would be a logical impossibility.'

With something very like a flounce, Freya turned to descend the hill. Her indignation at the gentleman's arrogance, his rudeness, his presumption, carried her all the way to the bottom; but once there, she thought about their last remarks, and suddenly realized the absurdity of her own and the truth of his. At once, she burst out laughing to the surprise of several passers-by, and continued her walk back to the inn at a more measured pace.

★ ★ ★

When she walked in at the front door, she was still smiling. She found Mr Bryce in the parlour having coffee. He rose courteously, and invited her to join him, and after a moment's hesitation, she took off her bonnet and laid it on a chair.

'Have you been for a walk, Miss Pascoe?' he asked her.

'Yes, I've been to look at the castle,' she said, forgetting her resolve to say nothing of her expeditions.

His eyes widened. 'Right up to the castle!' he exclaimed. 'Miss Pascoe, you must be exhausted!' She laughed.

'No indeed, on my honour,' she replied, 'it was most invigorating.' She recalled the encounter at the top of the hill, and found herself blushing.

'Well, it has certainly given you a most becoming colour,' said Mr Bryce. 'But are you sure that you were wise to go alone? Suppose some accident had befallen you?'

'Thankfully it did not,' said Freya, annoyed at hearing the views of the infuriating fair-haired gentleman repeated, however courteously. To change the subject, she encouraged Bryce to talk about London, which he did very readily, and she found herself obliged to say little more before she had finished her coffee, whereupon she rose to take her things upstairs.

In many ways she found Piers Bryce attractive. True, his dislike of the countryside and his love of town life might soon pall; and his assumption that she must be too delicate to indulge in vigorous country pursuits was a little irritating, but she had to acknowledge that it was rather refreshing as well. She had never before found that women of her stature brought out the protective instinct in men.

Smiling, she went to her room to tidy

herself up. That done, she looked critically at herself in the mirror. There was no doubt that she looked much better in her rather severe walking costume than she did when attired for the evening, and she found herself wishing, not for the first time, that she could always dress in such a manner.

This time, as she descended the stairs she heard voices inside the parlour, and detecting the sound of Miss Bryce's society drawl, she pushed open the door and walked inside. But she had not taken many steps into the room before she came to an abrupt halt, and stood staring at those present. Standing by the fire was Mr Bryce, but by the window, apparently engaged in intimate conversation, were Miss Bryce and Freya's unwelcome acquaintance from Mam Tor and Peveril Castle.

# 4

Miss Bryce and her companion turned towards the door, and when the former saw Freya, she smiled with an expression that seemed to Freya to convey both triumph and a little smugness.

'Ah, Miss Pascoe, do come in,' she said sweetly. 'I would like you to meet my very good friend — Lord Ravendale! Daniel, this is Miss Pascoe, who is acting as my companion.' Freya was almost tempted to look around and see if someone else was speaking. She could not remember Miss Bryce ever addressing her so courteously before. It also made her rather curious that Claudia should describe the earl as her friend, when she had been saying before that she was engaged to him. Ravendale came forward to take Freya's hand, and as he did so, there was a decided gleam in his eye, although what it signified, she would have been at a loss to say.

'Miss Pascoe,' he murmured in the deep tones that she remembered so well. 'It is a pleasure to meet you.' So he did not intend to divulge the fact that they had already met.

This suited Freya very well, and did not particularly surprise her. He would hardly want Miss Bryce to know that he had been hobnobbing with her companion. Freya acknowledged his greeting with the smallest possible curtsy, and only just managed to resist snatching her hand out of his grasp. 'Claudia has just been telling me how relieved she has been to have some female companionship on the way here,' he went on.

'Many ladies like to have a member of their own sex to converse with on a journey,' Freya replied in a neutral tone.

'No doubt to discuss the failings of us mere males,' suggested the earl.

'Failings?' queried Freya. 'I'm surprised you even admit to the possibility of having any.'

'I didn't, of course,' he answered, his eyes showing appreciation of her spirited reply. 'I merely suggested what you might have been discussing. I said nothing of the veracity of what you might have been saying.'

'Well, this is very amusing,' murmured Miss Bryce. 'Miss Pascoe, pray be so good as to fetch my shawl from my bedroom.' Freya excused herself and went upstairs, feeling very thoroughly put in her place.

Truth to tell, she was not sorry to have a few moments to herself before rejoining the company. Seeing the earl had been a double shock. For one thing, to see the gentleman at all after two stormy encounters with him had taken her aback. Up on the hillside, he had somehow acquired a certain unreality, like a kind of goblin or supernatural being, with no connections to ordinary life. Meeting him just now, in company with Miss and Mr Bryce, had given him a place in the real world which, however absurdly, she had not expected him to occupy.

The second shock, of course, had been to discover that he was Lord Ravendale. She had been conscious of feeling that there was something familiar about him, from the first moment that she had seen him clearly. She remembered Lady Terrington pointing him out that evening at the ball. 'His whole family crippled by his ruinous addiction,' she had said. Freya was conscious of a feeling of disappointment. Unable to find a reason for her feelings, she attributed it to a reluctance to see anyone, even someone as unsympathetic as Miss Bryce, fall into the clutches of one who would reduce his own dependants to penury just to satisfy his own craving.

As she picked up Miss Bryce's shawl, she caught sight of herself in the mirror, and suddenly she remembered how Ravendale had kissed her. Heaven forbid that Miss

Bryce should ever find out about that! Even though it had been entirely Ravendale's fault, she was sure that the lady would blame her for leading him on. Poor Miss Bryce, she thought. Her fiancé is a rake as well as a gamester!

Lacking further excuse for delay, she went downstairs with the shawl and found Miss Bryce sitting near the fireplace whilst Lord Ravendale and Mr Bryce looked out of the window at something in the street. As Freya laid the shawl about Miss Bryce's shoulders, she hear her employer say *sotto voce*, 'I would advise you to have a care, Miss Pascoe. I do not expect my companion to be putting herself forward in such a brazen way. Kindly remember your place in future!' Freya was so astonished that she almost said something, but the gentlemen came away from the window at this point, and Mr Bryce, seeing that Freya had returned, asked her if she had recovered from her exertions.

'Exertions? Don't be absurd,' drawled Miss Bryce. 'She has only just climbed the stairs!'

'No, my dear, you are mistaken,' he replied. 'She has climbed the hill to Peveril Castle! *And* come down again!'

'And made the return trip as well!' exclaimed Ravendale, looking at Freya with a twinkle in his eye. 'You astonish me!' Despite what Freya knew about him, she felt a terrible, almost overwhelming desire to giggle.

'Miss Pascoe is a woman of great energy,' said Miss Bryce, as if describing a great fault. 'It really does astonish me. I declare, she should have been a man.'

Freya could never hear such remarks without feeling hurt. Whether or not Mr Bryce sensed her discomfort could not have been determined, but immediately he said, 'But if she had been a man, you would not have had the pleasure of her company!' Freya smiled at him gratefully. His handsome face was alight with laughter.

'Well, for my part I cannot understand anyone's wanting to go all the way up there,' Miss Bryce said. 'I would by far rather stroll about the town.'

'Your preferences are well known, my dear,' said Lord Ravendale. 'But in Miss Pascoe's defence, I should say that my aunt has climbed to Peveril Castle more than once, with no ill effects whatsoever.'

'Ah, but your aunt is a *countrywoman*,' replied Claudia, as if she was talking about some strange species. The earl continued to smile, but his smile looked a little fixed.

'As you say,' he murmured.

'For my part, I suggest that we all have a

walk about the town this afternoon,' Bryce said after an awkward silence. 'I think it will not over-tax us, and a change of scene might do us good. Ravendale, will you take luncheon with us, and join us in our walk?'

'If it is permitted,' he answered courteously.

'Why, of course,' said Miss Bryce, laying her hand on his arm and speaking in such a caressing tone that Freya found herself wondering whether she had imagined her employer's derogatory innuendo with regard to the earl's aunt.

'Then I shall remain,' he said, smiling down at Claudia. 'No doubt a little gentle exercise will do me good as well.' After a slight pause, he went on, with a sideways look at Freya, 'You are probably wise not to venture up there anyway. Who knows, you might find yourself the object of gallantry from the ghost of some Norman knight.' Miss Bryce smiled then — a rare occurrence.

'Perhaps it is a good thing that Miss Pascoe climbed the hill and not I,' she said playfully. 'No Norman knight would dare to approach her.'

'Oh, some of these Norman knights were uncommonly bold,' answered Ravendale, 'and Miss Pascoe is the image of a healthy Norman maiden.' It would be hard to say who was the more astonished, Freya or Claudia.

At that moment, the maid came in to tell them that luncheon was ready. The meal with which they were served, which consisted of thick slices of ham, cheese, crusty bread, pickles and a cold steak and kidney pie, was well up to the high standard that Freya had come to expect of the establishment. Having taken exercise that morning, she did ample justice to what was provided, as did Lord Ravendale, presumably for the same reason. Both Miss and Mr Bryce's appetites were poor, however, and Miss Bryce toyed with her food, cutting it up into small pieces, pushing it around her plate, and consuming very little of it.

'What a lot you eat, Miss Pascoe,' she remarked, laying down her knife and fork as if they were both too heavy for her. 'I declare, it will be very expensive to keep you if you continue to consume food at this rate.'

Mortified, Freya put down her own knife and fork, her desire for food suddenly gone.

'Miss Pascoe has worked up an appetite,' said Ravendale. 'And besides, Claudia, you have probably pushed nearly as much around the perimeter of your plate.'

Freya could not help smiling at him gratefully, but the next time she looked at

70

Miss Bryce, she encountered a look on that lady's face that seemed to indicate that there might be another lecture to come about drawing attention to herself.

After the meal was over, the party set out for their walk around the town. Castleton was quite a small place, and it seemed to Freya that they would exhaust its possibilities quite rapidly. Miss Bryce took the lead, her hand tucked into Lord Ravendale's arm in a very proprietorial manner. Mr Bryce offered Freya his, and she took it rather than appear ungracious; but in truth she had always preferred to set her own pace rather than measure it to another's. As she had expected, Miss Bryce's speed of walking was a very dawdling one, and she constantly found herself having to slow down rather than step on her heels.

'Shall we look at the church?' suggested Lord Ravendale, turning to speak to Freya and Mr Bryce. 'It has one or two features of interest, I believe.' His fiancée did not look very enthusiastic, but Freya gladly agreed. She had observed the church from Peveril Castle, and welcomed the chance to discover a little more about it. Mr Bryce seemed to be almost as unenthusiastic about visiting the church as his sister, so it happened that Freya found herself walking with Lord Ravendale.

71

He did not offer her his arm, but without thinking, they both quickened their pace, until they had left Mr and Miss Bryce behind.

'That's better,' sighed Freya without thinking, then realizing the implied criticism that she had made of her employer and his lordship's intended, she added quickly, 'Oh, I beg your pardon!'

'Not at all,' answered Ravendale. 'I was just thinking the same. Neither of us, I believe, makes a very good saunterer, ma'am. Well, here is the church. Shall we go inside?'

'Perhaps we had better wait for the others,' suggested Freya. They walked around the outside of the church while they were waiting. 'How old is it?' she asked him.

'It isn't mentioned in the Domesday Book,' replied Ravendale. 'But look, you can see the Norman arches. It's probably about seven hundred years old. Has anyone told you about the Castleton Garland Day?'

'No,' replied Freya. 'Pray, what is it?'

Mr and Miss Bryce arrived at this point, and Lord Ravendale said in an amused tone, 'Perhaps you might ask Claudia to tell you about it.'

'What is this?' asked Claudia. 'What am I to tell Miss Pascoe?'

'Lord Ravendale was suggesting that you

might like to tell me about Castleton Garland Day,' replied Freya. A look of scorn crossed Miss Bryce's features.

'I cannot imagine why he should think so,' she said in a tone that perfectly matched her expression. 'He surely must be funning! I do not have the slightest interest in provincial entertainments.' She turned away to enter the church. Ravendale looked at Freya, his eyes full of amusement, but she refused to respond. She held no brief for Miss Bryce, but it seemed to her to be vastly unfair that Ravendale should take such pleasure in exposing his fiancée's weakness. It hardly seemed a healthy precursor to a happy marriage.

'I'll tell you,' said Piers eagerly as they entered the church behind his sister and the earl. 'It takes place on 27 May and is a commemoration of the restoration of the monarchy. The culmination of the festivities involves the hoisting of a garland to the top of the church tower.' Intrigued, Freya waited for him to say more and a few minutes later he did so, disappointing her by merely adding 'My sister's right, you know. It's just peasant stuff.' They wandered briefly around the church, but Freya found it difficult to give her full mind to it, when Claudia and Piers Bryce made it clear by their whole demeanour that

73

they were thoroughly bored with the proceedings.

They soon left the church to resume their ambling progress around the town. As they left the churchyard, Freya paused to look at the top of the tower, trying to imagine the garland being hoisted to the top.

'It is an interesting spectacle,' said a voice in her ear. She turned to see Ravendale standing next to her.

'You have seen it take place then, my lord?' Freya questioned him.

'Oh yes, on several occasions. I've even taken part in it once! It is not to everyone's taste, as I think you have discovered, but it's part of our history, after all.'

'I should like to see it,' admitted Freya.

'Well, perhaps you might still be here next time it happens,' he suggested.

'I do not think it likely,' murmured Freya. Before any more could be said, Mr Bryce called to them to come along. They walked back along the high street past 'The Castle' and in the direction of Mam Tor. Freya looked about her, noticing afresh how the town nestled amongst the hills.

'This must be a place where one is always conscious of nature,' she mused, as they paused to look at the great hill before them. It was a beautiful sunny day, and the few clouds that there were cast shadows on the hills around them as they moved across the sky.

'Just think of the poor folk of Edale,' murmured Ravendale. 'Until the 1600s, there was no church there at all. Imagine trudging three miles here and back in all weathers — and sometimes with a coffin, too.'

'Oh, for heaven's sake, Daniel, don't be so morbid,' complained Miss Bryce. 'No one wants to hear about such sad stuff. Shall we go back to 'The Castle' now? I for one have walked quite enough for today, and I think it is nearly time to begin changing for dinner.'

'We had better leave the caves until tomorrow, then,' said Ravendale.

'If you think that I am going to set so much as one foot in those horrid caves, you are very much mistaken,' declared Miss Bryce.

'What are they like?' asked Freya curiously. 'I have not read Mr Defoe's account of the caves; but I suspect that he probably did not like them.'

'Sadly, Mr Defoe does not seem impressed with Derbyshire at all,' the earl put in. 'I have read his account of his travels, and for my part, I am convinced that he must have had a severe bout of indigestion when he came here.'

This was very much Freya's view, and she was about to say so, when Miss Bryce said, 'If he disliked Derbyshire, then he must have been a man of sense. And as for the caves, they are dirty, dark and smelly and inhabited only by ignorant peasants. You may go in the morning if you wish, Miss Pascoe, but I am afraid that my sensibilities are a little too refined to endure it. And if you *do* go, for heaven's sake wash afterwards.'

'My sister is very right,' said Mr Bryce, offering Freya his arm. 'I am persuaded you would not care for it at all. It is not a suitable outing for a lady.' Freya half expected Lord Ravendale to make some contribution to the debate, but he said nothing. When they arrived back at 'The Castle', Miss Bryce invited him to dine with them, but he politely declined.

'I am staying with an acquaintance of mine who lives on the outskirts of the town,' he explained. 'I am engaged to dine with him tonight, so you will have to hold me excused.'

'Oh, very well,' replied Miss Bryce ungraciously. 'You must do your duty, I suppose. Can we take you up with us tomorrow afternoon? We can drop you at Ravendale.'

'You must forgive me, but I have tasks awaiting me at home, so I will go first thing in the morning,' replied the earl. 'Do you care to ride with me, Bryce?'

76

Piers shook his head. 'Your country hours don't suit me,' he replied with a grin.

'As you please,' said Ravendale in a rather curt tone. He bowed and took his leave.

'You should have gone with him, Piers,' Miss Bryce said after the door had closed behind him. 'I expect he wanted to talk about settlements.'

'Plenty of time for that,' answered her brother easily. 'I dislike talking business on horseback.'

Before dinner, Miss Bryce sent for Freya. When she arrived, her employer was engaged in looking carefully into a hand mirror, turning her face this way and that. 'Come in,' she said. 'I think that it is time that you and I had a little conversation.' Freya closed the door, and sat down in the chair that Miss Bryce indicated. After a long, last look at her flawless complexion, she laid the mirror down. 'It occurs to me that Lady Terrington must have allowed you a degree of licence which is unusual in a lady's relationship with her paid companion.'

'That may be so,' said Freya carefully, 'but — '

'Such licence is not a thing I have ever permitted,' continued Miss Bryce, as if her companion had not spoken. Freya realized that this was to be a very one-sided conversation. 'You must understand that familiarity with Lord Ravendale or with my brother cannot possibly be tolerated.' Miss Bryce got up from her dressing table, and began to pace slowly across the room and back. 'You are clearly of quite a good family, and perhaps you suppose that in my company you may possibly be able to attach some gentleman, and make a marriage which will remove the necessity of having to continue in your present occupation.'

Freya opened her mouth to protest indignantly, but Miss Bryce lifted one hand imperiously, commanding her silence. 'Do not think I blame you for this. I can quite understand such an ambition, and it may be that I might be able to help you. Reverend Tobias Simpkins, for example, is a clergyman who lives quite near my brother's estate. He is a respectable widower with five children, and he would probably be very thankful to find anyone who might be prepared to take them on, however unprepossessing she might be. But I must have it understood that my brother is not for you. He can do much better for himself. And Ravendale is mine. Is that clear, Pascoe?'

It was perhaps as well that at that moment, there was a knock at the door, and two menservants came in, carrying a large cheval glass. 'At last!' exclaimed Miss Bryce languidly. 'How I could be expected to dress properly without a full length mirror, I cannot imagine.'

While the mirror was being set down, Freya walked over to the window. She could not remember ever being so angry in her life before. The rudeness and sheer cruelty of the woman were astounding. *Damn the bet*, Freya fumed to herself. *This is not to be endured!* She would almost certainly have given her employer a piece of her mind and walked out immediately, when her attention was caught by the sight of a man walking down the street. He was so like her brother John, that for a few moments, she almost thought that the bank problem was solved, and he had come to fetch her.

The small mistake gave her pause. If John had let it be known that she had gone out of town with friends, then she must not do anything to appear to contradict his story. Her return to town earlier than expected might give rise to speculation that all was not well, and the tiniest rumour could be enough to disturb the delicate equilibrium that John was striving to maintain. No, she would just have to stick it out.

As the servants left, Freya made as if to follow them. She was arrested by her employer's voice. 'Well, Pascoe, is that clear?' Freya turned in the doorway.

'You have made yourself perfectly clear, ma'am,' she replied with calm dignity. 'But allow me, in my turn, to remind *you* of something. I am not a chambermaid or a groom, and I will not answer to anything other than *Miss* Pascoe.' Before Miss Bryce could answer, she whisked herself out of the room and down the passage to her own.

Before making her own speedy toilette, she badly needed to give vent to her feelings, so after mending her pen, she wrote everything down in a letter to Lady Terrington. As she wrote, she began to see the funny side of the business, and by the time she had finished her account, she was smiling. She hoped that her friend would find it similarly amusing.

While she was changing, she could not help reflecting that Miss Bryce was the most unsympathetic person she had ever met; and as she went down to dinner that night, she almost found it in her heart to feel sorry for Lord Ravendale!

# 5

There were times the next day when Freya wondered whether they would ever leave 'The Castle' at all. Although they had a journey ahead of them, neither of the Bryces stirred from their rooms until nearly noon, but Miss Bryce was awake long before then, and sent for Freya several times in order that some essential item might be purchased in the town. Freya's curiosity with regard to the caves had been further stimulated by the previous day's conversation, but there would clearly be no possibility of going that morning. She decided that if no opportunity of visiting them presented itself during her time with Miss Bryce, then she would make sure that she went there during her holiday with Lady Terrington. She was quite determined that she would earn that holiday. It was not just a matter of winning the bet with her friend, but of not allowing Miss Bryce to get the better of her!

The journey itself was picturesque, if not particularly comfortable. Some of the roads were scarcely made, and those that were threw the others into strong contrast. It made

Freya wonder why such a keen horseman as Piers Bryce had chosen to sit inside. Not that they were able to remain in the coach all the time, for sometimes it became necessary for them to get down in order to lighten the load for the horses.

Freya scrambled down very readily on these occasions, glad to have a change from sitting inside. Miss Bryce's abigail was obliged to do so, needless to say, and Piers got down willingly enough. Miss Bryce, however, remained seated in her corner, fanning herself languidly.

'*My* weight cannot possibly make a difference to the horses,' she declared. 'I'm sure they would not notice one way or the other if I were there or not! Now you, Miss Pascoe, built more robustly than myself, will certainly help them.' Little though Freya valued Miss Bryce's opinion, she could not help feeling hurt by such observations, and she comforted herself with thoughts of the day when, released from the constraints imposed upon her, she could retaliate in kind! For his part, Mr Bryce made no reference to his sister's comments, either to confirm or refute them. Freya was left wondering whether he was so used to his sister's spitefulness that he simply did not notice it any more.

Their journey took them out of Castleton and up Winnats Pass, so that they had a good view of Mam Tor. As Freya looked up at it, she could not help remembering her encounter with Lord Ravendale near the top. Today, it was bright and clear, and she thought regretfully of the excellent views that she would have seen from the summit, had she been able to climb it today.

'You see how high it is, Miss Pascoe,' said Mr Bryce as they walked behind the coach up Winnats Pass. 'I believe that when you reach the top of this road, you will concede that you will have walked quite far enough.'

'If you think that, then I can tell you that you do not know me very well,' replied Freya cheerfully.

'Perhaps not,' returned Bryce. 'But the walk to the summit is very strenuous. I have never attempted it myself, and I would certainly not advise any lady to do so.'

Freya suddenly thought of Lord Ravendale. When she had met him on the hillside, he had criticized her for climbing alone, and for moving about when the mist had come down; but never had he suggested that she should not be climbing at all. She drew her companion's attention to the outcrops of rock which towered over them on every side, at times blocking the view of Mam Tor itself.

'One can well imagine brigands hiding amongst these rocks,' she commented.

'Ah!' he exclaimed. 'Someone has fore-stalled me!'

'What do you mean?' Freya asked him.

'Simply that I have been deprived of recounting to you one of the most gruesome stories connected with this part of the world.'

'Oh, the young couple who eloped and were murdered here. Yes, I have heard the tale.'

'You are very matter-of-fact about it,' said he, surprised. 'I wonder whether you would be similarly unconcerned if you were stranded here at dead of night.'

'Possibly not,' she said crisply. 'So obviously it behoves me to avoid such a contingency. Anyway, why is everyone so certain that they were murdered? It seems to me to be far more likely that they laid a false trail for their pursuers in order to make their elopement easier, and went on their way with no one being any the wiser.'

'Then why would their spirits be heard on dark nights, begging for mercy when the wind is high?' asked Bryce with a gleam in his eye.

Freya glanced to the side of the road, saw a rather unpleasant-looking hole half hidden beneath the rocks, and barely repressed a shudder. Then her strong vein of common sense reasserted itself, and she said, 'Because the wind blowing in confined spaces makes strange noises.' At this point the carriage stopped for them to get back in and they resumed their journey.

Mr and Miss Bryce began to talk about some acquaintances of theirs who were unknown to Freya, so that meant that she was free to think her own thoughts. She had found herself thinking rather a lot about Lord Ravendale recently; but she told herself that that was only because he was the most uncivil man that she had ever met. Instead, she decided to think about Mr Bryce. He was certainly handsome, more conventionally handsome than Lord Ravendale, and his manners were more conciliatory. He had also chosen to travel in the coach, and despite the reason offered by Miss Bryce, namely that he did not want to talk about settlements with Ravendale, Freya could not help thinking that he might have chosen to ride inside in order to be near to her. Certainly, he had got out to walk with great alacrity, and his conversation had been sensible enough, even if his views about the robustness of women were rather conventional. He was hardly to be blamed for that, Freya told herself, living as he did with his sister and her notions of appropriate exercise for females. Perhaps a little acquaintance with herself would change his opinion!

If indeed he had sought her out because he was interested in her, then his interest was worth encouraging for at least two reasons. The first was that his interest could have nothing to do with her money. As far as he was concerned, she was plain, tall Miss Pascoe, the paid companion, not wealthy Miss Pascoe, of Pascoe's bank. Rather like the prince in the fairy tale, Freya liked the idea of having someone take an interest in her for herself and not for her fortune.

Secondly, as the years had gone by other debutantes had entered society, Freya had grown older, and all the fortune hunters had discovered that she was too astute to be taken in by their wiles and ploys. It was now somewhat unusual, therefore, for any young eligible man to devote any time to her, and she found that she was rather enjoying the novelty of his attentions. Suddenly the thought popped into her mind, *If Ravendale notices, all the better*, but she sternly repressed it, and forced herself to look at Miss Bryce, who was at that moment smiling at something that her brother had just said. To suppose that Lord Ravendale would ever look her way when he was as good as engaged to such a beautiful woman as Miss Bryce was clearly an absurdity; and to want him to do so was a piece of presumption.

Their route took them to Chapel-en-le-Frith — where they took some refreshment for themselves and for the horses — and from there to Tideswell. It was not the shortest route on the map, but the roads were comparatively better. The shortest but most difficult part of the journey was between Tideswell and the Bryces' house. In order to get there, they were obliged to turn off the main road, and to travel down what amounted to little more than a lane.

'I am sure you must suppose our coachman has mistaken the road,' said Miss Bryce, 'but I am afraid that such is not the case. This appalling little track does indeed lead to our house.'

The horses were forced to drop to a walk, and the jolting, which had been somewhat uncomfortable, became acute. It was on the tip of Freya's tongue to ask why they did not do anything about the road, since it appeared to lead only to their house, but she held her tongue. She was to have her curiosity satisfied very shortly.

After they had jolted and rattled along for what seemed to be some considerable distance, Freya noticed a magnificent Jacobean house half-concealed by trees.

'Is that your house?' she asked, hoping that the journey might almost be over.

'No,' replied Bryce, without even glancing in its direction. 'That's Ravendale Hall.'

'But that must be . . . ' began Freya.

'Yes, it belongs to Daniel,' said Miss Bryce pointedly. Freya received the distinct impression that she would have liked to add, *and Daniel belongs to me.* They got a better view of it as they travelled on a little further, and Freya was surprised to notice that it seemed to be rather neglected.

'I suppose you noticed what a bad state it's in,' Mr Bryce remarked, when they had gone past.

'Well, I . . . ' murmured Freya, unwilling to commit herself.

'I'm afraid all the money the family has ever had has gone on gambling and so on,' he continued. 'The Ravendales have always been wastrels.' The carriage lurched violently at this point, and Bryce laughed ruefully. 'I suspect you have been wondering why we do not do something about the state of this road, but the reason is very simple. It is partly ours, and partly Ravendale's, and he won't pay his share. There are times when I wonder if it will ever be done!' He fell silent. Freya glanced at Claudia, expecting to see some evidence of indignation at her brother's slighting reference to her fiancé; but instead, her pretty features seemed to bear a secret smile.

Freya was at a loss to understand her. If she bore any love for the man, surely she would leap to his defence; but if she held him in contempt, how could she contemplate marriage with him? What was more, how could Piers hand over his sister to such a man with equanimity? There had been something rather distasteful in the way that he had talked of the earl's financial difficulties so casually. For the first time, Freya began to have doubts as to the good nature of Mr Bryce.

Just as she was thinking that by the end of the journey she would not have a tooth left in her head, the woodland began to clear, the vista opened up, and a Georgian house, scarcely more than thirty years old, appeared before them. It was a great relief to step out of the carriage, and for a moment Freya felt as unsteady as if she was setting foot on dry land after a month at sea.

'Welcome!' exclaimed Mr Bryce as he handed her down. 'Welcome to our home!' They walked together up the steps into a light, cool hall, where servants were waiting to relieve them of their outdoor clothing.

'I shall take you straight up to your room, Miss Pascoe,' said Miss Bryce. 'I am sure that you will want to attend to your appearance, and so do I! If I have suffered anything like as much as you from the rigours of the journey, then I must look a perfect fright!' Not for the first time, Freya looked for and failed to find any spark of humour in her hostess's face; and as there was no trace of malice there either, she could only conclude that she had no idea how insensitive she was being.

The room that was to be hers was on the same floor as that of her hostess. This surprised Freya a little, for knowing how much importance Miss Bryce attached to form and precedent, she had half-expected that she might have been placed in some kind of attic room. Maybe Claudia had remembered her connection with the influential Lady Terrington. Or perhaps, more probably, she wanted to be certain that her companion would be easily within call at any time.

Freya's room was decorated in pale blue, and had a view which looked down on to the swiftly flowing river.

'But this is charming!' she exclaimed. 'What a pleasant view!'

'Yes, I have heard other people admire it,' drawled Miss Bryce wearily. 'The drawing-room has the same aspect, I'm afraid. For my part, I find it rather noisy, and there is always that unspeakable mill just a short distance away. I would much rather live in London.'

Freya smiled at the thought that the sound of a river could be considered noisy, and she could not help remarking, 'You cannot be averse to *some* noise if you like London, Miss Bryce.'

'I did not say that I was,' she replied. 'Simply that I do not like *that* noise.' She walked to the door. 'Come downstairs when you are ready, and we'll have some refreshment.'

After Miss Bryce had gone, Freya wandered over to the window to take a better look at the river. It seemed to be quite shallow at this point, and fast flowing. There were trees on the far bank, but the side nearest the house had been kept free of them, obviously so that someone who lived in the house could have an uninterrupted view of the water. Not Miss Bryce, Freya decided with a wry smile. Looking out of the window, she could see the river winding away to her left, but to her right and downstream, a big bend in the river obscured its view from her sight.

For her part, she would be very happy to live in such a setting, she decided. She began to wonder, not for the first time, what Mr

Bryce would be like as a husband. He had shown himself to be affable enough so far, even given her lowly status as his sister's companion; no doubt his affability would be even more marked if he found out about the Pascoe thousands. Not that she would want to censure him for that. It would take either a very wealthy man or a very altruistic one to regard her immense fortune with indifference. But was Mr Bryce the kind of man with whom she wanted to spend her life? Yes, he was handsome and friendly, but really, she knew very little of him, and the most recent conversation that she had had with him had been rather disquieting. Perhaps these next few days in his company would help her to make up her mind.

As she looked across the river to the woods beyond, she remembered another man who lived close by; but even as the name 'Ravendale' came into her mind, she sternly repressed her thoughts.

Suddenly realizing that she had spent more time in her room than she had intended, she hurried to the dressing table to check her appearance. She was a little untidy; but then, she had scrambled in and out of the chaise and walked a time or two, whilst Miss Bryce had remained sitting inside all the time.

Quickly, she remedied her appearance, then went downstairs.

Once in the hall, she found a servant who took her to where Miss and Mr Bryce were taking a glass of wine. Miss Bryce had taken the opportunity to change her gown, and was now dressed in the shade of pink which Freya always found the most trying. On Miss Bryce, it looked delectable.

'Miss Pascoe,' she murmured languidly. 'So you decided not to change.'

'Miss Pascoe always looks charming,' said Mr Bryce smiling as he carried over a glass of wine. Freya smiled back as she took it, but even while she took pleasure from his compliment, the practical side of her wanted to say, *No I don't! Don't be so absurd!*

After a brief silence, Freya wandered over to the window.

'In which direction is the mill?' she asked.

'Oh, over there,' replied Claudia, waving downstream with one hand. 'When the wind is in the wrong direction you can almost smell the wretched place.' From her admittedly brief experience of his character, Freya expected Mr Bryce to say something optimistic in response to this, but instead he merely sipped his wine, a slightly brooding expression on his face.

Dinner that night was a pleasanter affair

than Freya had dared hope. Mr Bryce, recovering his customary good humour, exerted himself to please, and even Miss Bryce, perhaps suddenly aware of her duties as a hostess, became quite affable. The meal with which they were served was well chosen and delicious and Freya, trying not to draw attention to herself by her healthy appetite, thoroughly enjoyed it.

'Breakfast can be served downstairs, or taken in your room, whichever you prefer,' Miss Bryce said before they retired. 'Pray do not think of disturbing me before midday. Until that hour you may amuse yourself as you please.' This news did not surprise Freya, and it was certainly not unwelcome. At least she would have a chance to explore the surrounding countryside!

# 6

As Freya had expected, she was the only one to take her place at the breakfast table the next morning. She had been unsure as to what attitude she might expect from the servants, but so far, they had all been perfectly courteous. She wondered whether they were quite glad to have someone about before noon.

After a satisfactory breakfast of eggs, bacon, toast and coffee, she set out to explore the grounds. She was tempted to go in the direction of the mill, but suspected that there might be a danger of her straying into areas forbidden to her, and interrupting work. She wanted to see the mill, but decided that it would be better to wait until Mr Bryce could conduct her there — although judging by his expression when the mill had been discussed the previous evening, he would probably take a bit of persuading!

Instead, she crossed the little bridge which they had driven across the day before, and entered the wood. She had not realized until now what a relief it would be to get out of the house and into the fresh air. Miss Bryce

95

would never normally be her choice of companion., but for the remainder of the day she would be obliged to spend time with her. Her employer was clearly one of those persons who constantly felt the need to establish their status over those whom they felt to be their inferiors. With a sigh of thanksgiving that her employment would be of very short duration, Freya resolved to dismiss that lady from her mind for the time being; but this scarcely led to brighter thoughts, for she soon found herself thinking about John and his situation.

John had not been so very old when their father had died; but thanks to his own financial acumen, and the help of some experienced advisers, he had shouldered the burden with surprising ease. It would be too bad, Freya thought to herself, if by some mischance things should go wrong now. A proportion of her own fortune she knew to be secure, and there was no danger that they would find themselves without means, but John's pride would be seriously hurt if the bank collapsed. Knowing John, however, Freya felt sure that this would hurt him less than the knowledge that those who had invested stood to lose all that they had. She had half hoped that there might be a letter waiting for her at the Bryces' with tidings, but there had been nothing. She would just have to be patient. The trouble was, she thought to herself, smiling ruefully, patience was not really one of her virtues.

She had now been walking for some time, and at last stopped to look around her. She had been half aware that she had recently ceased to climb; now she realized that she could not even tell which way she had come. She was hopelessly lost.

\* \* \*

'Daniel! Let me look at you! I declare, you are even more handsome than when I saw you last!'

Ravendale grinned. 'And you, my dear aunt, contrive to look prettier every time I see you,' he answered, before picking her up and swinging her around. Unlike her nephew, Lady Ravendale was tiny and dark, her raven hair only touched here and there by grey, her eyes still bright, although now surrounded by tiny lines, and her figure was excellent.

'Put me down at once, you naughty boy,' she cried. 'I cannot believe that this is how they behave now in London.'

'Well, not in the best circles,' he admitted, putting her gently back on her feet. 'Is all well here? How does it go?'

She tucked her hand into his arm and together they strolled into the saloon. It was a bright, sunny room, but the furnishings were not of the latest fashion. The curtains looked a little faded and the carpet somewhat threadbare, and there was a patch on the wall to show where a picture had once hung.

'Oh, we go on very well,' replied his aunt gaily. 'The hens are now laying prodigiously, and we are selling some eggs, as well as eating them ourselves; and Kingman is pleased with the sheep, I believe.'

Ravendale took hold of her shoulders and turned her to face him. 'Tell me the truth!' he said insistently, but gently. 'Have you been obliged to sell anything more?'

'No, no indeed!' she replied cheerfully. 'In fact, I have some good news for you.'

'Good news! That would indeed be welcome.'

Breaking away from him, she walked over to the sideboard, and picked up a square package wrapped in brown paper. 'I only acquired it yesterday,' she said. 'I was going to wrap it up more prettily for you, but you have saved me the bother.' She handed it to him, and he opened it carefully. Inside was a miniature. The beautiful, gracious face of his mother looked out at him from it. He swallowed hard.

'How? Where?' he managed to say.

'Devonshire found it in a little shop in Buxton,' she told him. 'He recognized it and asked them to put it on one side until I could come and see it. He was sure that it was your mama.'

'You don't know what it means to me to have it back,' he said smiling at her, his eyes very bright.

'Oh, I think perhaps I do,' she replied softly, after a short silence.

That evening as they sat at dinner, after all the desultory conversation and gossip of London had been exhausted, Lady Ravendale said, 'What brings you here this time, Daniel?'

'Why, the pleasure of seeing you of course, my dear.'

'Daniel,' she prompted.

He was silent for a long time, then he said, 'I think I've almost definitely decided to ask Claudia Bryce to marry me.'

'Oh, Daniel,' she said again, but this time, her voice was more in the nature of a wail.

'Hear me out,' he said, pouring himself another glass of wine after offering some to her, which she refused. 'There are many things to be said in favour of such a match. Firstly, she is disposed to like me . . . '

'Well, what woman would not, unless she

99

were entirely demented,' declared his aunt.

'Thank you! I am sure I shall value your very biased opinion just as I should,' said Ravendale ironically. 'Secondly, as she lives nearby, she is under no delusions about the state of my finances. Thirdly, I believe she already considers herself committed to me. Fourthly she is very pretty, as I'm sure you'll agree.' Lady Ravendale continued to look at him very steadily, her brows raised. 'Oh, all right then, she's also very rich, or at any rate, she will be,' added the earl roughly.

'Daniel, if you are so convinced that marrying her is the right thing, why do you need to give me so many reasons?' she said quietly.

He did not answer her directly. Instead, he said, 'You must know better than anyone that I cannot afford to marry a poor woman.' She turned away from him and for a few moments there was silence between them. Then she turned back towards him, and there were tears in her eyes.

'Daniel, forgive me,' she whispered.

'Forgive you?' He leaned over to clasp her hands. 'My dear, you are not to blame.'

'I cannot help thinking that I could have done *something*,' she said. 'But I did not know. How could I have been so stupid?'

'Enough of this,' he said in firm tones. 'We

have talked of this before. My grandfather halved the family fortune through his gaming. My uncle — your husband — did what he could to remedy matters, but when he died, my father contrived to waste everything that he had saved — and more! What part you played in that sorry business will always be a complete mystery to me.'

'Yes, I know,' replied his aunt, still looking distressed. 'But I cannot help thinking that if I had tried harder, I could have persuaded your poor mama to make economies.' Ravendale gave a crack of laughter.

'Aunt Rosie, I loved mama dearly, as you know, but it would, I think, have been as easy to persuade her to enter a nunnery as it would have been to induce her to economize! The only thing that I regret as far as you are concerned, is that Uncle Gervase did not make independent provision for you. It might have prevented my father getting his hands on your money.'

'He did not want to break up the estate any more,' replied his aunt. 'And besides, wise though he was in many ways he was very naïve with regard to your father's weakness; and truth to tell, I was no wiser. When Roger said that he had given up gaming, we both wanted to believe him. He was always your uncle's beloved younger brother.' They were silent for a few moments, each one absorbed by private recollections. Then Lady Ravendale said softly, 'He would have been so proud of you. We were never blessed with children of our own, but you are exactly as he would have wanted a son of his to be.'

'I'm not really so very admirable,' returned the earl, getting up from his place. 'Had I any sense, I would have sold out and been back here looking into how my father was conducting his affairs, rather than prancing about Europe in a red coat!'

'Daniel, don't be so absurd,' declared Lady Ravendale, also getting to her feet. 'You were doing your duty.'

'Exactly so,' he replied. 'So do not be surprised if I feel bound to do it now.'

Her shoulders drooped and she gave a little sigh. 'Very well,' she said. 'But promise me this — that you will not take this step without being absolutely certain.'

'I promise,' he agreed with a smile.

★  ★  ★

The following day, he joined his aunt at the breakfast table before going over the estate accounts. In his grandfather's day, the estate had employed a bailiff. There had been other estates, too, in the south of England, the profits of which had helped to support Ravendale. But the more profitable property had been sold before his time, and the money raised from them long since lost in late night transactions over a green baize cloth. Now, the earl acted as his own bailiff, and during his visits to London, his aunt held the reins for him. And she was right, he reflected as he got up from the desk and flexed his muscles. Things were beginning to turn round a little. But that little was not enough. While he waited for matters to improve, there were farms to be repaired, and wages to be paid, and a bad year could still ruin everything. Little though he relished it, there was only one possible solution.

Deciding that a breath of fresh air would do him good, he went in search of Lady Ravendale, in order to invite her to join him for a stroll in the gardens.

'No, thank you,' she answered. 'I have some letters to write which must not wait, and the housekeeper to see. If you're going for a walk, though, you might as well take Princess with you. She could do with some exercise.' Ravendale whistled, and his father's elderly greyhound, who had been lying on the rug with her head on her paws, struggled to her feet, her tail wagging.

'Come on, then,' he said, and walked out of

one of the side doors and on to the terrace. Lady Ravendale watched him as he went, then sighed and sat down at her desk, her important letters temporarily forgotten. Not for the first time, she wondered how life would change here at Ravendale once Daniel was married.

She remembered the day when he had left home, looking so young and proud in his regimentals. He had always been army mad, and to do him justice, his father had never tried to prevent his only son from following his chosen career. Now, Lady Ravendale wondered rather cynically whether he simply wanted to prevent Daniel from discovering the extent of his debts.

There had been a girl in Daniel's life once before, when he had joined the army, and for a time it had seemed that there might be an engagement; but it had all ended very abruptly, and Rosie had never discovered why. The earl, though very fond of his aunt, was a private person, and seldom spoke about his deepest feelings. After that episode, he had shown no interest in any other woman, until recently, when he seemed to have resolved to marry Claudia. She could only pray that Miss Bryce would make him happy, but she very much doubted it. The woman of her imagination whom she had dreamed he might marry bore very little resemblance to the mill-owner's sister. Sighing once more, she picked up her pen again and tried to get on with her letters.

As Ravendale stepped outside, he looked at his home as if observing it for the first time. All around him there was evidence of neglect. There was not sufficient money to employ enough men to care for the gardens, as well as to run the farms and look after the livestock, and so the gardens were having to wait for the time being. Near to the house, there was evidence that Lady Ravendale was doing what she could, but it was far too much for one person to manage. The terrace itself was not in a good state of repair, and he walked the length of it, testing the balustrade for safety, but all seemed to be secure.

Eventually he walked down the steps and crossed the lawn, Princess at his heels. He turned round and looked at the house. It was still a beautiful, gracious dwelling, despite the obvious neglect. He could just remember the Palladian mansion that his grandfather had sold, and was conscious of a feeling of thankfulness that Ravendale had remained, even though it had been the least profitable of the family estates.

This was the house which he had always thought of as his home. This was the house to which he had returned, and where he had spent his school holidays, sometimes with his pretty, fragile mother, until she died when he was fifteen, but always with his aunt, who had invariably been the strong, reliable presence in his life. Now it fell to his lot to care for her, as she had cared for him. He had often regretted the absence of brothers, sisters and cousins in his lonely boyhood. Now, he was glad that he only had himself and his aunt to provide for.

In some ways, there was no immediate need for him to marry; but marry he must, for there was no other heir, and to marry Claudia would be an easy solution. She was very ready to become the Countess of Ravendale; indeed, he had a suspicion that she already regarded the position as hers by right. There would be no necessity for expensive visits to London in order to seek her out and woo her, and there was no doubt that her undoubted beauty would set off what remained of the family jewels to perfection.

He had told himself these things before, but now for some reason they rang hollow. For the first time, he began to wonder whether anything would compensate him for the fact that he did not like Claudia very much. She did not seem to enter into any of his interests or concerns, and he was almost certain that he would have to fight very hard for his aunt's right to remain with them after the marriage.

He had never had an ideal of what his future wife should be like, except to think that in some way, she ought to be something like his beloved aunt. Now, as a kind of farewell to freedom, he tried to call to mind this mythical damsel. No clear picture came into his mind, but he found himself envisaging someone grander of spirit and bigger of heart than the mistress of Riverside. He had been in love once, but the object of his affections had cynically played him off against another suitor, finally choosing his wealthier rival. Well, Claudia was the wealthy one this time, and if she was only marrying him for his title, what did it matter? At least she was honest about it!

Abruptly, he turned away from his contemplation of the house, intending to walk a little way into the home wood; but to his surprise, he found himself looking directly at Claudia's companion. Perhaps because he had just been thinking of Claudia, it struck him as never before how unlike his betrothed-to-be she was. She was tall for a woman, and many would have said that she was too tall. She was bigly made, her dark hair was of an unfashionable shade, and her clothes were well cut but unremarkable. But her face was flushed with health, and although her hair was somewhat tousled, the effect was not unbecoming. Most striking of all, there was an animation and a vigour about her which threw Claudia's constant languor into strong relief.

'Oh! Lord Ravendale!' she exclaimed. She was clearly very disconcerted by the encounter. 'I beg your pardon!'

'Miss Pascoe,' he said, with an inclination of his head. At that moment, Princess came trotting up to Freya, her tail wagging, her tongue hanging out. 'Do you mind dogs?' he asked her, catching hold of the dog's collar.

'No, I like them,' she replied, bending to pat Princess as the earl released her. 'I used to have a dog very like this one.' He watched the confident way in which she scratched Princess behind her ears, and contrasted it to the manner in which Claudia had shooed the dog away distastefully during her last visit.

After a moment or two, because he could not resist, Ravendale said disapprovingly, 'Walking alone *again*' He shook his head, tutting. 'I would have thought that you would have learned your lesson by now.'

She flushed, standing up straight. 'I trust you do not intend to insult me again, sir,' she said.

'My intention on that occasion was to warn rather than to insult,' he replied.

'If so, then your warning was made in a singularly insulting manner,' she said swiftly.

'Forgive me, ma'am,' he answered her gently. 'But when I attempted to warn you in a less insulting manner, you took no notice.'

She flushed a little, rather mortified by the justice of this observation, but found the courage to say, 'It is only from my brother or perhaps from those I respect that I am willing to take such warnings.'

He grinned. 'That's put me firmly in my place, hasn't it? So you have a brother, Miss Pascoe?'

'Yes,' she said shortly. Then, afraid that such an abrupt answer might attract too much attention, she improvised, 'David is a tutor to a family in Hertfordshire.'

'Are you very close?' he asked her. 'It must be difficult for you when your employment does not permit you to meet frequently.'

'Yes. I do sometimes worry about him,' murmured Freya, thinking of John.

'Is he younger than you?' asked Ravendale.

'No, he is older,' she answered rather shortly. The obvious interest that he was showing was in marked contrast to the indifference of both Miss Bryce and her brother, neither of whom had shown any interest in her family whatsoever. His concern seemed almost out of place in one whose way of life showed so little thought for the needs of those dependent upon him; and yet it made her feel very guilty about lying to him.

'I beg your pardon for seeming intrusive,' he said, misinterpreting her taciturnity, 'but I suppose I am a little envious of those who have brothers or sisters. I was always an only one, you see.'

'Poor little boy,' she murmured involuntarily. Then, conscious that he was looking at her a little curiously, she went on quickly, anxious to deflect any further questions that he might pose with regard to her brother. 'Is that your house?'

'Yes, that is Ravendale Hall,' he answered her, turning to look at it. 'Pray come inside for some refreshment and meet my aunt, then I will drive you back to Riverside.'

'Oh no,' said Freya hurriedly. 'There is no need. I can walk back the way I have come, if you will only direct me.' She turned back towards the wood, then hesitated.

'Precisely,' said Ravendale dryly. 'The way down is rather difficult to find especially when the trees are in leaf. Even with my directions, you would probably miss your way. You will really be much better advised to come inside.' When she continued to hesitate, he went on, 'I'll drive you back directly if you prefer. Then as we go, you can tell me what I have done to make you disapprove of me.'

She gave a little gasp. 'Surely your conduct at Peveril Castle was sufficient,' she said as she walked with him towards the Hall.

'Possibly,' he replied. 'But do you know, I have the strangest feeling that there is something else?'

Freya looked at the beautiful gracious house which showed such obvious signs of neglect, and she was tempted to remind him that it was because of his profligate behaviour that his home was in such a deplorable state. Before she could say anything, however, they were approached by a small, dark elegantly dressed lady, who had come out on to the terrace, and was now walking towards them across the grass.

'I will find out what it is,' he said softly before the lady was within earshot. Then as they met her, he introduced Freya to his aunt.

'Miss Pascoe is Claudia's companion,' said Ravendale.

'Oh, my dear, I am so sorry!' exclaimed Lady Ravendale, who then, realizing the infelicitous nature of what she had just said, covered her mouth and whispered, 'I beg your pardon! I shouldn't have said that.'

Freya hastily suppressed a giggle, and

could not help glancing at Lord Ravendale to see how this implied criticism of his intended might affect him; but she could detect nothing either from his manner or from his expression. For her own part, she did not feel that she owed Miss Bryce any particular loyalty, but neither did she feel that a slighting attitude towards the woman who was supposed to be her employer was appropriate, so she contented herself with saying merely, 'I cannot say that I know Miss Bryce very well as yet.'

'No indeed,' answered Lady Ravendale, belatedly seeking to retrieve the situation. 'Of course, what I meant was that being at the beck and call of another person must be difficult to bear, however agreeable they may be. Have you walked all the way from Riverside?'

'Yes, I have,' replied Freya, bracing herself for a remark that would indicate either criticism or astonishment.

'It is some time since I undertook that walk,' said the countess, surprising her until she recalled that the earl had spoken of his aunt as a countrywoman who enjoyed walking. 'It is a pretty path at all times of the year. But the day is warm, and you must be quite tired. Come inside for a cup of tea or some lemonade.'

'I should not really stay,' she murmured. 'I was only out walking because Miss Bryce had not yet got up. But she will be rising soon, so I ought to return immediately.'

'You cannot possibly leave without having had something to drink. I will send a message to say that I encountered you on your walk and pressed you to join me for some refreshment,' said Lady Ravendale, tucking her hand into Freya's arm and beginning to walk toward the house. 'And if you tell Claudia to come and see me very soon, then that will please her.'

'You will do much better to do as my aunt tells you, Miss Pascoe,' said the earl as he walked beside them. 'I have always done so and have found it to be much the wisest course.'

'Do not listen to him,' put in his aunt in a lively manner. 'Very often, the only notice he takes of my advice is to do the opposite.'

Looking up then, Freya surprised a look which passed between aunt and nephew which was pregnant with meaning. She found herself wondering whether Lady Ravendale, who clearly held her nephew in great affection, had striven in vain to keep him from gambling to excess. Her attention was brought back to the present by the countess's saying, 'Do take care on these steps, Miss

Pascoe. They are not in the best possible state of repair.'

They entered the drawing-room and Freya noticed its shabbiness just as the earl had done. At the same time, however, she contrasted its welcoming character very favourably with the cold perfection and formality of the Bryces' residence.

'Will you have tea, Miss Pascoe, or would you prefer wine or lemonade?' the countess asked. Freya chose the latter, and while Lord Ravendale was sending for refreshments, her ladyship invited her guest to sit with her on a somewhat worn rose-patterned sofa. 'Do tell me, Miss Pascoe, for how long have you been in Miss Bryce's employ?'

'For a few days only,' replied Freya. She toyed with the idea of saying that it was only a temporary arrangement, but decided that it would be far too difficult to explain such an unusual situation without giving away something of her real circumstances. Instead, she went on, 'I have been lately accompanying Lady Terrington. When I heard that Miss Bryce was coming to Derbyshire, I seized the chance of visiting the Peak District. Such an opportunity has not come my way before.'

'And have you been able to take in anything of the Derbyshire scene?'

'Yes indeed,' murmured Freya. 'Miss

Bryce, as I believe I told you, is not an early riser, so I have been walking in the mornings, before she is up.'

'There are some fine walks around Castleton, are there not, Daniel?' said Lady Ravendale in all innocence.

'Indeed there are,' agreed his lordship, pouring himself some wine whilst the butler set down the ladies' lemonade. 'Have you tried any of them, Miss Pascoe?'

Freya was glad that she had not yet taken a sip of lemonade, or the sheer effrontery of the man might have caused her to choke. 'I would very much like to climb Mam Tor, but I am told that it would be inadvisable to do so alone,' she replied. It was then Ravendale's turn to choke!

'Oh Daniel, do be careful,' scolded his aunt unsympathetically. 'Drink your drinks more slowly.'

'Yes, Aunt Rosie,' he said meekly, as soon as he was able, which made Freya laugh again.

The brief time that she spent at Ravendale was wholly enjoyable. The countess, although much higher in degree than Claudia Bryce, showed no hint of condescension in her conversation, and although she did not ask questions about her visitor's family, Freya felt instinctively that this was owing to her innate sensitivity and not because of any lack of interest. After half an hour, when Freya said that she must be going, Lady Ravendale made no protest, and the earl went immediately to have the horses put to.

'My dear, I have very much enjoyed your visit,' said the older lady. 'Do, please, come again.'

'I should love to,' confessed Freya. 'But I feel that Miss Bryce's wishes must come first.'

'Oh, not in the early morning, surely,' answered the other in a way that made Freya laugh. 'In any case, I am going to give a ball now that Daniel has come home. I shall need someone to help me with the arrangements, if Claudia can spare you.'

'Gladly,' replied Freya. That must be the betrothal ball that Claudia had mentioned, she decided.

'By the way, pray tell Claudia that I would like to entertain her to tea tomorrow afternoon if she should be free,' added Lady Ravendale as they made their farewells at the door. Freya promised to pass on the message, and then she left, feeling that she had gained an agreeable friend.

Ravendale was waiting outside and helped Freya up into his gig, which, like the house and everything in it, did not look to be in the best state of repair.

'I'm afraid it's a bit shabby, but as you have seen the state of the roads, I'm sure that you will understand that it's not worth driving anything smarter around here.'

Remembering the conversation that she had had with the Bryces on the way to their house, she could not resist saying, 'I wonder you do not do anything about them, then.'

He glanced at her a little sharply, but merely said, 'I should like to do so, but sadly there are many other calls upon my purse at this time.'

'Yes, so I can imagine,' she answered a little tartly, thinking of his gambling.

Although he glanced at her a little sharply, he made no response to this, but instead changed the subject by saying, 'I am glad that you came in to see my aunt. She loves the Hall, but sometimes feels a little lonely here.'

'I can see that it is somewhat isolated,' agreed Freya. 'Does she never go to London?'

'She has not been for many years. When my uncle was alive, they used to go to London together, but since he died she has remained here.'

Freya could not help wondering whether he encouraged his aunt to stay in Derbyshire so that she would remain ignorant of his ruinous habits.

'Did you succeed your uncle?' she asked him.

'No, my uncle was the older brother, but he and my aunt had no children, so my father succeeded him. We are a very small family, Miss Pascoe. I had no brothers or sisters, as I have already told you so there is just my aunt and myself left.' They travelled on in silence for a short time, until the earl said eventually, 'Miss Pascoe, do you believe that a man should always do his duty — whatever the circumstances?' She looked at him in puzzlement. He smiled slightly. 'You are surprised at my question, and perhaps wonder that I should ask such a thing of someone whom I have known for such a short time.'

'Yes — yes, I am,' she admitted.

'Sometimes, it is easier to gain an unbiased view from someone who is not involved in a situation. And, forgive me for saying so, ma'am, but you strike me as being a person who does not allow other influences to sway her too readily.'

'I hope I am always ready to take advice — when it proceeds from a source that I respect,' she answered. His lordship's lips twisted cynically.

'I am left with the uncomfortable feeling that you do not respect me,' he murmured. At first she was at a loss as to how to answer him. She could not respect a man who gambled away his inheritance, and who made advances to one woman whilst being as good as engaged to another. But she had liked his aunt immediately, and Lady Ravendale's love for her nephew was undeniable, and this had to give her pause. Furthermore, the concern that he had shown for the well-being of one whom he believed to be a penniless companion had given her reason to think again.

'Your actions make respect a little difficult,' she said eventually.

'So then I have my answer.'

'Your answer, my lord?' she asked, wrinkling her brow.

'A man who does his duty must command respect from those who witness his actions. I would therefore hazard a guess that you would say that a man must always do his duty.'

'Whenever possible, I think he should,' she agreed.

He sighed. 'Sometimes I wish I'd never left the army,' he said. 'There, one's duty was clear. Here, it seems that two different courses of action are possible, and there is no one to give me orders as to which course I should take.' Again, silence fell.

'But since you talk of duty, you must feel

that one of those courses of action is the proper one,' Freya said eventually.

He laughed humourlessly. 'You are right of course,' he said. They were by now drawing up outside the Bryces' house. He looked straight at her. 'Very well then, so be it,' he added. Piers Bryce came out to meet them as Ravendale was getting out of the gig.

'Ravendale!' he exclaimed. 'Come in, come in! My sister will be very pleased to see you, I believe.'

'And I to see her,' replied the earl. He turned to Freya 'Thank you for your advice,' he said, before going inside. Bryce came forward and helped Freya down.

'What advice might that have been?' he asked her curiously.

'I have no idea,' she replied, walking towards the door.

'Wait,' said Bryce. 'I don't believe you've seen the gardens, have you? Allow me to show you around. I'm told that they are at their best at this time.' Freya allowed him to conduct her around the side of the house and into the gardens, where a beautiful assortment of roses made a fine show. They strolled around the gravel paths together, talking in a relaxed manner about these and other gardens they had known. Freya found herself comparing them in her mind to the gardens that she had seen so recently at Ravendale. There was no doubt that Piers Bryce's garden was far better tended; but there was a romantic dishevelment about the gardens at the Hall that Freya had found very attractive.

After a short stroll, they wandered back inside and going to the drawing-room, found Miss Bryce and Lord Ravendale standing close together. As they entered, Miss Bryce tucked her hand into the earl's arm and smiled, and her expression held a hint of triumph.

'You must be the first to wish us happy,' said the earl, smiling as well. 'Claudia has consented to become my wife.' Piers hurried to congratulate them both, and Freya, following his lead, did the same.

While Piers was embracing his sister, Ravendale turned to Freya and said blandly, 'Miss Pascoe, I must thank you for I owe this to you.'

'To *me*?' she exclaimed in a voice that was too loud. Fortunately Miss Bryce and her brother were too involved in their own conversation to take any notice.

'Why certainly,' he replied. 'Did I not thank you for your advice? You told me to do my duty, and I am doing it.' Then he turned away to speak to Miss and Mr

Bryce, and she was left staring at him, with a horrible feeling in the pit of her stomach that something dreadful had just been set in motion and that she was to blame.

# 7

After this, Freya did not see Lord Ravendale for some days. She was not sorry. Her feelings about him were far too confused for her to resolve them easily. She tried very hard to believe that he and Miss Bryce were welcome to one another, but part of her refused to be convinced. For one thing, there was the obvious affection in which he was held by his aunt, and the affectionate respect with which he treated her in his turn. For another, there was the fact that despite all his failings, some instinct deep inside told her that at bottom, he was good and honourable, and that there was something in him that was worth saving.

If she saw less of Lord Ravendale, she certainly saw more of Piers Bryce than she had expected. Claudia kept to her established pattern of remaining in bed until noon. Her brother, however, began to appear at the breakfast table, and soon Freya found that she seldom ate her breakfast alone, an arrangement which she found agreeable enough. She and John had always broken their fast together, chatting about the plans for the day ahead, so a silent table felt very strange to her.

Mr Bryce, she found, made pleasant enough company, and if his opinions were predictable and his conversation rather shallow, he was perfectly amiable. The only subject which seemed to bring out a less agreeable side of his personality was that of the mill. He certainly resented the fact that the terms of his inheritance meant that he must take an interest in it. At first, Freya had tried to ask him about the business, but clearly he concerned himself in it no more than he was bound to do.

If he disliked the mill, however, there was something in him which enjoyed the deference with which he was acknowledged by his workers by reason of his position. He and Freya took one or two walks together, and on these occasions, the respect with which caps were doffed to him obviously pleased him greatly, although he never had any idea who the people might be who acknowledged him thus.

'It must please them very much to see you in the vicinity,' Freya ventured on one occasion.

'Well, I'm glad it pleases someone,' he replied frankly.

'Do you not have any desire to discover

more about the work that is done in the mill?' she ventured.

'Good God, no,' he answered. 'As long as they all come to work and none of them runs away, why should I bother?'

Freya was at a loss to discover why he had such a desire for her company. In the end, she decided that it could only be because she was a novelty to him, or because she was the only single woman in the vicinity. At times, she wondered whether against all logic he was actually attracted to her, but if he was, he kept his gallantry very much in check, and never strayed over the boundaries set by good taste.

Now that the engagement had been announced, Claudia seemed to be in a much better humour; and if she was not markedly more polite, she was certainly no less so. Freya had expected that Lord Ravendale would ride over every day to see his betrothed, but he did not do so. This surprised Freya until she learned that he had been invited to spend some time at Chatsworth at the duke's behest.

Afternoons at Riverside were usually spent in the drawing-room, situated at the back of the house, looking away from the river. For her part, Freya would have chosen to sit in one of the rooms from which the river could be seen, but knowing Miss Bryce's tastes, she was not surprised at her decision.

Sometimes Freya was obliged to read to her employer, sometimes they both sat and sewed, and sometimes they strolled in the gardens at the kind of dawdling pace that suited Miss Bryce the best. Mr Bryce generally found something else with which to entertain himself in the afternoons, but he always joined them for tea.

Freya found this way of life very irksome, and she longed for news from John to tell her that she was free to go home whenever she liked. Although some days had passed since they had left for Derbyshire, she had heard nothing; but the newspaper that was delivered to Mr Bryce from London contained not a hint of difficulties with the bank, so she was forced to be content.

One day, as they were having tea in the drawing-room, Bryce announced his intention of going to Buxton on the morrow.

'Would you care to accompany me?' he asked his sister.

'Good God, no! Why on earth should I want to be shaken over country roads simply in order to visit a backward provincial town?' was her reply.

Freya saw Bryce glance at her, and the thought struck her that he might be tempted to ask her to go with him. Of course, to accept such an invitation would have been out of the question; but something in his expression meant that she was not entirely surprised when he said to her later, in his sister's absence, 'I am sorry that you will not be going to Buxton tomorrow. It is an interesting town, and I should have enjoyed showing it to you.'

'Perhaps there may be another opportunity,' replied Freya politely.

'I hope so indeed,' said Bryce in a more intense voice, so much so that Freya felt more than half inclined to glance over her shoulder and see if he might be looking at someone else. For the first time, there was something in his eyes which made her feel a little uncomfortable. As she was wholly without acquaintance in Buxton, a visit there without the presence of Claudia would have meant that she was entirely dependent upon Mr Bryce. It struck her that this might have proved to be rather an unnerving experience.

That evening, Miss Bryce said, 'I have just remembered, Miss Pascoe, that Lady Ravendale expressed a desire to see you. She has decided that the ball that she was to give anyway is to be my betrothal ball, and as she needs some help with organizing it, I offered to send you to her to do what you can. You might as well go in the morning. She appears to keep the same peculiar hours as you do.'

Remembering that Lady Ravendale herself had predicted just this eventuality, Freya had to bite back a smile, but she merely agreed to go.

The following day, Mr Bryce left for Buxton quite early, and Freya was on her own once more at the breakfast table. The day was fine, and as she set out to walk to Ravendale, she decided to take the path that followed the course of the road, rather than risk getting lost in the wood. She found the Hall without difficulty, and when she arrived, the countess was outside cutting flowers and putting them in a basket at her feet. She greeted her visitor with great pleasure.

'Miss Pascoe!' she exclaimed. 'How delighted I am to see you again!'

'Miss Bryce told me that you would like some help with the arrangements for the betrothal ball,' answered Freya, picking up the basket and holding it so that Lady Ravendale would not have to bend. The countess pursed her lips.

'I do hope that Claudia made it clear that I wanted to see you for your own sake,' she said firmly.

Freya smiled, but merely said, 'I always think that these tasks are far more agreeable when done with a friend.'

Belatedly, it occurred to her that this might sound presumptuous when they had only met once before, but the countess immediately said, 'Exactly so! Thank you for holding the basket for me. I think I have picked enough flowers now. Let us go inside and have some refreshment, then we can decide how to proceed.'

They went inside, and Freya was struck as before by the faded grandeur of the place. Lady Ravendale sent for lemonade for them both, and then she conducted her guest into the same room in which they had sat on the last occasion. This time, the countess invited Freya to sit at a desk in the window.

'You can be my amanuensis,' she said brightly. 'Now let us make a list of all the things that need to be done. On this occasion, more than any other, I want everything to be just right. *No one* must be allowed to say that anything was not as it should be.' She mentioned no names, but Freya was sure that her ladyship was thinking of Miss Bryce. Obediently, she sat down and the next half-hour was occupied in making lists of guests, and of things to be done. Eventually, Lady Ravendale gave a sigh. 'That is enough for now,' she declared. 'Let's just sit for a while.' She looked around her. 'I love this room. My husband and I used to sit here often.'

'Is it long since your husband died, ma'am?' Freya ventured.

'He died nine years ago,' was the wistful reply. 'He was out supervising some work on the estate when a bridge collapsed beneath him. He was killed immediately.'

'I am so sorry,' said Freya with quick sympathy.

'You are very good,' replied the countess. 'I can assure you that for the most part, I am quite reconciled. It is only sometimes . . . ' Her voice drifted off, and a moment or two later, she said in a different tone, 'Some more lemonade' Freya gratefully accepted, as the day was warm, and Lady Ravendale poured them both some more from the jug which the butler had brought earlier. 'For my part, I cannot understand how gentlemen can drink alcohol in the morning,' she confided. 'If I do so, I always find myself falling asleep in the afternoon, and an afternoon nap is one thing I cannot abide! If I should chance to fall asleep in my chair, I always wake up feeling like death.'

Freya smilingly agreed, and thought briefly of her employer. Miss Bryce always lay down on her bed for an hour in the afternoon, even though she had probably only risen three hours before. They were silent for a short time, and Freya glanced around the room once again.

'I can see what you are thinking,' said her hostess. 'The old place is not in the best state of repair, is it?'

Freya protested that those had not been her thoughts at all. 'I would never be so uncivil as to suggest such a thing,' she added.

'No,' agreed the other. 'But admit that the thought *has* come into your mind, if not now then at some other time.' Freya said nothing, and for a few moments, silence reigned. Then, eventually, Lady Ravendale said, 'Although we have not known one another for very long, I believe that you are a trustworthy person in whom I can confide without fear of indiscretion.'

'I have had to be discreet before,' admitted Freya, thinking about the anxiety concerning the bank.

'I knew it.' She was silent again. 'Gambling has always been this family's demon,' she said at last. 'My husband escaped the taint, but he was rare. You cannot imagine what it is like, living in a house where nothing is safe; where at any moment, you might find that a dear possession has been taken, if it can be sold, in order to provide money for gambling.' She paused again 'I suppose I should not say this, but Lord Ravendale even took and gambled away his mother's wedding necklace, replacing the jewels with paste in an effort to conceal his crime.'

'Oh no!' exclaimed Freya distressfully. It was one thing to suspect Ravendale of such crimes, but another to have his infamous deeds confirmed by one in a position to know the truth of the matter.

'I am afraid so. Indeed, had it not been for — '

Freya was not to hear the end of her sentence, for at this point the door opened and Lord Ravendale came in. Knowing what she did about him, Freya half expected him to look pale, lined and degenerate. It seemed quite unfair, almost hypocritical, that a man who had been so profligate should have such an erect bearing and so healthy a complexion. She was suddenly seized with such rage at his behaviour that she wondered how she could possibly be civil. It was, therefore, a relief when after greeting her briefly, he turned to his aunt and said, 'I find that I am obliged to ride into Buxton. Is there anything that you need me to procure for you?'

'No, I thank you,' she replied, smiling at him in an affectionate way. 'Certainly, I shall be needing supplies from there very soon, though, for Miss Pascoe and I have been very busy this morning, and all for your benefit!'

'For me?' he asked, looking at Freya, his brows raised. A smile still lingered about his mouth. 'I am obliged to you both. In what cause have you been so busy?'

'We have been making preparations for your betrothal ball,' replied his aunt. His smile disappeared, but he turned to Freya and bowed courteously.

'Then I am doubly obliged to Miss Pascoe.' Lady Ravendale wrinkled her brow.

'Doubly obliged? Why so?'

'It was Miss Pascoe who encouraged me to . . . ah . . . press my suit,' he responded. Freya glanced quickly at Lady Ravendale, and surprised on her face an expression of reproach. 'However, if you have no commissions for me *now*, I shall be on my way,' Lord Ravendale went on. He smiled at his aunt again, and she smiled back at him. Freya found herself wondering at the ways of families, in which individuals could behave quite scandalously towards other family members, and still manage to retain their affection.

'If you are leaving now, you will not be able to escort Miss Pascoe home,' her ladyship protested. 'Can you not delay your journey?'

At the present moment, Freya felt that she would rather die than be obliged to him in any way, so she was relieved when he said, 'Sadly not. However, I will order the gig for Miss Pascoe if you wish it.'

'By no means,' said Freya hastily. 'I enjoyed the walk here, and shall enjoy the return journey just as much.'

He nodded briefly, and with a polite farewell, he was gone.

'His business must be pressing,' said Lady Ravendale concernedly. Freya could not help wondering, with a sinking feeling, if his aunt suspected that he was going to Buxton to indulge his craving for gambling. Even in a provincial town, there must be others who shared his addiction. Suddenly, she had no desire to talk further about the earl's failings, and so she turned the conversation to interesting places in Derbyshire.

The morning passed very pleasantly, and when the time came to leave, Freya was amazed at how long she had stayed.

'You will come again soon, won't you?' begged Lady Ravendale. 'You have clearly had experience of organizing these kinds of functions before, and your help and advice is invaluable. And I hope you don't mind my saying so, but I cannot remember the last time I took to anyone so strongly on so short an acquaintance.'

Freya felt very much the same, but

although she expressed a similar pleasure, she was conscious of a feeling of constraint about going back to Ravendale Hall.

The truth was, she acknowledged to herself as she walked back, that she did not want to spend any more time in Lord Ravendale's company than she had to. She found him unsettling. He took such a high-handed attitude towards her with regard to her behaviour, whilst his own life clearly did not bear very close scrutiny. And yet she was forced to admit, if she were honest, that at other times, he could be agreeable, conversable, sensitive, even attractive.

She halted so suddenly that if anyone had been following close behind, they would certainly have fallen over her. There! She had admitted it! She found him attractive! A gambler who had stooped to taking his own mother's jewellery, a man who put the very home of his aunt at risk; a man who was as good as engaged to one of the most unpleasant women of her acquaintance, and whose sole reason for becoming engaged was probably to acquire more funds to support his ruinous habit.

That settled it, she decided as she walked back into Riverside. She was clearly becoming unhinged, and the sooner John managed to set affairs in the bank to rights, the better.

Then she could leave this place and, with any luck, never set eyes on Lord Ravendale or his future wife again.

★ ★ ★

Desirable though such an eventuality might be, Freya found that that evening, she was obliged to sit at table not only with Miss Bryce and her brother, but also with Lord Ravendale. Lady Ravendale had been invited as well, but the earl made his aunt's excuses.

'Unfortunately, she has a severe headache,' he explained, 'and has asked to be excused.'

'How annoying,' replied Miss Bryce, somehow conveying the impression that Lady Ravendale's indisposition was a deliberate act in order to cause the maximum inconvenience to her hostess's arrangements.

'Yes, indeed,' agreed the earl blandly. 'Possibly the most annoying aspect of the business is the lack of vision in one eye and the flashing lights in the other. When I left her, she was barely able to speak for the pain.'

'Very tiresome,' drawled Miss Bryce, apparently oblivious to his sarcasm.

'Oh, poor Lady Ravendale!' exclaimed Freya quickly. 'My brother sometimes suffers from migraine, and for him there is no solution but to lie down in a darkened room.'

Ravendale turned and smiled at her, and despite herself, she felt her heart give a little lurch. 'That is my aunt's remedy,' he replied. 'Also a tisane, which the housekeeper prepares for her.' Then he went on, disconcerting her, 'I trust that your brother's migraines are not too frequent. It cannot be easy to accommodate such a complaint in a busy tutor's life.' Freya coloured at this reminder of her deceit.

'No . . . no, not too frequent,' she stammered.

'Oh, your brother is a *tutor* is he?' exclaimed Miss Bryce with a great air of condescension. 'How ghastly.'

'I detested all my tutors, and led them a merry dance,' laughed Piers.

To her surprise, Freya felt her anger rising, as if her brother really had been engaged in that occupation. Before she could open her mouth to speak, however, Ravendale said smoothly, 'Then you were very misguided. They might have taught you much, and they were certainly worthy of some respect.'

'Oh, don't be so stuffy,' declared Claudia. 'Tell me instead if your business in Buxton prospered today.'

'Yes, come to think of it I saw you in the town today,' put in Bryce, oblivious to the set down that he had just received.

137

'Oh, you were there too, were you? No, sadly my business was not successful. I hope that you had better fortune, Bryce.'

'Quite satisfactory,' replied Bryce. He glanced at Freya, and again, she received the impression that he would have liked to have invited her to go with him, but she really did not want to think about that now. For the first time, she was feeling acutely uneasy about her masquerade, and she began to consider what might be the reaction of those she was deceiving when her true identity was revealed.

Once at the dinner table, Claudia seemed determined to make up for the time lost to her whilst her fiancé had been away by monopolizing him completely. She gave him her sweetest smiles, laughed at all his pleasantries and in general, conducted herself very much in the manner of an acknowledged beauty, who knew the art of entrapping a man, and was determined to employ it to the full. Ravendale, Freya observed cynically, seemed completely bowled over by her performance. Her lack of sympathy for his aunt's complaint might never have been expressed.

No one observing Miss Bryce on this occasion could possibly realize what an unpleasant young woman she could be. Freya thought it a pity that the laughing good humour that she displayed at the table would only last for as long as she and Ravendale were in the same room. *She'll lead him a dance*, Freya thought to herself, and tried to feel satisfaction at the notion; but the idea only made her feel strangely depressed.

'Have you had your fill of Derbyshire yet, Miss Pascoe?' asked Piers, breaking in upon her reverie.

'By no means,' she replied. 'There is so much to see, so much beauty to be appreciated.'

'But it's all the same,' he protested between mouthfuls of fish. 'Just trees, fields and hills, you know.'

'Yes, but they are constantly changing,' she protested. 'Why, a hill can be any shade of green, brown or purple, depending on the season. And a tree's shape varies as it grows, and as it buds, flowers, or sheds its leaves. Why, the very woods above your house here — '

'Not bad for shooting,' put in Bryce thoughtfully. 'Care to take a gun out sometime, Ravendale?'

'We'll see,' smiled the earl, but he was looking at Freya rather than at his host.

As Freya had expected, Miss Bryce's smiling charm lasted until the dining-room

139

door closed behind them when they left the gentlemen to their port.

'Fetch my lace handkerchief from my bedroom,' she said before drifting into the drawing-room. Freya climbed the stairs unhurriedly. Miss Bryce's lack of courtesy might be infuriating, but at least the errand meant a few minutes less of her company!

The men did not linger over their wine for very long, and when they entered the drawing-room, it was Bryce who looked the more flushed. Claudia rang for the tea tray and whilst they were waiting for it to be brought, Ravendale wandered over to the window, where he was soon joined by his host.

Soon, the conversation between the gentlemen fell to sporting pursuits. Whilst they were talking, Claudia turned to Freya and, with her sweetest smile, said, 'I do trust that this detestable habit of yours of flirting with Ravendale will cease immediately. It is quite inappropriate for one of your station.'

'Flirting?' said Freya in mystified tones.

'Yes, indeed, miss. Don't think that I was blind to those eyes that you were making at him across the table.'

'Miss Bryce, we were only talking together!' declared Freya, but Claudia did not allow her to finish.

'I have already told you that Ravendale is mine,' she went on, 'and he knows it as well as I. Or perhaps you had forgotten that very soon his ring will be on my finger? If you cherish any foolish dreams that he might turn to you from me, then have a look in your mirror, and ask yourself whether such an overgrown, plain creature as yourself could ever attract such a man as he!'

Freya looked at the face of her employer. Her expression was still all sweetness, so much so that it was hard to believe that such unkind sentiments had just come from that rosebud mouth.

Not trusting herself to say anything in response without her voice shaking, whether from anger or from hurt she could not tell, Freya got up from her place and walked over to one of the windows. As she did so, she caught sight of herself in one of the mirrors. All that Miss Bryce had said was true. Freya knew it, and it had not been necessary for Claudia to point it out.

Nothing that Claudia had said was new to her, but the spitefulness with which it had been expressed was outside Freya's normal experience. She smiled a little wryly. Flirt with Lord Ravendale? It had never occurred to her to do such a thing; and as for attracting him, she had not considered such a

141

possibility. So why did Miss Bryce's blunt assertion that such a thing would be impossible cause her even the smallest distress?

That night, in her room, she seriously considered the possibility of handing in her notice and leaving immediately. She felt that she owed no particular loyalty to Miss Bryce, and Mr Bryce, though handsome, seemed to be a man without high aspirations or deep sentiments. As on previous occasions, the thought of not letting John down gave her pause, but now she had another reason for staying. It had not escaped her notice that Lady Ravendale did not care for Claudia, and from odd remarks that she had let slip, Freya had gathered that the betrothal ball was going to be a considerable ordeal for her. For the sake of her new friend, even if for no other reason, she resolved that she would remain until the ball was over. Then, quietly, she would inform Lady Ravendale of her real identity, and assure her that she would be a very welcome visitor if ever she wanted to escape from her new niece-in-law!

One question did rather intrigue her. Even though she, Freya, was under some compulsion to remain, Miss Bryce was under no compulsion to retain her. Why, then, had she not dismissed her companion immediately upon feeling the suspicion that she was flirting with her fiancé? Freya could only suppose that as she needed a companion for form's sake, she might as well have one who threw her own fragile prettiness into strong relief. Even Miss Bryce could not have seriously thought that her companion and Lord Ravendale were flirting. Perhaps, then, her accusations had simply been a means of warning Freya off for the future.

Whatever might be the reason for Miss Bryce's hostility, however, to live in this kind of atmosphere, in which she felt that she was just a small step away from disapproval, was entirely new to her. It made her wonder what kind of childhood Claudia must have had in order to make her into the kind of person that she was. This idea turned her thoughts once again to Lord Ravendale. She remembered the kindness that he had shown to her, and decided that his loving aunt must always have had a considerable influence upon him. *Such a man must be redeemable*, she told herself again; and then she realized where such thoughts were taking her.

*Oh John!* She exclaimed, punching the pillow and turning over restlessly for what seemed like the hundredth time. *Please write soon, or come and get me out of here!*

# 8

The following day, Freya received a letter from Lady Terrington, which she opened and read eagerly. It was full of news and gossip, and caused her to chuckle more than she had done since arriving in Derbyshire. In it, her friend reminded her that the time allotted for their bet would soon have expired.

> . . . *so you will no doubt be claiming your due penalty! I would have thought that you would have had enough of Derbyshire by now. Indeed, since you left London, I have heard things about Miss B. that have made me sorry that I ever challenged you. 'Spiteful, idle and shockingly untruthful' were the comments that I heard.*

Freya smiled ruefully. Had she had enough of Derbyshire? More than enough of this particular corner, certainly. And as for Miss Bryce, Lady Terrington's informant was certainly accurate in part, although, to be fair, Freya had not caught her employer in untruthfulness, although she did remember that Claudia had told her that the ball would be to celebrate her betrothal, when in fact at that time, Ravendale had not yet proposed. She read on.

*I chanced to see your brother at a concert last night. He looked to be tired but in good spirits. I don't suppose he's written to you — remember, I have brothers so I know the species — but I did ask him if he had any message for you. He said 'I've no news — but tell her that no news is good news, so they say.' Make of that what you will.*

Clearly nothing had changed at the bank, either for better or worse. She would just have to be patient for a little longer.

The day followed the same pattern that Freya had now come to expect. She breakfasted, took her morning walk, then occupied herself with seeing the housekeeper and the cook. Miss Bryce had delegated these duties to her, declaring that they were far too fatiguing and tedious.

Eventually, Claudia emerged. It seemed as though she might have realized that she had gone too far in what she had said the previous evening, for she eyed Freya a little warily, and was as cordial as Freya had ever known her.

She even thanked her companion for the tasks she had performed.

'I declare, I do not know where you find all your energy,' the beauty said frankly as she lounged on one of the sofas in the salon. 'I am not sure how it can be, but whereas in London I find myself to be quite energetic, and ready to be up and about at all hours, in the country I can hardly find enough energy even to breathe.'

'It is quite the reverse with me,' responded Freya.

'That is just as well, as I wish you to make preparation for some guests who are to arrive tomorrow. They are coming for my betrothal ball, of course.'

'How many guests will there be?' Freya asked her.

'One couple, Mr and Mrs Siddall. Mrs Siddall is my particular friend, and we shall have plenty to say to one another, so I shan't be needing you much. There is a possibility that Mrs Siddall's mother, Mrs Baxter, may be coming too. She is a sickly sort of woman, so she may need some attention from you, but from past experience she will probably spend much of her time in her room. That will free you to give every assistance to Lady Ravendale.'

Freya readily agreed. It had been clear

right from the beginning that she and Miss Bryce were never going to be boon companions, whereas she had immediately felt herself to be in sympathy with the countess. As long as she did not bump into the earl too frequently, the course of action proposed by Miss Bryce would suit her very well.

Mrs Siddall proved to be as small and dainty as Claudia, although not quite so pretty, and very much inclined to admire her friend, all of which, as might have been supposed, went down extremely well with her hostess. On being introduced to Freya, Mrs Siddall opened her rather protuberant brown eyes very wide and exclaimed, 'Good heaventh! A gianteth!'

Freya, who was quite certain that she had been prompted beforehand to make such a remark, longed to knock the two young ladies' heads together. Instead, she contented herself with a thin smile, and asked whether the Siddalls had had a good journey.

'Yes, thank you, very good, until the last half a mile or so,' replied Mr Siddall 'But after careful examination, I think that all my teeth are still in place!'

Freya laughed. 'I love the countryside, but getting about can sometimes prove to be difficult,' she agreed. Mr Siddall was a tall, sensible-looking man, and Freya could not help wondering how he had come to choose such a very silly woman for his wife.

Mrs Baxter seemed very pale and rather unsteady on her feet, and she certainly looked as if she had found the journey trying. Mrs Siddall appeared to be quite unaffected by her mother's obvious discomfort, and it was left to Freya to help the older lady upstairs to her room, and send for tea to soothe her.

When she came downstairs, having left Mrs Baxter in the care of her maid, Mr Siddall and Mr Bryce had gone to the stables to inspect the horses. She was about to enter the drawing-room when she heard her name mentioned.

' . . . Miss Pascoe, poor dear, throwing herself at Ravendale in a manner that would be positively humorous if it were not so pathetic!'

'I thuppothe she mutht be at her latht pwayerth,' replied Mrs Siddall. 'One should weally pity her.'

'Oh, I do, believe me,' sighed Miss Bryce. 'But I pity Ravendale more. The poor man finds it very embarrassing, and of course he does not wish to be rude.'

Freya did not wait to hear any more. Leaving the house by a side door, she went into the garden in order to cool her hot cheeks. Throw herself at him! She had never done such a thing, had she? True, she had walked to his house and met him, but that had been purely by chance, and the second time, she had gone to see his aunt and not to see him. Naturally she had conversed with him, but was not aware that she had done so in a forward manner. What had she done for Ravendale to find her embarrassing?

It could be that Claudia was lying, of course; but what reason would there be for her to do that? She had not been aware that she and Mrs Siddall were being overheard after all. All that she could think of was that he was in some way taking his revenge for the way in which she had spurned his advances at Peveril Castle. Whatever his reasons, however, he would from now on be left in no doubt that his way of life, his manners and his morals, and above all his boundless conceit, filled her with absolute disgust!

At that moment, she would have been delighted to have given the objectionable earl a piece of her mind, but when she turned round to walk back to the house — her furious, energetic pacing having taken her some distance from it — she encountered not Lord Ravendale, but Mr Bryce. He was alone, and as he met her, he smiled warmly in greeting.

'Miss Pascoe! You are taking advantage of this fine day, I see. Are you going on one of your long walks, and if so, may I accompany you?' She was about to decline, when it occurred to her that if she went inside, she would have no excuse for not joining Miss Bryce and Mrs Siddall.

'I was just exploring the gardens,' she answered.

'Then let me escort you, and show you some of its beauties which perhaps you had not seen before.'

'But what of Mr Siddall?' Freya asked, looking round.

'Oh, Siddall has gone riding. He'll be gone for a while yet.' They began to walk.

'You did not wish to accompany him, then,' said Freya.

'No, I had other plans,' he answered, glancing at her, but not in such a pointed way that she could be certain that he meant that he had planned to see her.

'Are the gardens old?' Freya asked him when they had walked a little way. 'They look to be very well established.'

'Yes, they are older than the house,' he answered her. 'The house that stood on the site originally was Elizabethan; very draughty and inconvenient. My father had it pulled down, and the present house built. My contribution will be to have the garden remodelled, when I get round to it.'

'Oh no,' exclaimed Freya. 'It is lovely as it is. And you yourself spoke of its beauties not long ago.'

'Perhaps,' he agreed. 'But its day is gone. And if I am obliged to stay here for part of the year, then I may as well make the place as I want it to be.'

Thinking of Mr Bryce's obligations prompted Freya to say, 'And do you have plans to alter the mill too?'

His handsome features took on the disgruntled expression which always adorned them when the mill was mentioned. 'Alter it? Would that I need never see it again, curse it!'

Freya looked startled.

'Forgive me, but I hate the way in which things have been left. By the terms of my grandfather's will I cannot sell it, knock it down, burn it up, or even give it away without losing everything else that he left, including this house. Not only that, but by the terms of his will, I have to spend a certain amount of time here every year, overseeing a business that I hate, about which I know very little and desire to know even less. Given the choice, I would spend all year in London, but what can I do? My hands are tied.'

Freya agreed that it was an awkward

business; but she could not help thinking that if he would just make a push to discover more about the work of the mill, he might find it more interesting than he supposed.

They had by now reached the far end of the cultivated part of the garden, which was separated from the surrounding fields and the woods beyond by a ha-ha.

'The end of my domain, Miss Pascoe. Does it please you?'

'Very much,' answered Freya. They turned to wander back.

They had not gone far when Bryce said, 'I don't suppose you have seen the sunken pool?' Freya shook her head, and her escort led her to a square pool with steps down to it. There was a small fountain in the centre, adorned by stone fish, and it was surrounded by trees on every side.

'How delightful!' Freya exclaimed.

'I used to fancy that the trees might come to life, and take the form of tall, willowy woodland goddesses,' he said. 'But today, ma'am, I am convinced that my fantasy has come true. You look quite enchanting.'

Freya turned to look at him in surprise, and before she could collect her thoughts, he had pulled her into his arms and swiftly kissed her.

'Mr Bryce!' she declared stepping back.

'You forget yourself.'

'By no means,' he answered seizing hold of her once more. 'Look me in the eyes and tell me that you didn't enjoy my kiss.' He began to pull her towards him again, but before she had time to struggle, there was a sound of a throat being cleared, and they both turned to see Lord Ravendale watching them from the other side of the pool.

'Dammit! How long have you been here?' asked Bryce angrily.

'Long enough to know that I am de trop,' he answered ironically. 'I heard voices and came in search of you. But I will remove myself.'

'There is no need,' declared Freya, her face flaming. 'I was going inside anyway. Excuse me.' She hurried away in the direction of the house, but before she had gone far, she heard footsteps behind her. Thinking that it might be Bryce in pursuit of her, she turned to reprimand him, and found herself confronted with Lord Ravendale.

'What do *you* want?' she said. She spoke rather more rudely than she had intended because she was flustered.

'I seem to be forever in a position of having to warn you,' he replied. 'This time, however, it is not about your walking alone, but about the nature of the company you keep.'

'And what business is it of yours?' Freya demanded.

'Perhaps none; but Bryce's reputation — '

'Oh yes?' interrupted Freya sarcastically. 'And what gives you the right to criticize anyone's reputation?'

'I am not aware that I have yet offered any criticism of anyone,' he said.

'Except for me, of course!'

'I don't criticize you. God knows you are entitled to walk with and talk with anyone you choose. If you don't give a fig for your reputation, you're entitled to kiss any man you like within the privacy of his garden . . . '

Freya curtsied. 'Thank you for your permission, my lord,' she simpered, with an insincere smile, 'but — '

'Oh be quiet, woman, and listen, won't you?' his lordship stormed at her. 'If you are so careless of yourself as to choose to allow Bryce to take liberties with your person, then who am I to stop you? But before you do so, I must and will tell you with what kind of man you are dealing. He does not have a good reputation. He makes a habit of exploiting those who are either powerless to resist him, or to insist upon redress. His only interest in you is because there is no other single woman about to flirt with. Even if you were middle-aged, plain and shapeless, he

154

would pursue you just to amuse himself. If you think that his kissing you means that he will ever marry you, then you are very much mistaken. Bryce has an eye to a fortune, and he will never sell himself for less than £5,000 a year. Do I make myself clear?'

During his speech, Freya turned as white as she had been red. 'Perfectly clear,' she said angrily. The fact that Mr Bryce's kisses had been uninvited now seemed much less important than Ravendale's arrogant judgement of her morals. 'I suppose you are now going to accuse me of throwing myself at him in the same way that I have been throwing myself at you?' she went on.

'What the devil do you mean by that?' he demanded. 'Who says that you have been throwing yourself at me?'

'You do, apparently,' she replied.

'Balderdash!' he declared. 'Of what else do you want to accuse me?'

She took a deep breath. 'You see fit to criticize Mr Bryce and myself for the kiss that you saw, but you forget, sir, that you have not been entirely blameless in that respect. Of the propriety of your referring so detrimentally to one who is to be related to you by marriage, I will not speak. Furthermore, Mr Bryce has at least been civil to me. *He* did not call me middle-aged, plain and shapeless. *He* did not refer to me as a kind of . . . of last resort . . . '

'No, he called you a willowy woodland goddess, and said that you were enchanting, and a fine piece of nonsense I thought it, too.'

'Oooooh!' exclaimed Freya and she turned to leave, but he caught hold of her arm and pulled her round.

'I never said you were plain or middle-aged,' he declared exasperatedly. 'You dress appallingly, but that's another matter. And any man who thinks you shapeless wants his eyes testing. You aren't enchanting either; that's a stupid word to apply to you. Magnificent would be better; and a flowery, floaty woodland creature isn't you at all. For heaven's sake, he doesn't even have the wit to see that the only goddess that you could possibly be is Juno.' For a long moment, they stood staring at each other. Then with an inarticulate murmur, she tore herself free, ran the rest of the way back to the house, went inside and hurried up to her room. Joining Miss Bryce and Mrs Siddall was out of the question until she had composed herself.

*How dare he! How dare he!* She stormed to herself over and over again. It was some little time before she realized that the person whose daring she condemned was not Bryce for kissing her, but Lord Ravendale for misunderstanding the situation and for making her feel cheap. He had been so condemnatory of Bryce's reputation. What of his own? *He* was the one who had gambled away his family's possessions. *He* was the one who had behaved like a libertine. After all, Bryce, unlike the earl, was not an engaged man. He was free to kiss her if she permitted him to do so.

On the other hand, she had not permitted it at all, she reminded herself as she sat down on the bed when the worst heat of her fury had gone. He had taken her by surprise and kissed her. But then, so had Ravendale on a previous occasion. But oh how different were the two kisses. The one, the most recent, had been pleasant enough, but quite forgettable. Whereas the other . . .

Enough of this, she declared forthrightly, getting up. She would go and join the ladies. As she walked across the room, she caught sight of herself in the mirror, and stopped to look at her reflection. Ravendale was right. Her clothes were deplorable. But for the first time, she caught a glimpse of what the earl had referred to — the lustrous hair, the glowing complexion, the shapely figure. Could he *really* have thought her Junoesque?

As she closed the door, another thought occurred to her. He had denied saying that she had thrown herself at him. Part of her wanted to assert that of course he would deny such a thing; but another voice inside her pointed out that Lady Terrington had written that Claudia was untruthful. Could this be an example of her mendacity?

'Ah, Miss Pascoe,' said Claudia when they met for tea. No one could have supposed from her manner that she had been saying spiteful things about her companion behind her back. 'I have just been telling Maude about that sky-blue material that we saw in the window of that shop in Castleton. Do you remember it?'

'Yes indeed,' answered Freya.

'I have decided that it would be the very thing to add the finishing touches to my gown for my betrothal ball,' she went on. 'Would you be so good as to take the gig into Castleton tomorrow and purchase it? Maude and I would find the journey much too fatiguing, and Piers would be sure to buy the wrong stuff.'

'Of course,' answered Freya She had no intention of complaining. A day away from this vicinity would do her good, and already she was making plans for her entertainment.

'Don't hurry back,' said her employer carelessly. 'The horses will need a rest.'

# 9

The following day, Freya got up early, in order to set off in good time. It had occurred to her that if she could execute her commission quickly, she might have time to explore the caves. She would have to go alone, but the idea only gave her a moment's pause. When staying at Castleton before, she had been up Mam Tor and Peveril hill alone after all. In the caves, there would be guides to lead her. There was no reason why she should not go alone; but just in case anyone should object, or see fit to reprimand her, however little they might be entitled to do so, she decided to tell no one about it, either before or afterwards.

To make sure that she was properly equipped for her expedition, she put on stout shoes, and serviceable clothes. She also took with her a cloak which she did not really need outside, because of the clement weather, but which she was quite sure she would need in the caves. Having made her preparations, she set off for the stables.

The gig was ready, since she had been round to the stables the previous day to let the head groom know her intentions. Freya had never cared for horses, but she did not mind driving as opposed to riding. One of the grooms was accompanying her, so she knew that she would not have to do anything for the horses other than handle the ribbons, and this she had been taught to do by her father some years before.

The track was just as rough as she had remembered, but because she was in the open air, and concentrating on the road, the time passed more quickly than before. The groom was a local man, and once he had discovered that Freya was interested in the countryside about them, he had many helpful observations to make. In fact, Freya reflected, he was a far more agreeable travelling companion than Claudia!

The day was fine and warm, and the late morning found them drawing into the stable yard of 'The Castle'. Freya left the horses in Merrill's hands, and made her way to the shop that Claudia had mentioned. The material was no longer part of the window display, but the shop assistant soon found it, and Freya told her how much of it she wanted. Having arranged to collect it later, she left the shop, then set off once more in the direction of Mam Tor, for the caves were situated at that end of the village.

In order to prepare herself, she had turned once more to Daniel Defoe before she retired the previous night. Unfortunately, she had found him as disappointingly condemnatory of the caves as of anything else in Derbyshire, merely saying that they might be considered wonderful if they were the only caves to be found in the world, but as they were not, there was nothing special about them. Impatiently, she had thrown the little green volume down on the floor next to the bed before settling down to sleep. *Annoying man!* she thought to herself now, as she walked down the street. *I declare you and Miss Bryce would make a fine match of it, as miserable as you are!*

The thought made her smile, and as she walked briskly up the high street, she imagined several amusing scenarios, in which the two of them might meet, possibly on a desert island, on which they might be served by Mr Defoe's creation, Man Friday.

In no time at all, she was standing before the entrance to the caves, which was indeed, as Defoe accurately described it, 'a large opening very high, broad at bottom and narrow, but rounding, on the top, almost the form of the old Gothick gates or arches which come up . . . to a point; the opening being upwards of thirty foot perpendicular, and twice as much broad at the bottom at least.' It seemed to be very dark indeed, when viewed from outside in the light of the morning sun.

Freya stood looking at the cave and hesitating. She was not without courage, but climbing a great hill suddenly seemed to be a very different matter from plunging into the earth beneath one. Her opinion was confirmed when a ragged, dirty, wild-looking man stepped out of the entrance and, in a thick accent, called out to ask her if she wanted to view the caves. She did not say anything. She did indeed wish to view them, but felt a certain reluctance about doing so with only this strange individual to bear her company. She was about to refuse when a figure whom she had not noticed before stepped forward from where he had been lounging against the rocky wall a short distance from the entrance.

'Miss Pascoe! Now why am I not surprised?' It was Ravendale.

In her first surprise at seeing him, Freya was conscious of a feeling that was something very like pleasure. Then she recalled their previous encounters, and squaring her shoulders she said waspishly, 'I do not know why you are not surprised, Lord Ravendale! Perhaps it is because you are a mind-reader!'

He burst out laughing. 'Certainly not,

ma'am,' he said. 'But it would have surprised me very much if as intrepid a traveller as you have proved yourself to be did not at least want to take a look at the caves.'

More pleased than anything else at hearing herself described as intrepid, Freya said more mildly, 'No doubt you are here to advise me not to enter them. But I am of age, sir, and may go into them without your permission.'

'Indeed you may,' he agreed, walking closer to her, his hair shining golden in the morning sun. 'I had a suspicion that you might wish to do so, especially when I discovered that Claudia was sending you on a commission to Castleton today. Knowing that this would be your opportunity and being obliged to come to the town myself for reasons of my own, I decided to come here, and if you appeared, I would offer you my escort. So here I am, at your service.' He gave a slight bow.

'You think me incapable of looking after myself, in fact,' she said accusingly.

'By no means,' he replied, lifting his hands as a disclaimer. 'It is simply that I fear you may not understand the local dialect!'

Freya looked at him indignantly for a moment, then her sense of humour asserted itself, and she laughed. 'Very well, sir,' she said. 'I am not so intrepid with regard to confined spaces as I am to open ones, I must confess.'

'You astonish me, ma'am,' he murmured as they approached the entrance. 'I thought that your intrepidity embraced everyone and everything.' She looked at him suspiciously, but his expression was perfectly bland. Together, they turned to walk to the entrance, but before they got there, Freya paused.

'You do not think that escorting a paid companion would be beneath your dignity,' she asked him, curious to discover what he might say. He looked at her blankly.

'What the deuce has that to do with anything?' he asked.

Feeling unaccountably cheered by his words, she said, 'Nothing, I suppose.'

'Besides,' he added as they reached the caves, 'It's dark in here, so no one will see us.'

Freya looked up at him and seeing the twinkle in his eye, she was forced to laugh again.

The wild man seemed markedly more impressed at the advent of Ravendale, called him 'm'lord', and touched his forelock, all of which convinced Freya that with the earl present, she would receive much better treatment. They followed their guide into the cave. Freya glanced behind at the sunlight, strangely reluctant to leave it behind; then Ravendale was at her side, offering her his arm.

It seemed as if they were entering another world. By the light of the candle that Ravendale had been given, and which he now held aloft, Freya could see to the right, crowding against the wall of the cavern, what appeared to be a tiny village, with cottages around which women worked and tiny children played. In front of them, there were big wheels set out in order and in the middle distance, Freya could just make out others. Some men and women were standing by the wheels, engaged upon some task.

'What are they doing?' Freya asked curiously.

'They are making rope,' replied Ravendale. They watched the workers for a time, then the earl said, 'Do you want to penetrate further into the cave, or have you had enough?'

'I want to see all there is,' Freya answered firmly.

'Very well, then' agreed Ravendale. 'On we go.' Led by the ragged man, who was as silent as he was unkempt, they walked away from the daylight, until only a few rays penetrated weakly into the blackness. As they walked forward, they gradually progressed at the same time down an incline, until at last they reached a low door, where an old woman gave Freya a candle.

'Mind yer heads,' she warned in a raucous tone. 'The next part is low.' Still following their guide, Freya and Ravendale did as they were bid, and found that for a short time, they had to stoop in order to move through the passage. When they reached the end of it, their efforts were rewarded, however, for they found themselves in a vast cavern.

'I wish we could see better,' said Freya regretfully. 'One can sense the size of it, even though one cannot see it.' She held her candle high, in order to see as much as she could, and Ravendale did the same.

'I believe it is very large,' he agreed. 'Would you like me to ask our guide to let off some gunpowder so that we might see better?'

'No, indeed!' exclaimed Freya, barely repressing a shudder. 'I will content myself with my imagination, thank you!'

Ravendale chuckled in the darkness. The sound echoed round them, giving rise to a rather sinister effect.

Shortly afterwards, their guide conducted them to an underground river, where some little boats were moored, each lined with straw. The guide made some grunting sounds, accompanied by gestures, which Freya took to mean that she should get in. This she did and sat down, waiting for Ravendale to enter as well.

'No, Miss Pascoe,' said Ravendale from the bank, his face looking somewhat sinister by the light of the candle. 'You must lie flat in the boat, whilst your guide tows you. The passage through which we are to pass is so low that in places it almost touches the water.' Freya looked at the water, then at what she now realized, to her horror, was the passage which was to take them deeper into the caves.

'What's the matter'?' he went on. 'If you're afraid, we can go back.'

Freya squared her shoulders, as he had known she would.

'Afraid! Certainly not! But the candle . . . ' She looked down into the boat. 'The straw . . . '

'As long as you hold it up, everything will be all right,' Ravendale said reassuringly. 'Give me the candle, whilst you lie down.'

She hesitated, put her candle into his outstretched hand, then lay down reluctantly. As she held out her hand to receive it again, she said, trying not to sound anxious, 'You'll come too?'

'Yes, I'll come in the next boat. Look, another guide is here to tow mine. I'll be just behind you.'

Freya experienced a strange feeling of loss as he stepped away from the boat, then her guide pushed away from the side, and they were moving towards the passage. Gradually the roof lowered, until, as the earl had said, there was barely any space between the boat and the roof. Freya stared at the lowering, moist grey stone above her, and tried not to think about the great weight of rock and stone of which it was only a fraction. She gripped her candle as tightly as she could, and began to think that this was what it must be like to be buried alive. She opened her mouth to scream, suddenly remembered how foolish it would sound, closed it, but made a rapid exhalation of breath, and with that, her candle went out. She gave a small whimper; but fortunately, that part of the journey was practically over, the shore was reached, and Ravendale was soon springing forward to relight her candle. Involuntarily, she clung to his wrist as he did so.

'Are you all right?' he asked her concernedly. 'I thought I heard you cry out.'

'Yes, I . . . I am now,' she said breathlessly. 'But now that it is over, I will confess that it is an experience that I do not ever want to repeat!'

Ravendale, reflecting that she would either have to repeat it on the return journey or stay underground for ever, prudently remained silent on that score for the time being, saying merely, 'Come! You wanted to see wonders, did you not?' They followed their guide along a little path, beside which Freya was entranced to see many different shapes and colours of rock formations, some resembling plants or animals.

'This is beautiful,' she exclaimed. 'If only one could sketch down here!'

'You will just have to commit it all to memory,' said the earl. 'Damned if I'm going all the way back to the shops in Castleton just to buy you drawing paper!'

Soon they came to a second river. There was no need for a boat this time, but clearly anyone who walked across would get their feet wet. The guides stepped forward to carry them on their backs, but Ravendale waved them back. 'Allow me,' he said, before sweeping Freya up into his arms as if she were a featherweight. She opened her mouth to protest, but to insist that she be carried by one of the ragged, dirty guides seemed a trifle absurd. She could feel her heart beating a little faster, and put this down to the unfamiliarity of the experience; for she had certainly not been carried by a man in such a way for many years, and never by anyone other than her brother or her father. In order to cover her embarrassment, she said, 'I hope you do not expire under my weight!'

'I can see no reason why I should,' he answered cheerfully, smiling down at her. 'You don't seem particularly heavy to me. Don't drop the candle!' The stream was not wide, and soon Freya was on her feet again. Away from the sunlight, it was decidedly chilly, and she was very glad that she had brought her cloak with her. The path ahead of them was wet and slippery, and it was as well that they were both wearing stout shoes. Soon, Freya became aware of a lovely melodious sound coming from somewhere in the distance.

'Oh, what is that, pray?' she asked their guide.

'Wait and see,' he replied with unusual loquacity. Soon they did, for they found that very close to them, water was falling from the rocks above them. They stepped back to protect the candles, and admired how the light cast by them glistened in the droplets. It was the falling water that had caused the melodious sound that they had heard. They kept to the narrow path and as they went, they caught glimpses of other openings on either side, which clearly led to other caves. Freya's ready imagination could not help but toy with the idea of how lost they might become, did their guides suddenly decide to desert them!

They reached the end of the path, and walked into another cavern, whose dimensions reminded Freya of nothing so much as some of the paintings of exotic temples which she had seen in some of the volumes in her library at home.

'Why, this is magnificent!' she exclaimed, examining it as well as she could by the light of her candle, and that of Lord Ravendale, which he held high for her benefit as before.

At last, they had had their fill of looking, and Ravendale said, 'There is little further to go, — and no more to see. The last part of the caves is impenetrable, except on hands and knees. I suggest we return now. Unless, of course, you wish to go further.'

'No, I am satisfied,' replied Freya. 'Let us return.' It was not until they reached the shore of the first river that they had crossed that Freya realized that she would have to get into the shallow little boat once more and endure the oppression of the low ceiling. Involuntarily, she shrank back, found herself against something solid, and put out her hand to grasp hold of the fine woollen cloth of which Lord Ravendale's greatcoat was made.

'I can't,' she whispered, shaking her head. 'I can't!'

'My dear girl, you must — or stay here.'
She looked around her, then down at the boat
again, and to her shame, found herself
trembling. Ravendale sighed faintly, and
turned to the guide. 'We'll both go in the one
boat. There's just room, I think. Take my
candle.' He handed his candle to the guide
and helped Freya into the boat. 'Lie down
over to the side,' he told her. Then he climbed
in himself. The guide held out the candle, and
Ravendale said to Freya, 'You hold the
candle. I'll hold you.' Then he lay down and
put his upper arm around her.

She took the candle and held it carefully, so
that it would not go out this time. Then the
guide pushed off from the shore and they
were once again moving under the low
ceiling, formed by solid rock, miles thick.
Freya glanced up and felt a shudder all
through her frame. Then, just as surely, she
felt Ravendale's arm tighten around her. 'It's
all right,' he said. 'I've got you.' The darkness
was no less dark, and the rock was no less
thick, but suddenly she was conscious of a
lightening of her spirit.

As soon as she became less afraid of her
environment, she became suddenly aware of
the intimate proximity of the man who held
her. She had never, before this day, been held
in such a close embrace by a man unrelated

to her. Today, within a short space of time, Ravendale had held her twice, and no previous experience had ever affected her in this way. Moments earlier, she had been feeling cold, despite the warmth of her cloak. Now, she was beginning to feel rather warm, and the heat appeared to be emanating from every point at which her body was touching that of the earl. At the same time as she realized this, she remembered him saying that any man who described her as shapeless would have to be demented. Was he thinking of that now?

In order to banish these disturbing thoughts, she reminded herself — not for the first time — that this man was a gamester, and, furthermore, engaged to her employer; but even these salutary recollections did not appear to make any difference to the effect that Ravendale was having upon her. The wisest thing to do at this point would be to put some distance between them, but this was clearly impossible. The boat was far too small for her to do any such thing, and in any case, to start wriggling might convey the very opposite impression to the one which she intended.

Thankfully for her peace of mind, the journey was soon over and Ravendale, taking the hand of the guide, scrambled ashore then put out his own hand for Freya to take. She did so, and was immediately struck again by that same sensation of heat which seemed to run all the way up her arm. Thankful that the darkness prevented him from seeing her colour increase, she murmured a word of thanks and turned to leave the caves as quickly as possible.

'Take care,' warned Ravendale. 'The floor is apt to be treacherous.'

'Among other things,' she muttered to herself, thinking not so much of Ravendale as of her own heart; but she slowed her pace and, before long, the welcome sunlight was beginning to penetrate the darkness of the cave. Freya hurried outside. Whilst in the cave, it had seemed to her that they were in some entirely separate world, where different rules of behaviour applied. Now, standing in the warmth of the sunshine, it was hard to believe that that underground world even existed. She turned to look back at the entrance to the cave. Lord Ravendale had stopped to thank their guide and to give him some coins. As Freya watched, he emerged, blinking, into the bright morning, and a shaft of sunlight brought out the gold of his hair, making it shine. *Why*, thought Freya, *he's not handsome; he's spectacular.* At once, she repressed the idea and turned away in disgust, but the thought remained at the back of her mind, ready to return at some inconvenient moment.

Angry with herself at this further evidence of his attraction for her, she stalked back into the town, intending to collect Miss Bryce's material before going to the hotel for some luncheon. His lordship calmly kept pace just behind her, and however hard she tried to forget about him, his solid presence was impossible to ignore.

'I think I've discovered how a prince consort feels,' he murmured as they reached the shop. 'But too much association with royalty can give one a pronounced feeling of inferiority, so I will leave you, ma'am, before my sensation of unworthiness completely overcomes me.' He bowed politely, and left her. She could not help but smile at his remarks; and she reflected as she went inside and waited to be served that the earl always seemed to be able to make her laugh, even when she was most angry with him. It occurred to her that this might be the most dangerous thing about him.

She had half expected to discover that when she went to 'The Castle' for lunch, Ravendale would be there too. She was conscious of a sensation that she told herself was relief, but deep down inside, it felt far more like disappointment.

# 10

Rather to Freya's surprise, Miss Bryce was pleased with the fabric, which she said was just the right colour, and thanked her companion for fetching it.

'You must have had a very tiresome day,' she said. 'Did you have lunch at 'The Castle'?'

'Yes,' answered Freya, reflecting that this must be the first time that her employer had enquired about anything she had done. While she was debating whether or not to say that she had met Lord Ravendale, Mrs Siddall changed the subject, and she decided to say nothing of the matter. It was hardly likely that the earl would speak about their encounter. After all, he had not revealed on an earlier occasion that they had met at Peveril Castle. She recalled how they had lain together in the boat in close embrace, and she coloured; but fortunately Miss Bryce and Mrs Siddall were too absorbed in their own conversation to notice.

'I hope you have something special to wear for my betrothal ball,' Claudia was saying. 'It is to be a costume ball, you know.'

'I guethed that it might be,' replied Mrs Siddall. 'Tho I have come pwepared. Henwy wefutheth to wear any thort of cothtume, of courthe.' Freya, listening whilst she was sewing in one corner, suddenly felt a strong desire to hit the silly, affected woman over the head with her tambour frame. Genuine speech afflictions could not be helped; but she had heard Mrs Siddall giving her maid a good dressing down without any trace of an impediment. 'What ith Mith Pathcoe to wear?'

Freya looked up in surprise. She knew that she was to help Lady Ravendale with the preparations, but had not expected to be invited herself.

'Well, I am not at all sure,' answered Miss Bryce. 'As she is so very big she cannot possibly borrow or even adapt anything of mine.'

'No, indeed,' replied Mrs Siddall laughing merrily. 'She would need two dwetheth of yourth jutht to make one for her!'

Freya smiled dutifully, but the smile did not reach her eyes.

That evening, Lord Ravendale and his aunt dined with them. Miss Bryce looked positively ethereal in a gown of white with an overdress of delicate lace. To Freya's eyes, it seemed a little on the elaborate side for what was after all a country dinner among friends; but since she herself looked perfectly dreadful in a high-waisted blue gown with fussy trimming, she knew that she was in no position to criticize.

Mrs Siddall, though by no means as pretty as her friend, was charmingly, and far more appropriately dressed in a gown of sprigged muslin. Mrs Baxter, who certainly appeared to enjoy indifferent health, pronounced herself well enough to dine downstairs that evening. Freya had already found herself obliged to entertain Mrs Baxter on one or two occasions when Miss Bryce and her friend were otherwise occupied. She had found the older lady to be cheerful even in discomfort, and with a wry sense of humour which she seldom expressed in the context of larger gatherings.

Freya could not help but laugh to herself when they came to sit at table. Obviously, Miss Bryce was determined to have a man either side of her, despite the fact that there were only three men to go round amongst them. Lord Ravendale, predictably, was placed on her right, and Mr Siddall was seated on her left. Naturally, at the other end of the table, Piers had Lady Ravendale on his right, as befitted her rank, but who to put on his left? Of course, Freya was too lowly to have that honour, so that left Mrs Baxter or Mrs Siddall. Seniority might demand that it should be Mrs Baxter, but that would mean that Lord Ravendale would have to have either Freya or Mrs Siddall next to him. To put Freya there was obviously unthinkable; and even Mrs Siddall, though a friend, and married into the bargain, could not be depended upon not to flirt with the earl. Therefore Mrs Baxter found herself on the earl's right, whilst Freya was in between Lady Ravendale and Mr Siddall.

This resulted in a very agreeable dinner. Mr Siddall took an interest in politics, and enjoyed talking about issues of the day. After an animated discussion about the Regency bill, he said to her, 'You know how to hold your own, ma'am. It's very agreeable to be able to talk with an intelligent woman.' Whilst accepting the compliment gracefully, Freya knew that she had not said anything particularly startling, and she could not help reflecting that intelligent female conversation might be somewhat lacking in his own home.

Lady Ravendale, too, proved to be a pleasant dinner companion, unsurprisingly enough. 'When are you coming to Ravendale again?' she asked Freya. 'I could do with your help, for the ball is not many days off, now.'

Freya promised to visit her the following day.

After the meal was over, the gentlemen did not linger for long over their wine, and soon joined the ladies in the drawing-room.

'Extraordinary that the mill should be so close by, yet impossible to see from here,' remarked Mr Siddall, wandering over to the window. 'Is it visible from any of the upper rooms?'

'I have no idea,' replied Bryce. When Siddall looked at him curiously he added, in a slightly resentful tone, 'The servants' quarters are up on the top floor. You surely don't expect me to go up there, do you?'

Ravendale wandered over to join them. 'I confess that in your place, I should be curious to see the view,' he said.

'Why, have *you* been up to *your* top floor?' asked Bryce dubiously.

'I certainly have.' Ravendale grinned at his aunt. 'I've even been on the roof as well,' he went on. 'But I was caught and given the punishment I deserved for my daredevil behaviour.'

'You were indeed,' agreed his aunt, smiling back. 'I think I gained more grey hairs over that episode than over anything else you did in your boyhood.' Freya smiled as well, and found herself wondering curiously what other pranks the earl might have got up to in his youth.

Evidently Claudia's interest was not similarly caught, for she said placidly as she poured the tea which had just been brought, 'I don't see that it matters. I have no desire to see the wretched place from any of my windows. I had just as soon it didn't exist at all.'

'Exactly so,' agreed Bryce. His glass had been refilled more frequently than anyone else's at dinner and he was beginning to become a little belligerent.

'Surely that would make life rather difficult for you,' said Ravendale mildly.

'It's all very well for you,' answered his host resentfully. 'At least your inheritance was not left to you with the condition that you ran a mill!'

'Perhaps not,' agreed the earl. 'But my estate is there to be run, after all. What do you suggest I do with it instead? Allow it to collapse about me?'

Sensing a degree of tension between the two men, Siddall said quickly, 'Have you been to the mill on this visit yet, Bryce?'

'Good Lord, no,' Bryce exclaimed. 'I put it off for as long as I can. Why on earth should I *want* to go there?'

'Perhaps to safeguard your investment,'

suggested Ravendale. 'I think I'd rather like to see round your mill, Bryce.'

Siddall grunted in agreement.

'Why?' asked Bryce, completely mystified.

'Possibly because we're both curious fellows,' suggested Ravendale, with a grin at Siddall. 'What say you show us round one of these days?'

'Haven't you anything better to do?' asked Bryce, still incredulous. 'I could think of any number of things!'

'My dear Bryce, nothing would please me more than a morning spent in your company,' said Ravendale with exaggerated courtesy, bowing with his hand on his heart.

Bryce did grin at this. 'Oh, if you must,' he conceded. 'But don't blame me if you're bored to extinction.'

Freya had listened attentively to this conversation. She felt that she would very much like to see the mill herself, but could hardly express such an idea uninvited. She glanced at Lord Ravendale, and for a moment, their eyes met.

'Perhaps the ladies would like to go,' he suggested.

Bryce looked dumbstruck. 'I hardly think so,' he replied doubtfully.

'Let's ask them,' pursued the earl. 'Claudia, my dear?'

Miss Bryce could not have looked more horrified if he had suggested she actually work in the mill, rather than just visit it.

'Certainly not,' she answered. 'The idea is quite disgusting. And Maude will not wish to go either.' Mrs Siddall nodded vigorously, her ringlets bouncing at the side of her head.

'Enough of this, then,' said Bryce. 'Anyone for cards, and a little wager?'

Freya found herself hoping that Ravendale would refuse, but he and Siddall both accepted, and the three men went into the next door room to enjoy their game. Freya surprised a look of anxiety on Lady Ravendale's face, which she determinedly banished, as soon as she realized that she was observed.

'I'm sorry, my dear, I cannot help but be anxious,' she confessed, in low tones. 'Seeing him go off into the card room brings back unpleasant memories, I'm afraid.'

'It's quite understandable,' replied Freya, just as softly, but with an angry glance towards where Ravendale had gone.

Lady Ravendale smiled at her. 'You're very kind,' she said. 'Forgive me for being so foolish. I know that there is no cause for anxiety.'

No doubt they would not be playing for high stakes in such circumstances, Freya reflected, which was why her ladyship was not overly concerned. But how dreadful to live one's life in such a way, never knowing if one's very home might be put at risk by one man's recklessness.

Whilst Ravendale was in the card room, Freya found it very difficult to concentrate on anything. Fortunately, Lady Ravendale and Mrs Baxter had discovered a number of mutual friends, and were soon deep in conversation. She thought about the different sides of Ravendale that she had seen. Arrogant and overbearing, as she had discovered on Mam Tor; flirtatious and rakish at Peveril Castle; a gambler who was prepared to marry the most objectionable woman just to get his hands on her money. Yet at the same time, he was strong, vigorous, knowledgeable, and could be kind and sensitive; she only had to think of how caring and thoughtful he had been in the caves to realize that. Which was the real Ravendale? She kept looking at the door into the card room. Illogical though it might be, she found herself praying that he would not drag his noble name more deeply in the mire than he had done already.

Later on, she noticed that Mrs Baxter was shivering a little, despite the warmth of the evening, and she excused herself to go and fetch her a shawl. It was while she was coming back down the stairs with Mrs Baxter's shawl over her arm that she saw Lord Ravendale in the hall. Because she was surprised to see him, she found herself saying the first thing that came into her head.

'So you have finished your game, then.'

'Apparently.'

'Have you fleeced them both, or does your effrontery not extend to beggaring a man in his own house?'

Ravendale's brows snapped together.

'And what is *that* supposed to mean?' he asked her tersely.

'You know very well,' she replied, descending the last few stairs so that she stood level with him. 'Or do I need to remind you about the way that you have reduced your family's fortune to nothing by your ruinous habits?'

'From whom had you this?' he asked quietly.

'It is common knowledge,' she flared back at him. 'Everyone knows about it.' He was silent. 'I deduce from your silence, my lord, that you have nothing to say in your defence?'

'Would it avail me anything if I did?' he said quizzically. 'You have clearly appointed yourself judge and jury. Incidentally, perhaps I should remind you that it was not I who suggested that we should play cards.'

'Don't prevaricate,' she replied.

'I'm not doing so. Why should it matter to you what I do with my own money, anyway?'

'It matters to me because your actions affect more than just yourself. How can you be so unfeeling as to treat Lady Ravendale as you do? I expect you thought that your theft of your mother's necklace was a secret, but believe me — '

He seized hold of her shoulders then. 'My WHAT?' he demanded.

'You know very well,' she retorted. Both of them were now so absorbed in their own conversation that they were quite oblivious to the possibility of interruption. 'How can you be so uncaring of her feelings? What must she think every time she looks at you? That she must keep her jewellery box locked away for fear you steal something of hers? And what of . . . ' She had been about to say something about the impropriety of fleecing his future brother-in-law when he tightened his grip and shook her hard.

'Now let me make sure that I understand you,' he said, his voice shaking with rage. He was a little white about the mouth and his eyes glittered. 'Are you calling me a thief?'

Reaching up with her arms, she struck him away with all her strength. 'Certainly a thief, probably a liar, and for all I know, a cheat as well.'

He seized hold of her again.

'Add to that, a libertine and a scoundrel,' she went on. 'Unhand me immediately!'

'By no means,' he declared, dragging her into the shadows of the staircase. 'Have you not heard? There are no lengths to which I will not sink!' So saying, he pulled her into his arms and kissed her savagely, his powerful grip making nonsense of her struggles. When he eventually let her go, they were both breathless, and she was shaking. He took a step back. 'Were you a man, you would be answering to me across twenty yards of turf with a pistol in your hand for the things that you have just said. As it is, I will simply bid you goodnight.' Turning on his heel, he re-entered the drawing-room, and shortly afterwards Freya heard the ringing of the bell which signified that Ravendale's carriage was to be sent for.

Slowly, because she was still trembling, she climbed the stairs again and went to her own room, Mrs Baxter's shawl still in her hands. She doubted if she would be missed. Even if she were, she was beyond caring. Suddenly, she had an overwhelming desire just to put this whole adventure behind her and simply go home.

* * *

The journey home for Ravendale and his aunt was at first a very silent one. Earlier in the evening, the earl had appeared to be positively genial, treating Bryce with courtesy even though the countess knew that her nephew had no respect for him, and behaving towards his betrothed exactly as an engaged man should. When her nephew had returned to the drawing-room after a brief absence, however, and declared in tones that were only just the polite side of curt that it was time they were leaving, the countess had been very surprised. Not being enamoured of the Bryces' company herself, she acquiesced readily enough, and stood nearby as Ravendale made his farewells to his fiancée.

'My aunt is rather tired, so I think we must go,' he said austerely.

Claudia, laying a well-kept white hand on his arm, murmured, 'My dear Daniel, I quite understand. We all have to be at the beck and call of our elderly relations from time to time.'

'You mistake the matter,' he replied coldly. 'I am not at my aunt's 'beck and call', as you put it. Nor is she at all elderly. A moment's reflection must tell you that, and a mere pinch of courtesy would prevent you from saying such a thing.'

Claudia glanced up at him warily. She disliked Lady Ravendale, and had every intention of having her ejected from Ravendale Hall as soon as possible; but insensitive though she was, she realized that she had gone too far. She pouted a little, and looked up at him through her lashes.

'You are not very gallant, sir,' she said accusingly. 'What has happened to put you in such an ill humour?'

He laughed humourlessly. 'Just an encounter with that tiresome companion of yours,' he answered. 'How the deuce do you put up with such a plain beanpole?'

Claudia laughed. 'She serves my purpose,' she replied. 'I must admit, it pleases me to find that you are not attracted to her.'

'Attracted to *her*?' he said with automatic gallantry, lifting her hand to his lips. 'When *you* are present?'

Claudia smiled with satisfaction, and bid farewell to the earl in a very good humour. Ravendale returned her smiles, but after they had left the house, he was conscious of a sense of some disquiet.

Once they were sitting in the carriage, he sighed, uttered, 'At last,' and lounged back in his seat in brooding silence. Lady Ravendale settled back into her own place and sat in silence for the first part of the journey.

Eventually, she said, 'Quite a pleasant evening.' She was rewarded with a grunt. 'I was delighted to meet Mrs Baxter,' she went on. 'It appears that she went to the same seminary as my very good friend, Henrietta Perry.' Another grunt. 'Mr Siddall was very agreeable, I thought. His wife seems a very silly woman, though.' She was rewarded with 'Mmm' by way of contrast. 'Claudia was in great beauty,' she said tentatively. This time he said nothing, but merely nodded. She was silent for some time. Eventually, she said, 'I am so glad that Miss Pascoe has come to live here. I like her very much.'

'Then you must have windmills in your head,' he responded curtly.

*So that's who's upset him*, she thought to herself. Out loud, she said calmly, 'You do surprise me. I thought you liked her. You certainly gave that impression before.'

'That was before I discovered what she was really like. A more self-willed, opinionated, prejudiced, exasperating female I have yet to meet in the whole of my life.'

'What has she done to set you all on end?' she asked.

'What has she done? *What has she done?* She has insulted my name, she has doubted my word, she has accused me of . . . of . . . in short, ma'am, she has made me lose my temper!'

'So I see,' she replied. 'I suppose you don't want to repeat what she said.'

He snorted. 'I wouldn't soil my lips. Thank God I'm not marrying *her*, that's all I can say!'

'Well if you wanted to have your revenge upon her, then you have certainly found a way of succeeding,' said her ladyship evenly.

'What can you mean?' asked Ravendale, his brow wrinkling.

'You don't suppose that Claudia will be able to resist repeating that remark about Miss Pascoe's being like a plain beanpole, do you?'

The earl grunted.

'I cannot imagine anything more likely to cause her pain than that.'

'She has caused me pain,' he retorted. 'Why should she not suffer some herself?'

The countess made no other reference to the subject. Neither of them spoke again until they arrived back at Ravendale manor.

* * *

As Freya got ready for bed, she thought about the conversation that she had had with Lord Ravendale. She admitted to herself that she had been hoping that he would deny the accusations and give a rational explanation of the rumours that were circulating about him. True, he had been very angry. She fingered her mouth as she recalled the brutality of his kiss. How very angry he had been! He had said that had she been a man he would have challenged her to a duel; that had been a reaction to her accusation that he was a cheat. Gentlemen, she knew, were very sensitive about that particular imputation, even whilst they might be committing all kinds of injustices against their family without a qualm. She tried to feel satisfied about the way in which she had brought him to book; but she only succeeded in feeling vaguely uneasy and rather ashamed.

# 11

Freya woke the following morning conscious of a feeling of oppression. At first she could not think why, but then she recalled the things that she had said to Ravendale the previous evening. The night was supposed to bring counsel, or so she had read; but if it had, the counsel that it brought was that she had been terribly mistaken in speaking so hastily. After all, she had had no justification in calling him a cheat. The information that he was a thief was based on Lady Ravendale's testimony alone; and whilst she ought to know what she was talking about, there might be some other explanation. She spent some time trying to imagine all the mitigating circumstances that there might be, but could reach no conclusion about the matter.

A brisk walk to the top of the hill behind the house and back exercised her limbs, but did not ease her mind. Whilst she was sitting at luncheon with Miss Bryce and Mrs Siddall, however, a conversation took place which had the effect of diverting her thoughts in the most unwelcome way. It was when the meal was halfway over that Miss Bryce suddenly said, 'Miss Pascoe, I believe I have found the solution to the problem of what you should wear for the ball.'

Feeling that something was expected of her, Freya looked up briefly from her plate and said, 'Indeed, ma'am?'

She detected a knowing look passing between Claudia and her friend, so she was not altogether surprised when her employer said, 'A most fortunate circumstance. You may have noticed that my housekeeper is very much of a height as you. I have prevailed upon her to lend you her second best uniform.'

'I am obliged to her,' said Freya evenly. 'I shall do my best to keep it clean.' The silence that followed told Freya that this was not quite the reaction for which Miss Bryce had hoped.

'I am hoping to introduce you to Reverend Tobias Simpkins at the ball,' went on Claudia, calmly taking another piece of bread and butter. 'He wanted to meet you before, but has been rather ill with a putrid sore throat. The housekeeper's gown will strike an appropriate note of sobriety for one who might become a clergyman's wife. And anyway, I'm afraid that that was all that I could find. You are such an awkward shape.'

'Awkward in what way exactly, ma'am?'

asked Freya, only controlling her temper by sheer effort of will.

'Well, so tall, and . . . well . . . so shapeless,' drawled her employer.

'Like a beanpole,' giggled Mrs Siddall. Freya looked at her in astonishment.

'Now, now,' said Claudia in minatory tones. 'You must not repeat Ravendale's every light comment.' Freya's eyes met hers, and saw the malice in them. Suddenly, her anger disappeared, and instead she felt completely deflated. She got to her feet.

'Perhaps I may be excused,' she said in a colourless tone.

'Certainly,' answered Claudia calmly. 'And don't forget that Lady Ravendale wants your help tomorrow.'

'I shan't forget,' replied Freya, before she went out and began to climb the stairs to her room. Briefly, she paused on the stairs and looked down. It had been on this step, or perhaps the next one, where she had been standing when she had seen Ravendale come out into the hall. She remembered some of the things that they had said, and what had happened at the conclusion of their argument.

Why had he kissed her if he thought her so unattractive, she wondered? There had at times been something in his eyes which had told her that he was in some way drawn to her; and she, despite herself, had felt similarly drawn to him. But if this was true, why had he spoken of her in such derogatory terms? Funnily enough, it was the fact that he had referred to her in that way, rather than that a silly woman had repeated it, which hurt her the most. She tried to tell herself that he was the last man whose good opinion she cared to have, but she could not shake off the fact that he had criticized her for something that she could not help. Furthermore, the remarks that he had made to her only a day or two ago in the gardens told a very different story. Whatever might be his true opinion — and she told herself firmly that she was far from caring which it might be — it seemed that his word could not be relied upon. And to think that she had been feeling guilty for possibly misjudging him!

She thought again about that kiss. Was it the kind of thing that gentlemen did if they were very angry? Briefly, she asked herself what might happen if she provoked him to anger beyond all reason; but before her thoughts could range beyond what was proper, she hurried up the rest of the stairs, and went to her room, resolved on writing to her brother. The time of the wager would be up two days after the ball. She would leave as soon as she could, and find somewhere to stay discreetly from where John could collect her when the threat to the bank was past.

When she was about halfway through her letter, there was a knock at the door, and the housekeeper entered self-consciously with a gown over her arm. It was, as Freya had suspect, of a plain design, and dull grey in colour.

'I'm sorry to interrupt you, miss, but Miss Bryce sent me with this for you to borrow.'

Freya smiled at her. After all, it wasn't the woman's fault. 'Thank you very much,' she said. 'I promise that I shall take great care of it.'

'I've no doubt of that, miss,' replied the housekeeper. It was a crying shame that old sourpuss couldn't find anything better for her companion, she thought to herself. At least, Miss Pascoe treated the staff with courtesy, which was more than could be said for some as she could mention. 'I'll have one of the maids come and fold it for you, then Lady Ravendale's woman can press it for you when you get there.' Freya thanked her again. As the housekeeper was leaving she turned back towards Freya. 'I'm very sorry, miss,' she said again; and they both knew that she wasn't talking about her interruption of Freya's letter writing.

Freya looked at the gown after she had gone. It was at least as bad as she had expected. What she would not have given to startle Ravendale with something more becoming than the housekeeper's gown! For a brief moment or two, she indulged these thoughts, then sternly repressed them. What call would Lord Ravendale have to admire any woman other than his fiancée at their betrothal ball? That being so, she ought to be glad that the gown was dull enough to mean that she would be able to blend into the background, so that he — and hopefully Reverend Tobias Simpkins — wouldn't notice her at all.

★ ★ ★

The following day proved to be a very busy one, and as far as Freya was concerned, one of the most enjoyable since she had come to Derbyshire. She had been a little uncomfortable about the possibility of encountering Lord Ravendale at first, but once the countess had assured her that business had taken him away for most of the day, she was able to relax.

Lady Ravendale asked her to supervise the arrangement of the flowers in the ballroom.

'I have decided to use what we have plenty

of in the gardens, rather than buy in yards of silk with which to drape the room, when we will have no further use for it afterwards,' she said. This was a task which was exactly to Freya's taste, and it seemed that no time at all had passed when a footman came to tell her that a light luncheon had been laid out in the breakfast parlour.

'Do excuse the unexciting nature of the fare,' said the countess apologetically. 'Every corner of the kitchens is needed to prepare the supper, so we are making do.'

Freya replied that making do with home-made bread, butter, cheese, pickles and a dark fruit cake suited her very well, and the ladies chatted amicably about the preparations for the ball. Eventually, Lady Ravendale leaned forward and said impulsively, 'Oh Freya, my dear, how I wish it could be you marrying Daniel!'

Freya was completely unprepared for such a comment, and was quite unable to think what to say. On the one hand, part of her wanted to say that Lord Ravendale was the last man on earth whom she could consider marrying. But on the other, to her horror, there was a part of her that felt a similar regret to that expressed by Lady Ravendale! Instead of laughing off her comments, therefore, she just stared at her friend, her face aflame, before looking away.

After a few moments' silence, her ladyship said in another tone. 'But you must show me your costume. I am longing to see it.'

The housekeeper's second best uniform had been pressed and hung up in the bedchamber which had been set on one side for Freya's use. The maid who had prepared it had done her best, but nothing could make it look other than what it was. Lady Ravendale looked at it for a few moments in horrified silence.

'Freya, you do not mean to tell me that that gown was all that that . . . ' She struggled to find a suitable epithet, and in the end finished lamely, 'That Miss Bryce managed to find for you.' Freya meant to laugh it off, but to her horror, she found herself close to tears, and merely nodded. 'You cannot *possibly* wear that,' the countess declared in tones of disgust.

'Well, there is nothing else,' stated Freya, trying to sound indifferent, with only partial success.

'I wouldn't be so sure of that,' answered the other. 'Daniel's grandmother was tall, and it may well be that there might be some of her gowns stored in the attic. She never threw anything away, you know. Let us send for Potter, my maid. She will help us.'

A few moments later, Potter was also standing and looking at the housekeeper's gown.

'Potter, that will not do for Miss Pascoe,' said the countess.

'I should think not, my lady,' answered Potter disgustedly. 'Do you want me to look in the trunks in the attic for something more suitable?'

Lady Ravendale clapped her hands. 'Didn't I tell you that Potter would help us?' she exclaimed. 'Potter, if you can find some of the things belonging to his lordship's grand-mother, I think that they might do.'

'That they may,' agreed Potter. 'If your ladyship and Miss Pascoe have other things to do for the ball, then I'll go and see what I can find.'

Lady Ravendale stared again at the housekeeper's gown. 'I don't care what we do,' she said in determined tones. 'She is not wearing that.' Both Lady Ravendale and Freya went back to their appointed tasks. A little less than an hour later, Potter came hurrying to find them, her round rosy face even more flushed than usual.

'Oh my lady! Miss Pascoe! Do, pray, come! I think I have found the very thing!' Catching her enthusiasm, they accompanied her back to the bedchamber. 'I've brushed it and pressed it, but I must say, her old ladyship's woman knew her work, if it was she who put it away. It's in a very good condition.'

A short time later, Freya stood in front of the long glass in her room, staring at her reflection in disbelief. She was wearing an open robe of deep red satin, with a cream petticoat, embroidered with tiny flowers of the same red as the overdress, each one with a sparkling centre. The dark colour of the fabric brought her complexion to life, made her lips seem redder, and gave rich lights to the darkness of her hair. Furthermore, there was something about its design which made her look not an inch too tall but, to the contrary, just right.

'Potter, it's . . . it's wonderful,' she breathed. 'You're a miracle worker.'

'I did nothing but find it, ma'am,' said Potter, looking pleased. 'The stuff is such good quality that it hasn't spoiled with time. I just need to strengthen the stitching on some of those beads and check the hem, then it'll be ready for you. You must be the same size as his lordship's grandmother almost to the inch.'

'I never thought that I would have cause to be thankful to Claudia,' said Lady Ravendale when they were going downstairs after Potter had helped Freya out of the gown. 'I thought

202

that a costume ball was a dreadful idea, and I know that she only suggested it so that she could come dressed as a shepherdess. But if it gives you an opportunity to wear something so becoming, then it has all been worthwhile.'

'I must admit, I did not think that I could look so well,' replied Freya.

'I can't wait to see Claudia's face when she sees you,' said her ladyship, echoing Freya's own thoughts. Then she added, in a more subdued tone, 'My dear, I feel it only fair to warn you that Claudia's reaction to your gown is not likely to be a favourable one. She is not used to being outshone, you see; and to be outshone by you, her companion, would be more than she could bear.'

'Outshone?' exclaimed Freya incredulously. 'My dear Lady Ravendale, Claudia is beautiful!'

'Outshone,' repeated the countess firmly. 'Claudia is very pretty, of course; but *you*, my dear, are beautiful.' She paused for a moment to let the words sink in, while Freya looked at her amazed, not knowing what to say. 'I do not want you to misunderstand me,' her ladyship went on. 'I want you to wear that gown, of course I do, and it is not that I am in any way concerned about what Claudia may think, or if her feelings will be hurt, because, forgive me for saying so, I don't think that she has any feelings. But after the ball is over, you will still be dependent upon her. I have no knowledge of your circumstances, but I am afraid that she may no longer wish to employ you after tonight.'

She paused again, her face distressed. 'There is nothing that I should like better than to keep you here with me as my companion; but our finances are not such that . . . ' She broke off for a moment, then went on resolutely, 'To invite you to remain here, much though I should love it, would be to give the marriage such a bad start, when . . . when . . . '

Freya smiled. Never had she been more tempted to reveal her identity and her true circumstances. But for all that she was fond of Lady Ravendale, she had no way of knowing how discreet she was, and she dared not risk endangering John's position.

'I am not completely without means,' she said at last. 'Don't distress yourself, ma'am. I have already discovered that Miss Bryce and myself cannot agree for long, and had intended to leave at the end of the week in any case.'

Lady Ravendale sighed thankfully. 'You do relieve my mind,' she said. 'If you need a reference, or any help at all, please let me know. And do say that we will continue to be friends. Perhaps, when a little time has elapsed, you may come and stay for a while.' Freya thanked her, but decided privately, that to have Lady Ravendale to stay at *her* house might be a more comfortable arrangement.

They went together into the long gallery, which was to serve as a ballroom on this occasion, and inspected the effect produced by the flowers.

'This is delightful!' exclaimed the countess. 'I am so glad that I entrusted this task to you.'

'It was a task that I was very happy to perform,' replied Freya, 'especially with such beautiful blooms available for my use. But I do not need to tell you that, ma'am, for I understand that the garden falls to your care.'

'Yes, indeed,' replied the countess. 'The garden has always been my joy and my solace as well. Of course, after the wedding, this house will have a new mistress, who will be wanting things done in new ways, no doubt. But I hope that she will allow me to continue to manage the gardens.' Freya looked at the older woman in sympathy. For the first time, she found herself wondering what it would be like for her to live in this house, of which she had once been mistress, and to see Claudia make all kind of changes, probably not for the better.

'In my experience, Miss Bryce is extremely indolent,' Freya said comfortingly. 'No doubt she will be very glad to leave a number of things in your care.'

'Indolent she may be, but she does like to have her own way,' replied the countess. Freya said nothing, but mentally, she could not help but agree. After this, the two ladies were kept busy, making sure that all the other rooms were ready for the different activities for which they had been assigned. One of the smaller rooms had been prepared for cards, with tables set out ready with fresh packs on them. Freya wondered how the countess felt about putting a room to such a purpose, but concluded that in fairness to the other guests, she could not very well ban a form of entertainment which, though a snare for the earl, provided harmless enjoyment for so many.

Before getting ready for the ball, Freya went down to have a last look at the long gallery to make sure that all was well. Even though she had been involved in its preparation from the beginning, she could not repress a gasp of delight. The beautiful old wood panelling had been polished until it shone, and its glow reflected the light of the candles which had already been lit, even though the room was by no means completely dark. The flowers decorated the room in lovely profusion, and their scent lingered on the air, giving the impression to anyone coming in that he was entering not so much a room as a garden.

She moved to the far end of the room, and bending, drank in the perfume of one perfect white rose. It had been her inspiration not simply to use flowers, but to use only white flowers. Up in her room she had been assailed by doubts as to the wisdom of this; but now, seeing the effect for herself, she realized how right she had been.

The little orchestra engaged for the evening was in place. Its members had arranged their manuscripts, tuned their instruments, and checked how their music would sound in a room of just these dimensions. They played snatches of one piece then another, and Freya closed her eyes, swaying a little in time to the music, imagining for a few moments what it might be like to dance around the room, partnered by someone who would not make her look like a giantess. The partner of her imagination was strongly built, and although not classically handsome, he was very striking to look at. In fact, he bore more than a passing resemblance to Lord Ravendale, surely the last man with whom she wanted to be dancing!

Giving herself a little shake, Freya opened her eyes, only to discover that standing a short distance away from her, almost as if she had conjured him up by her thoughts, was Ravendale himself. Refusing to be decked in any kind of outlandish costume, such as that of a pirate or a gypsy, he had simply donned his old dress uniform. In the red and gold of his mess dress he looked every inch the gallant soldier. Reluctantly, Freya was forced to admit that he appeared like the embodiment of her girlhood dreams. He bowed politely.

'Good evening, Miss Pascoe,' he said. 'I understand from my aunt that the decorations in here are your work.'

'Lady Ravendale asked me to take responsibility for them,' she replied defensively.

'And thereby showed keen discrimination,' he answered. 'I have seldom seen my home look lovelier.' She caught her breath at his tone.

'I was very glad to be able to help her,' she said. He turned from contemplation of the flowers and looked at her.

'I'm very glad that you wanted to. It's just as well that one member of my family meets with your approval,' he said ironically, raising his brows. Almost despite herself, she found that she was opening her mouth to protest, although if asked, she would have found it very difficult to say why.

She was saved from this dilemma by the voice of a housemaid who put her head around the door and said, 'Beg pardon, my lord, but Miss Pascoe must come and get ready now, or there won't be enough time.'

'Excuse me, my lord,' murmured Freya with a curtsy.

'By all means,' he replied with a bow. 'We will *resume* this conversation later.' Freya hurried away, resolving not to be alone with him for the rest of the evening.

The little housemaid was clearly very excited at the prospect of playing lady's maid, and entered into her task with an enthusiasm which made Freya smile. When the housemaid had done as much as she could, Freya dismissed her with thanks, and stood looking at herself in the mirror. Lady Ravendale had promised to send Potter later to dress her hair and add the finishing touches. There was no doubt that the colour made all the difference to her, and as she looked at her reflection, she revelled in the sensation that for once, she was able to feel nothing but pleasure in her appearance. A thought came into her mind that a certain gentleman would be quite unable to refer to her as a beanpole on this occasion, but she repressed it.

In a very short time, Potter came in to dress her hair, and Freya watched with great interest as the abigail worked with it, dressing it in the fashion of a bygone age.

'It's fortunate that you've kept your hair long, miss,' said Potter, as she deftly fastened some red roses in the finished arrangement. 'If you'd had it cut short in one of the modern styles, it would have been quite difficult to get the right look.'

'You would have had to have found me a wig,' Freya replied.

'Not in those trunks,' answered Potter. 'I'm afraid the wigs didn't last as well as some of the other things. You'd have looked as if the mice'd been at you.'

Freya laughed. 'Thank you so much, Potter,' she said. 'You've worked wonders this evening.'

'It was a pleasure, miss,' answered Potter, flushing a little. 'You're one that pays for dressing, as they say. You should always wear strong colours, though. Those pale shades don't suit you at all, if you don't mind my saying.'

'No, I don't mind,' answered Freya, standing up. 'I have wondered the same thing myself in the past, but never had the confidence to follow my own instincts. I can see that when I leave here, I shall have to buy a whole new wardrobe.' It was not until later that Freya realized that with these words she had given away something about her circumstances; but after a moment or two's thought, she simply shrugged. Potter would probably make nothing of it, and she would be leaving very soon now anyway.

She glanced at the clock. Although it was past the time when the guests had been bidden to arrive, she sat down and waited for a while. Lady Ravendale had not suggested that she should stand with her and her nephew and help to receive their guests, and it would clearly have been inappropriate for her to do so. On the other hand, it would also be absurd for her to go outside the door and come back in to be welcomed along with the other guests. She certainly did not want to stand about in the empty rooms downstairs and wait for people to join her, so she decided to slip in amongst the guests after a good number of other people had arrived. Before she left her room, she glanced at the mirror and smiled wryly. There was no denying the fact that her new costume was very striking, though whether it would suit Reverend Tobias Simpkins's ideas of what was suitable for a clergyman's wife was doubtful. Of course that was all to the good, but on the other hand, if she had really hoped to be able to mingle unobtrusively, she would have done better to have worn the housekeeper's gown!

As she arrived at the top of the stairs, she realized that she had made a miscalculation. Many guests had arrived, but Lord and Lady Ravendale were still welcoming the rest; and in a small group, having just been admitted, were Claudia and Piers Bryce, and Mr and Mrs Siddall. Miss Bryce was dressed as a shepherdess in pale blue, and Mrs Siddall was in pink. They were both staring at Freya as if they could not believe their eyes, and Claudia's mouth had dropped open. But it was Lord Ravendale's reaction which caught and held her attention.

He stood completely still, his expression one of stunned admiration, and for a moment, it felt as if they were completely alone. He took a step towards her as she reached them, but before he could say anything, Claudia spoke.

'Miss Pascoe!' she exclaimed waspishly. 'I see that the costume with which I provided you was not good enough.' Had Freya wished for confirmation that she was looking her best, she only had to look at Miss Bryce's face. The beauty was flushed rather unbecomingly, and her expression was one of chagrin; and for once, the pale shade that she had chosen for her gown looked a trifle insipid.

'No, indeed, it certainly wasn't,' said Lady Ravendale, before Freya could say anything. 'No doubt you did your best, Claudia my dear, but you do not have the advantage of an attic full of splendid materials which have never been thrown away.' Claudia made an unbecoming sound, very like a sniff. Mr Bryce walked over to Freya, dressed in a highwayman's costume, which became him to admiration, a fact of which he was clearly only too well aware. On his face was a smile which was not entirely respectful, and his eyes roved over her costume in an openly salacious way. Suddenly becoming aware of how low cut it was, she put her hand to her throat. He took her other hand and bowed over it gracefully, never taking his eyes off her face.

'May I say that you look charming; quite delightful, Miss Pascoe!' he declared, rather more fulsomely than she liked. 'I positively must have the first dance with you.'

'Piers, what are you thinking of?' said Claudia coldly. 'Miss Pascoe may be far more finely dressed than is appropriate for her situation, but she still has less right to the first dance with you than almost any other lady of your acquaintance. And in any case, I had arranged for her to dance with Reverend Tobias Simpkins.'

Ravendale laughed out loud. 'Simpkins! My God, Claudia, what has Miss Pascoe done to deserve such punishment?'

Claudia glared at him. 'He is by far the most appropriate person to dance with someone of her station,' she declared.

'At a costume ball, questions of protocol surely go by the board,' said Lord Ravendale pleasantly, but with a note of steel in his voice. 'I see no reason why Miss Pascoe should not dance with whomsoever she pleases.' Then turning to Freya, he went on, 'I may be mistaken, but I seem to recognize that gown from one of my family portraits.'

'I understand that it belonged to your grandmother,' Freya said, grateful for the slight change of subject. 'Lady Ravendale lent it to me. She said that it would be all right, but . . . '

Ravendale waved his hand dismissively. 'I am very far from condemning an action which has yielded such desirable results,' he replied smoothly. 'Dance with whom you please, Miss Pascoe; and I trust that you will save one for me later.'

Freya curtsied in reply, and as she rose, she saw that Miss Bryce had fixed her with a look of venomous dislike.

When the dancing began, Freya tried to keep out of Bryce's way. She had not enjoyed the way in which he had looked at her, and although she enjoyed dancing, she felt that she had rather dance with someone whose admiration was expressed in a less disturbing way. As she had suspected, however, her gown made it impossible for her to fade into the background. Furthermore, she could see that Claudia, despite what Ravendale had said, was coming towards her with a rather bandy-legged clergyman of uncertain age in tow. When Mr Bryce approached her, therefore, she was unable to think of an excuse for not dancing with him which did not involve taking Mr Simpkins instead, so she quickly accepted his invitation.

After the dancing had begun, she looked around and saw that, quite properly, Ravendale was partnering Miss Bryce. The beauty seemed to have recovered her complexion, and was looking extremely pleased with herself. For a moment, Freya recalled the daydream that she had had earlier, in which she had imagined herself partnered in the dance by Lord Ravendale. She dragged her attention away from them, vexed to feel herself flushing; and when she looked at Mr Bryce, she saw that he was regarding her with an unpleasantly knowing expression.

'It's too late, I'm afraid,' he said. 'Ravendale's already spoken for.'

'What on earth do you mean?' she replied unhesitatingly; but as the movements of the dance parted them, she became aware that for some unaccountable reason, her heart was beating uncomfortably fast. She hoped that he had not noticed how much his comment had disconcerted her; but when they came together again, she could tell at once that her hopes were in vain.

'Why, nothing at all,' he answered lightly. 'I'm only rather mystified as to why you have chosen to reveal yourself as a beauty on this particular evening.'

It would have been difficult to receive this compliment without any pleasure at all, especially when, as far as Freya was concerned, such comments were almost unprecedented, so she smiled slightly, and said, 'Surely a costume ball is the perfect opportunity to change one's style, Mr Bryce.'

'But to change so dramatically would argue a powerful reason,' persisted Bryce.

'Or a friend with good ideas,' put in Freya. 'It is thanks to Lady Ravendale that I have this to wear.'

'Well, whatever the reason, I shall never quite regard you in the same light again,' he murmured. There was that in his tone which made Freya very glad that she would soon be leaving the shelter of his roof. She was not quite sure how this new light in which he said he regarded her would affect his behaviour towards her, and she remembered his uninvited kiss, and Ravendale's comments about his reputation.

That evening proved to be very different from any similar entertainment which Freya had experienced. The mirror told her that she was a desirable woman; and if she did not believe the evidence of her own eyes, she could surely have deduced it from the reactions of the men who were present. Previously, she had always spent most of the time sitting at the side of the room. On this occasion, she was in demand as a partner for every dance.

In one sense, this seemed a little strange; for even if she was now dressed in a colour and style that suited her, she had certainly not decreased in height, and she was still taller than most of the men in the room. She could only deduce that the romance of wearing strange and unusual costumes released the guests from some of their usual inhibitions and anxieties.

This certainly seemed true of Reverend Tobias Simpkins. He had chosen to retain his usual clerical dress, but from what Freya could observe of him, he appeared to be particularly drawn to ladies with low-cut gowns. This tendency became more pronounced after he had drunk several glasses of Lord Ravendale's excellent champagne. After a while, it became quite amusing to observe how at his approach, ladies who had previously been seated would spring to their feet in an effort to prevent him from peering down at their bosoms.

Since the reverend gentleman was shorter than Freya by at least six inches, it was not difficult to prevent him from indulging in such an activity, and for much of the evening, she managed to avoid him completely. But later on in the evening, she was obliged to give assistance to Mrs Siddall, whose hem had come down, and when she returned to the ballroom, Simpkins was waiting for her.

'Miss Pascoe!' he exclaimed in a squeaky voice, which had become squeakier with every glass he had drunk. 'You cannot deny me any longer. The next dance is a waltz, and I positively must dance it with you.'

Freya looked at him aghast. 'I did not think that you would approve of waltzing,' she said, hoping desperately for an escape.

'Normally, I do not,' he answered, 'but in your case, I have received every encouragement to proceed.'

Freya could well imagine from whom, but she had no intention of falling in with Miss Bryce's plans, and was about to make an excuse, when Lord Ravendale spoke from behind her.

'Unfortunately, you are too late, sir,' he said. 'Miss Pascoe has already promised this dance to me.'

The clergyman opened and shut his mouth once or twice, then said, 'But Miss Bryce . . . '

'I am sure Miss Bryce will be charmed to dance with you if you ask her,' replied the earl smoothly. 'Now, if you will excuse us . . . ' He put out his hand to Freya, and as she took it, she was conscious of that current of feeling which always seemed to surge through her whenever he touched her. She wondered if it was the same for him.

Despite Lord Ravendale's request earlier, she had had no expectation that he would really dance with her. Naturally, his first duty was to his betrothed, and after that, there were other ladies who could quite reasonably expect that he would dance with them. The betrothal announcement had taken place a short time before, and the couple had been circulating, receiving the congratulations of their friends and acquaintances.

'Do not think me ungrateful for your

timely rescue,' she murmured as he led her on to the floor, 'but surely you should be dancing with Miss Bryce.'

'I've already done so. Besides, she is now showing off her ring to all her friends, and is far too busy to have time for me.'

'Then perhaps Miss Waterford, or Lady Garstone . . . '

He gripped her hand more tightly. 'Freya, I *need* to dance with you,' he said. It was the first time that he had called her by her Christian name. She looked up at him in surprise. He looked not so much like a man who had just been receiving the good wishes of all his neighbours, as like someone drowning. Wordlessly, she allowed him to lead her into the dance.

Dancing with him was all that she had imagined it would be. Although he was a big man, he was light on his feet, and they were so well attuned to one another in their movements, that it seemed strange that they were dancing together for the first and probably the last time. To those observing them, they looked a magnificent couple, both dressed mainly in red, both towering head and shoulders over many of the other dancers present.

For a time, they danced together silently; then it occurred to both of them that to have no conversation at all would occasion some remark, and both of them began to speak at once. Ravendale stopped at once, and signalled for Freya to speak first.

'I was about to congratulate you on your engagement, my lord,' she said.

He inclined his head. 'You are very good,' he answered. 'But you must take your share of the credit for it.'

'Credit?' she asked, mystified.

'Why, yes, indeed, ma'am,' he said promptly. 'After all, as you very well know, you were the one who advised me to become engaged to Miss Bryce.' Freya was conscious again of that dreadful sinking feeling in the pit of her stomach. 'No, my lord, I did not,' she protested.

'You told me to do my duty,' he replied. 'That amounts to the same thing.'

'My lord, you cannot blame me for that,' she replied, indignation overcoming every other feeling. 'I would never do such a thing! I may have encouraged you to do your duty, but how could I possibly have imagined that you would interpret doing your duty in such an appal . . . in such a way,' she concluded, swiftly correcting herself.

'So you think my engagement appalling, do you?' he drawled. 'Hmm.'

She coloured painfully. 'I . . . no, of course

not! I merely meant . . . ' Her voice faded away as she found herself at a loss to find any interpretation for her words other than the correct one.

'Go on, Miss Pascoe,' said the earl patiently, as they continued to dance. The gold of his uniform sparkled as they turned in the light of the candles. 'I find that I am fascinated to discover why you consider it to be appalling. Is it upon Claudia's account, or upon mine?'

'My lord, please,' begged Freya, glancing round and willing the music to end.

'I should imagine that you consider Claudia to be the main sufferer,' he continued in a conversational tone. 'After all, you had quite a number of sins to lay to my account when we last spoke together, didn't you? Of what sin do you want to accuse me now? Of fortune hunting? Well, I plead guilty to that. Do you imagine that Claudia doesn't know? Or that she cares?'

Freya looked up at him, her expression half bewilderment, half distress.

'No . . . no, indeed my lord,' she protested.

'We both gain from this alliance. She gains my title, and I gain her money. So you see, she's just as unscrupulous as I am. Not a bad bargain, eh? But you must agree with that. I imagine that you think we deserve each other.' They looked into each other's eyes, and in Ravendale's Freya could see immediate comprehension that that was exactly what she *had* been thinking. A look of what could have been pain crossed his features. 'I see,' he said expressionlessly, as they whirled into the final few moments of the dance. 'There is, of course, one final sin of which you haven't yet accused me — marrying without love. But you, of all people, must know that that's true — mustn't you?'

Freya never knew afterwards how she got off the floor at the conclusion of the dance; nor did she have any recollection of the rest of the evening. Her mind was full of what Ravendale had said. Although she told herself over and over again that it must not be so, she could not help but realize that Ravendale could only have meant that he was in love with her. Worst of all, she was forced to realize that, whatever he had said, whatever he had done, and to whomsoever he might have become engaged, she loved him in return.

# 12

Freya went down to breakfast the following morning feeling very little refreshed by the sleep that she had had. They had not returned from the ball until the early hours of the morning, and it might have been supposed that after such a busy day, Freya would have fallen asleep the moment her head had touched the pillow. Sleep had been very slow in coming, however, and when it did, it was fitful, and punctuated by confusing and unsettling dreams.

She could not forget the conversation that she had had with Ravendale while they were dancing, and the look of pain that she had detected in his eyes. She had tried to tell herself that his expression had been just a trick of the light; but deep down, she knew that her conclusion about his feelings for her was correct. Of her conclusions about her own feelings, she tried not to think at all; but the effort of *not* thinking about them made sleep impossible.

When she entered the breakfast parlour, she was surprised to find Mr Bryce and Mr Siddall there already. Both men got to their feet, and Bryce hurried to pull out a chair for her.

'Miss Pascoe! Welcome!' he cried. 'You are up betimes today.' Repressing the urge to say that she was only up at her usual time, and that he was the one who had clearly risen early, Freya thanked him with a smile, and sat down. As she did so, he tucked her chair in, and when she glanced over her shoulder to thank him, she found his face to be closer to her than she had expected. Again, she recalled how he had kissed her in the garden and to her annoyance, she coloured fierily. Mr Bryce's smile widened and he wiggled his brows at her, then went to his own place and sat down.

'We have a fine day for our visit,' said Mr Siddall. If he had noticed the interplay between the other two occupants of the room, he gave no sign of it.

'Visit?' murmured Freya.

'Yes, indeed,' answered Mr Siddall. 'Bryce has promised to take us round the mill today.'

'God knows why,' said Bryce frankly. 'I must have been devilish drunk at the time. I don't even remember doing so.'

'You were,' laughed Siddall. 'It was just after supper that you said you would do so. But for all that, I should still like to see it.'

'Is the visit only for gentlemen, or are

ladies permitted to come?' asked Freya. Anything rather than brood over last night's events, she thought to herself.

'Why, certainly you may come, if you really wish to do so, Miss Pascoe,' said Bryce in some surprise.

'I should like to very much,' answered Freya. 'Who else is to be of the party?'

'Myself, Bryce of course, Ravendale, and Claudia and Maude if they wish to come — which is extremely doubtful,' said Siddall. Freya's heart gave a queer little jump at the news that Ravendale was to be among the party.

Briefly she toyed with the idea of making her excuses, only to dismiss it. She had shown her pleasure at the invitation too clearly for such excuses to sound genuine. Furthermore, in spite of all that had happened, she *did* want to see what was done there. She would be very foolish to allow Lord Ravendale's presence to prevent her from taking this opportunity, which might not come her way again.

'At what hour are we to go to the mill?' Freya asked, glad to have something to talk about.

'At eleven o'clock,' replied Bryce. 'Ravendale is to meet us here at that hour. Can I help you to some eggs, Miss Pascoe?'

After breakfast, Mr Bryce and his guest went down to the stables, and Freya retired to the library to write another letter to Lady Terrington. Shortly before eleven o'clock, she went upstairs to get her bonnet, then joined the two men in the hall. But before they had time to walk out, they heard footsteps above them, and turned to see Claudia descending, dressed enchantingly in a sprigged muslin gown and a charming chip hat. They must have all looked completely stunned, for Miss Bryce said defensively, 'I've decided to come. You don't mind, do you?'

'Mind? Of course not,' answered her brother. 'But I thought you hated the idea as much as I did!'

'Well I do, of course,' she answered carelessly. 'But why should you be the only sufferer?' She smiled and gave her hand to Mr Siddall. 'Maude is staying here to write a letter, and Mrs Baxter is lying down yet again,' she said. She nodded briefly to Freya, then led the party outside. Instantly, she was all smiles, for at that moment, Lord Ravendale was getting down from his horse and handing the reins to a waiting groom.

'Claudia, my dear,' he said, taking both her hands and kissing each one in turn. 'I hardly dared to think that I might have the pleasure of seeing you today, after last night's excitement.'

'I thought I might as well come also if you are so desperate to see it,' she replied.

'We needn't go at all if you had rather not,' said Ravendale. 'We can stroll in the gardens instead, if you would prefer.'

'Nonsense!' declared Siddall, before Claudia could say anything. 'You know you want to see the mill. Come along, man!'

'Please yourselves,' said Bryce. 'But I know that Miss Pascoe wishes to go, so I shall take her.' So saying, to Freya's great astonishment, he offered her his arm.

'Oh, very well, then,' said Ravendale. 'Let us go, after all.' Claudia laid her hand on the earl's dark blue sleeve, and smiled up at him. Ravendale smiled back at her, then as the smile faded from his lips, he looked at Freya over Claudia's head, and their eyes met and held for a long moment *'I'm marrying without love . . . you know that's true . . . .'* That was the gist of what he had said the previous night; and in a flash, in the expression in his eyes, she saw that message now, and its meaning was the same.

They walked the short distance from the house to the mill. It was a bright sunny day, and heavy coats were not necessary. Freya wore a stout pair of shoes, but Claudia was wearing dainty slippers and she found it necessary to lean heavily on Ravendale's arm for support. The engaged couple gave every appearance of regarding each other with the utmost cordiality, and they enjoyed an intimate conversation for most of the journey. For some reason, this meant that Freya had to respond to Mr Bryce's mild sallies with amusement, and to listen attentively to anything that he might say.

Although the mill was only a short distance from the house, it was screened from it by a generous planting of trees, and a bend in the river meant that there was no direct view between the two. There was a path which meandered along the bank of the river, and it was along this path that the little party walked.

'There must be another way from the house to the mill — for transportation and so on,' remarked Siddall.

'Oh yes, it goes around the back of these trees,' replied Bryce. 'By the way, do you care to go shooting one day? We could go out one morning, if you've a mind for it.'

The mill, when they reached it, was a large, long rectangular building, about five storeys high, with rectangular windows each made up of small panes of glass. There were a few people in the yard in front of the mill, and they eyed the party curiously, touching their caps when they realized that 'the master' had come. Almost immediately a door at the end of the building closest to them opened, and a respectable-looking man of about thirty came out.

'Good morning, Mr Bryce,' he said in tones of considerable surprise. 'We did not expect to see you today.' (Or even ever, his tone seemed to imply.)

'No, no, you are quite right,' replied Bryce airily. 'My friends expressed a desire to see the mill, so I have brought them.' He turned to his companions. 'Well, here it is. Hideous, ain't it?' They looked at the outside for a minute or two, then Bryce said, 'Shall we go back now?'

'I should very much like to go inside,' said Siddall.

'Go inside?' exclaimed Miss Bryce, her tone as incredulous as if he had suggested that they go to the moon. 'But why?'

'It really isn't a place for ladies or gentlemen,' protested Bryce. 'I suggest we wander back for luncheon.'

'I should like to see it as well,' said Ravendale. 'And as for the reason, well I seem to remember saying that I have always been a curious fellow.' He turned to the manager. 'Is it possible for us to look around, or would it disturb the business of the mill too much?' The manager looked stunned. Clearly, no other guests had ever made this request; and Freya could not help wondering, in view of his often-voiced antipathy, how frequently Bryce himself visited the mill.

'Why . . . why certainly,' stammered the manager. 'I should be most happy! That is, if . . . ?' He turned towards Bryce a little anxiously.

'Oh, very well Smithson,' he said carelessly. 'If they must look around, who am I to stop them?'

Miss Bryce then declared in horrified accents that nothing would persuade her to go round the mill. 'Ravendale and I will just stroll around for a little outside,' she said.

Ravendale smiled ironically. 'My dear Claudia, you had the chance to stroll around the gardens and did not take it,' he said gently. 'And, moreover, you might recall that I have already expressed a desire to look around the mill. Not to do so when we have come for that very purpose would appear to be a little perverse.'

Claudia sighed. 'Then Miss Pascoe shall keep me company,' she said. 'We can go back to the house and wait for you there.' Freya opened her mouth to protest then closed it. It was Ravendale who spoke again.

231

'Claudia, I believe that Miss Pascoe would like to see around the mill also,' he said.

Claudia stared at him, then at Freya. 'Would you?' she asked incredulously. 'I suppose I should not be surprised, given your unladylike vigour. Naturally, nobody is in the slightest degree concerned about *my* comfort.'

Ravendale held up his hand. 'Enough,' he said. He turned to the manager. 'Mr Smithson, is there somewhere quiet and . . . er . . . genteel, where Miss Bryce may sit whilst we go round the mill?'

'If Miss Bryce would care for it, she can sit in my house,' said the manager tentatively. 'My wife always takes tea at this hour, and she would be honoured to entertain you.'

Claudia looked from Ravendale to the manager, her mind wavering between settling for the comfort that was offered, and the need to assert what she saw as her rights. Comfort won the day, and she nodded briefly at the manager.

'I'll stay with her then,' she said. '*Anything* would be better than the noise and smell of that dreadful place.'

Ravendale looked at her coldly. 'You forget yourself, my dear,' he said. Turning to the manager, he went on, 'My fiancée is a little overcome by the . . . ah . . . rigours of the journey, and has forgotten her manners. She will be charmed to sit with your wife, Mr Smithson.'

Claudia opened her mouth to protest, then realizing that to do so would only expose her to more of the earl's criticism, closed it again; but the glance that she cast at him was full of fury, all the greater because it was unexpressed. The manager bowed slightly in acknowledgement, then conducted her inside his house where there was no doubt that her welcome would be more gracious than the manner in which she had accepted the invitation.

When Smithson returned, he conducted them towards the entrance to the mill.

'With Mr Bryce's permission, I'd better tell you about some of the things that you will see before we go in,' he said apologetically. 'Once we're inside, it will be rather difficult to talk.' Bryce looked exasperated, but as the others all looked as if they agreed to this notion, he waved a hand in acceptance, and held his peace. 'Would you like me to tell them something of the history of — ' Smithson went on.

'Oh, go on, man, for heaven's sake,' said Bryce impatiently.

'Very well. The mill was built about thirty years ago by Mr Bryce's grandfather; but it has been extended and altered somewhat since then, thanks to modern inventions. It . . . ' He cast a glance at Bryce's bored countenance, his voice faltered a little, then he went on. 'Well . . . well perhaps you might like to ask me some questions later. I will take you round the mill so that you can see the various processes in order. First, the raw cotton comes to us in bales. It has to be disentangled, cleaned and blended before it can go to have a loose twist put into it. We'll go there first, then I can explain what you'll see next. It isn't too noisy in there, so we'll be able to talk.'

'We don't want to spend all day at this wretched business, Smithson,' said Bryce as they walked in. He had offered Freya his arm and she had felt obliged to take it; but although she still thought Bryce handsome, she did not in any way want to be associated with his ungracious manner or his lack of interest.

'I don't see why not,' said Ravendale, following behind with Mr Siddall. 'What else do you propose doing?' Inside the room were large bales of cotton which men, women and children were pulling at and sorting.

'No two bales are the same, so the contents have to be mixed to make a uniform yarn,' said Smithson. Some of the workers looked up from what they were doing, but under the watchful eye of a thickset man, they quickly got back to work. 'All right, Jethers?' Smithson asked him.

'Doing nicely thank you, sir,' replied Jethers, touching his forelock.

'From here on it gets noisy,' Smithson said. 'We go now to the carding-room, where the fibres are straightened. Then we see a small twist put into the thread. After that I'll show you the thread being spun. It's then put on to the frame for weaving. That's putting it very simply. I could tell you in more detail, but . . . ' he cast a glance at Bryce. 'Well, let's go round.'

The most abiding impression that Freya received was the noisiness of the place. She now realized that the hum of the machines had been there in the background as they conversed outside. Once inside the mill itself, she wondered how anyone could endure a whole day of the incessant rattling and clattering. The other thing that struck her forcibly was the dust in the air. It made her cough from time to time, and she could not help but wonder how anyone could manage to breathe in such an atmosphere day after day, week after week, year after year. The possibility of getting dusty clothes, to which Claudia had referred, seemed a very small inconvenience in comparison.

The third thing that she noticed was the preponderance of children. There seemed to be so many of them, some as young as seven, and there were both boys and girls. One or two of them looked up curiously from their work — for visitors were a novelty — but knowing that they were under the watchful eyes of an overseer, one of which had charge of each room, they soon turned back to their work.

Bryce soon abandoned any pretence at interest, and hung back, separating himself from the proceedings, and looking out of the window whenever possible. By way of contrast, both Ravendale and Siddall took a close interest in everything, occasionally exchanging comments with the manager, whenever the level of noise permitted.

One of the noisiest rooms was what Mr Smithson referred to as the 'mule room'. Freya could not help smiling, for her imagination peopled the room with obstinate, four-legged creatures kicking up their heels. In fact, the room contained huge machines for stretching and twisting yarn into thread. The machines were operated by men, but women were there ready to mend any broken threads. To Freya's horror, she noticed that a child was crawling beneath the machine as it was running.

'Look!' she exclaimed, pointing. It happened that the manager was at her side, and seeing what had caught her attention, he leaned forward to speak to her. Bryce was at his usual post, looking out of the window, while Ravendale and Siddall were watching the workings of the machine. Not catching what the manager said the first time, she gestured to him to repeat his words.

'Cleaning,' he said. 'They have to clean off the dust while the machine is working.' Freya looked anxiously at the child, and could not help thinking that surely the machine could be turned off so that her work could be done more safely. The girl was now crawling under the machine close to where they were, and Freya perceived another danger; for as if aware of being discussed the child looked up, their eyes met, and for a few perilous seconds, her attention was taken away from her task. The mechanism shot back, and it seemed as if they would be the witnesses of an appalling tragedy. But before Freya had a chance to take in the danger properly, or even to scream, Ravendale had dropped to one knee, leaned under the machine at his own imminent peril, and dragged the child to safety.

The mule was stopped then, and to all present, used as they were to the constant noise of the place, it felt like complete silence.

'Good God, Ravendale, what on earth happened?' exclaimed Bryce, coming belatedly from the window.

'Lord Ravendale saved this child's life,' replied Siddall in incredulous tones. 'My God, Ravendale, I don't think I've ever seen such a brave act.'

'Certainly brave,' agreed the manager fervently. 'Even foolhardy. These machines are very powerful, my lord. You could have lost your arm.'

'You make too much of it,' said the earl tersely. 'An arrangement to have the machines turned off from time to time so that they could be cleaned would be more to the point.' The manager glanced at Ravendale, then at Bryce.

'It is never done,' he replied simply.

'Well, at least you've saved me a pound or two,' said Bryce carelessly. 'Brats cost money, you know. Have you seen enough now?'

Suddenly, Freya had seen quite sufficient of the inside of the mill, and nodded.

'There's just one thing that I would like to see, and that is the water wheel,' said Siddall.

'I'll take you there at once,' said the manager quickly, and led them out of the

238

room. Freya turned to get a last glimpse of the girl, and saw that she had caught hold of Ravendale's hand. With a smile, he gently released her before turning to follow the rest of the group. Behind him, the machines roared back into life, and as Freya saw the mule roll across the room, she imagined how the earl might have been cruelly maimed, and she shuddered.

Mr Smithson took them to the lowest level of the mill, to where a man stood wiping his hands on a dirty rag.

'Everything going as it should, Heap?' Smithson asked.

'Turning as sweet as ever,' replied Heap. Then he touched his forelock to the party, and stepped to one side. 'Take a good look sirs and madam,' he went on. 'But keep your hands out of the way. That beauty there can do a lot of damage as well as a lot of good.' They all moved forward to look at the massive wheel.

'How wide is it?' asked Ravendale.

'Thirty feet or so,' replied Heap. They looked at it for a while in silence, and even Bryce appeared to be impressed.

'What a quantity of water must pass over it in a day,' murmured the earl. Freya nodded, but she could not dismiss the scene in the mule room from her mind, and as she thought again of the dreadful consequences that might have been the result, she swayed a little. At once, she found her hand caught in a comforting grasp. She looked up and saw Ravendale looking down at her.

'Are you all right?' he asked her in an undertone.

'Yes, I am well,' she replied. 'I was just thinking about . . . in there.'

He held her hand for a few minutes more, a little longer than was necessary, and when he released it, she felt strangely bereft.

After looking at the wheel, they emerged into the sunlight and all felt some measure of relief at leaving the noise and the dust behind.

'How many children work in the mill?' Freya asked Bryce.

'Don't ask me,' he replied, gesturing towards Smithson.

'About a third of the workers are children,' responded the manager.

'But there are so many! Surely they cannot all come from around here?'

'No, they come from workhouses in the city,' he said. 'They are lodged in the apprentices' house, which is not far away.'

'They seem so young,' murmured Freya,

'Well, what else can the brats do?' asked Bryce carelessly. 'At least they have a roof over their heads. And before you ask, no, we're not going to see where they're lodged. I've had enough of this damned place and its inhabitants to last me a lifetime. I'll go and get my sister then we can walk back and get the stench of this place out of our nostrils.'

After Bryce had gone, Smithson turned to the other members of the party.

'Thank you for your interest,' he said. 'It's rare that . . . ' Suddenly aware that what he was about to say might be construed as criticism of his employer, he fell silent then added rather lamely, 'Well, thank you.'

When Claudia and Bryce had rejoined the group, they turned to walk back to the house. Clearly, Mrs Smithson had been acceptable enough company, for Claudia seemed to be in a reasonable frame of mind, and she had either forgotten her disagreement with Ravendale, or she had decided to make nothing of it. Needless to say, the topic of the earl's bravery came up. When Siddall told her about what her fiancé had done, she replied, 'Well, thank God you didn't lose your arm, that's all I can say. I cannot bear deformity of any kind.'

'What a mercy I was not wounded in the war then,' he said ironically.

'That at least would have been something to boast about,' Miss Bryce replied, oblivious

241

to the tone of his last remark. 'But as for risking yourself over a mill brat that is surely quite replaceable, what a waste of effort!'

She made as if to take the earl's arm once again, but Ravendale, with a smile on his face but a steely look in his eyes, said, 'Give your brother the pleasure of your company this time, my dear, and I shall talk to Siddall about estate matters.'

'Dull stuff!' she exclaimed, and did as he suggested. Brother and sister walked on ahead, leaving Freya to walk back with Ravendale and Siddall; and soon the two men were talking about the different ways in which land could be used to pasture animals.

Freya, walking beside them, showed an interested countenance, but in reality her thoughts were dominated by the actions of Ravendale in the mill. She could not imagine looking at one of those machines again without a shudder, and her admiration of his courage knew no bounds. As for Miss Bryce's reaction, that could only arouse her disgust, and from his decision not to walk with his fiancée back to the house, she was certain that the earl had felt the same.

# 13

That evening, the heavens opened and the rain fell in torrents, causing the river to flow even more swiftly than usual.

'How tiresome,' sighed Miss Bryce, as if the very weather had gone out of its way to annoy her. 'But then I always think that the weather is far worse here than in London.'

'Yeth indeed,' agreed Mrs Siddall. 'Thertainly the countwy ith alwayth wetter than the town.'

Freya bit her tongue so as to prevent herself from arguing with this piece of absurdity.

'I do hope that it stops before tomorrow,' went on Miss Bryce. 'We are expected at the Manners' for the day. It will be too bad if we have to put it off.'

'Yeth indeed,' said Mrs Siddall. 'It will be too bad.'

Freya reflected that if Miss Bryce had hoped that she would be the kind of companion who agreed with everything that she said, as Mrs Siddall appeared to do, then she must be sadly disappointed.

Shortly before they were due to retire, the

butler came in with a message for Mr Bryce from the mill. He cast his eyes heavenward, then with an air of great reluctance, got up from his chair and left the room.

'Poor Piers,' murmured Claudia. 'It is too bad that that wretched little concern should make all these demands on his time.'

Freya, her eyes on her sewing, found herself mouthing the words, 'Yeth indeed,' at the same time as Mrs Siddall said them, and gave herself a mental smack on the hand, for she had very nearly spoken them out loud!

It did not take Mr Bryce long to deal with the matter, and he soon returned to the drawing-room, an irritated expression marring his handsome features.

'One of the wretched brats from the mill has run away,' he said as he sat down. 'Devil if I know what I'm supposed to do about it.'

'On such a night as this?' exclaimed Freya, looking out into the gloom. They could not see the rain now in the darkness, but they could still hear it. It was as relentless a downpour as Freya could remember.

'Exactly,' replied Bryce, misunderstanding her meaning. 'I cannot be expected to go riding out in this weather to look for a mill brat. We'll set the dogs on the trail tomorrow.'

That night, Freya lay in her bed listening to the rain and thinking of the child who was out there somewhere, probably without shelter. He or she must have been quite desperate to flee on such a night; yet when Freya recalled the noise and the dust of the mill, and the ever-present danger of the machines, she could not feel entirely surprised that someone would wish to escape from such a life.

Such a reflection, unsurprisingly, caused her to think again about the child whom Lord Ravendale had pulled from beneath the machine. Did this child know the one who had escaped? For what kind of miserable existence had Ravendale saved the life of the mill child?

The following morning dawned bright and clear. Mr Bryce, at his sister's insistence, rode up to the top of the track, and pronounced the roads fit enough for the excursion to Chapel-en-le-Frith. Miss Bryce, making what was clearly, for her, an inordinate amount of effort, emerged from her bedchamber not long after ten o'clock, and the party, consisting of Mr and Mrs Siddall and Mrs Baxter and their hostess, set off as soon as they had breakfasted.

Freya was surprised to find that Mr Bryce was not going with them but he said that he had business to attend to. Freya wondered doubtfully if this business was anything to do with the runaway child; but as soon as the carriage had disappeared out of sight, he said to her, 'At last! Miss Pascoe, I wonder whether you would mind stepping into the library with me? I have something that I would like to discuss with you.' Remembering all that had passed between them, Freya was conscious of some feelings of misgiving as she followed him into the library. True, she had found him attractive at one time; now, she had no desire for an intimate interview with him, but she could see no way of avoiding it.

He closed the door behind them, gestured for her to be seated in an upright chair in front of the desk, then walked behind the desk to look out of the window, his hands behind his back. Freya waited patiently, and eventually, he turned and sat down opposite her, very much at his ease.

'I have a suspicion that you may have guessed why I have sought this interview with you,' he said at last.

'No sir, I have no idea,' Freya replied frankly.

'You surprise me. I thought I had made my feelings plain. When are you due to leave my sister's employ? In a day or so, isn't it?'

Freya was trying to elucidate the meaning of the first part of his speech, and found herself rather disconcerted by his sudden change of subject. She therefore answered, in a more flustered manner than was her wont, 'I believe so . . . That is, I had not given it any thought.'

'Then let me encourage you to think about the matter further. If you had hoped that she would consider employing you for longer, then allow me to enlighten you. She will certainly not wish to have you about the place after the end of this week.'

Freya said nothing, but she must have been looking at him with question in her eyes, for he shrugged his shoulders and went on.

'The explanation is quickly given. You will probably have realized by now that my sister is easily bored, and is always looking for something new to entertain her. She needed someone to come to Derbyshire with her, and to provide some company until the Siddalls arrived. They are now here. She also needed someone to be on hand to help Lady Ravendale in the preparations for the ball, and that is done.

'You may have noticed that Claudia is very indolent. Had you not been here, she would have been obliged to offer help herself. Your presence has relieved her of the necessity. But now the ball is over and she has others to entertain her, she won't want you in the way.'

Freya stared at him. It occurred to her that

if she had really been in a position where she depended on others for employment, and was hoping for an extension of her present work, then this information would be distressing indeed.

'I can see that you are disappointed,' he said kindly. 'But surely it's better to discover this now, rather than to hope for more work and then to find that you must go?'

'Yes . . . yes, I suppose so,' Freya agreed.

'Anyway, I have a suggestion for your future occupation, which I hope you will find agreeable.' *Oh heavens*, thought Freya. *Never say that he is going to ask me to marry him.*

There had been a time when, if she was honest, she might have welcomed such a proposal from this handsome young man. Further acquaintance had revealed his shallow nature and his lack of concern for his workers in the mill, however, and now she could only regard such a proposal with abhorrence.

'I have noticed how much you like Derbyshire, and have thought of a way that you might remain here, at least for part of the year,' he went on. 'I often have cause to visit Buxton, and it has occurred to me that if I were to find you an agreeable house there, I should have twice as much reason for going. I should put a sum of money at your disposal for housekeeping, clothes and so on, and no doubt little presents of one sort or another would come your way. I would continue to support you as long as the connection lasted, and I see no reason why it should not last for some time.'

He leaned towards her. 'I must say, I had no idea how desirable you could look until the night of the ball. You certainly cooked your goose then with regard to future employment with my sister, and probably with regard to Simpkins, too. Oh, I know his eyes were out on stalks as he looked at you, but sober reflection will tell him that someone capable of being so flamboyant at a public occasion is not suitable to be the wife of a clergyman. But as far as I am concerned, since then, I have been unable to get you out of my mind.'

Freya stood up, at first completely dumbfounded at what she had heard. Then, slowly, she said, 'Let me be quite sure that I have your meaning correctly. Are you asking me to become your mistress?'

Bryce stood up also, and came round the desk to stand very close to her. 'You are overcome by the generosity of my offer,' he said smiling. 'And no wonder! But . . . '

At this point, Freya regained her tongue, and drawing herself up to her full height, she exclaimed, 'How dare you?'

'Love makes a man daring,' he replied with something very like a smirk. He took hold of her hand. 'It's true that your beauty is not of a conventional kind, nor yet, to be honest, of a kind that I've ever admired very much. But you've plenty of spirit, and I've always liked a woman with spirit.'

'I can't believe that you are making this suggestion,' said Freya, too amazed for the moment to disengage her hand.

'That is quite natural,' replied Bryce, still smirking. 'It is not surprising that you should be overcome by my generosity. But — '

At once, Freya came to herself, and snatching her hand from his, she interrupted his self-satisfied speech. 'Kindly say no more, sir. You have already insulted me sufficiently by making me such an offer.'

'Insulted?' he queried, puzzled.

'I am a lady, sir, and you have not treated me as such.'

He laughed. 'A lady? By God, that's rich. To start with, you're a paid companion, and you can't afford airs and graces. You're obliged to work for your living. Well, you might as well do so in a pleasurable and well-paid way. And for another thing, if you're such a lady, why are you forever making eyes at Ravendale?'

She turned pale. 'I have never done such a thing!' she exclaimed.

'Well, m'sister certainly thinks you do. Why else should she tell Mrs Siddall? It's of no consequence, anyway. He'll never want you when he can have Claudia. You haven't her money as an inducement, my dear. And to be honest, without money to buy the kind of clothes you wore on the night of the ball, you'll never be anything but a plain Jane.'

She winced a little at his cruelty, but she refused to give him the satisfaction of knowing that he had hurt her, and instead, she said spiritedly, 'If I am so undesirable, why make me such an offer?'

'I told you, I like a spirited woman. Anyway, looks don't matter in the kind of connection I have in mind. And like Claudia, I'm a trifle indolent. I'm prepared to settle for what I can get.'

Freya listened to his words with an ever-increasing sense of disgust. 'Then sadly, you will have to find someone other than myself. You may be prepared to settle for what you can get, but I am not. I am a good deal too nice in my notions, I'm afraid, to settle for a man without wit, intelligence, manners or sensitivity!' She turned to leave.

'Why, you insolent hussy!' he exclaimed. 'Do you realize what you've rejected?'

She smiled slightly. 'Yes, I believe I do. Good day, sir.'

'Don't expect me to repeat my offer,' he called after her. 'And don't expect me to recommend that my sister keep you on. She can turn you out immediately, for all I care.'

'You relieve me extremely,' she added. Then making a small curtsy, because she couldn't resist it, she left the room.

Suddenly feeling stifled, she hurried upstairs to get her bonnet, resolving not to think about the conversation that had just taken place until she was out of the house. So it was that it was not until she was walking along the front of the house angrily tying the strings of her bonnet with hands that were not completely steady, that she allowed herself to think about the scene in which she had taken part.

The replies that she had finally given him afforded her some satisfaction; but the hurt that his disparagement of her had caused still remained. What would she have done, had she been indeed a paid companion, in expectation of being dismissed, she wondered? Would she have found herself obliged to enter into a loveless physical union, from which her lover would release himself the instant he tired of her? The very thought made her shudder.

As for making eyes at Ravendale, she had never done such a thing. To her shame, she had to acknowledge her love for him, despite her knowledge of his profligate life; but he was an engaged man, and she had never consciously tried to attract him. There came into her mind the idea that if Ravendale had made her such an offer, she would have found it much harder to resist.

In order to banish such thoughts from her mind, she lengthened her step, and before she realized where her journey was taking her, she found that she had almost reached the mill. To get any closer to it might be to draw unwelcome attention to herself, so instead, she took a path which led up the hill behind it. She glanced briefly at the river, swollen now, and much higher due to the heavy rain that had fallen the previous night. Turning away from it again, she began to climb the hill.

The ascent was a steady and gentle one, and it was not long before she reached a large house, with vegetable gardens around it. Outside, an untidy-looking maid was hanging washing on the line. This must be the apprentices' house, Freya decided. She remembered the apprentice who had run away, and wondered whether the child was regretting exchanging this sturdy shelter for a night out in the rain.

She began to think about the lives of the children who resided in the apprentices' house: long hours of work, followed by much-needed sleep, with little time for anything else. She contrasted this with her own happy childhood, and slowly there came into her mind the notion that when this whole adventure was over, she would use some of her fortune to provide care for children who needed it.

This decided upon, she walked on briskly; but it was not long before she started to think once again about her own troubles. Her heart had leaped that morning at the sight of a letter for her in John's handwriting, but its contents had been disappointing. Although he had seemed optimistic about the future of the bank, he had not given permission for her to disclose anything about the bank's situation or her own. Nevertheless, because of the morning's events, if for no other reason, she was now resolved to leave as soon as possible. If need be, she would stay privately and discreetly in the vicinity until she had better news from John; but to remain in the Bryces' home any longer than she had to was clearly quite impossible now.

Pausing for a moment or two to catch her breath, she caught sight of a very pretty flower a short distance from the path, and she went over to look at it and see if perhaps it was an orchid. As she crouched down to look at it, she saw that next to her was a large tree with a hollow at its base. At first, she thought that someone had placed a bundle of rags there; but when she moved closer, she saw that it was a child asleep and at once she guessed that it must be the runaway apprentice. Clearly, the child had decided to shelter from the rain, rather than put a greater distance between itself and the mill and get soaked through.

She paused in indecision. Part of her wanted to aid the child in its escape; but she was not at present in a position to offer alternative accommodation, and it seemed to her that those responsible for it should be informed of its whereabouts. She was still wondering what to do, when the child woke, looked at her with wide and frightened eyes and began to scramble out of the tree.

Freya could now see that it was a girl with long, unkempt red hair; and as they looked at each other, it was as if each one felt a stab of recognition. It was the child whom Ravendale had rescued from beneath the machinery in the mill. The child looked around in panic, and seeing that she was on the point of flight, Freya caught hold of her hand. For a few moments, the child struggled desperately, then Freya took her other hand, and crouched down in front of her.

'Look at me!' she said compellingly. 'Look at me, child.' The little girl ceased her struggles and did as she was bid. 'You recognize me, don't you? I was there when Lord Ravendale saved you from the machine.'

For a moment or two, the child looked silently at Freya, then she spoke again, whimpering, 'Please, ma'am! Oh please!'

'What's your name, child?' Freya asked her.

'Beth, ma'am,' she answered.

'Well, Beth, if I let go of you now, will you promise me not to run away?' The child nodded, and Freya let go of her. 'Why are you up here?' The child stood twisting the corner of her pinafore into a screw.

'I wanted to see him,' she replied eventually.

'Him?'

'Him that saved me. His lordship.'

'You thought you would see him up here?' Freya asked her.

'He rides up here sometimes,' she answered. 'I've seen him from th'ouse. I daresn't cross the river for fear of being seen.'

Freya nodded. 'Why did you want to see him?' she asked.

'I hate th'mill. I don't want to work there

no more.' With that she began to cry.

Freya took out her own handkerchief and gave it to her. She allowed the child to cry on for a little while, then eventually she said, 'I'm sorry that Lord Ravendale hasn't come as you hoped, but I'll do my best to help you if I can. What is it you want me to do?'

'I don't want to go back to th'mill,' the child repeated. 'Oh please, please ma'am, let me go somewhere else!' Freya looked at her and thought hard. To take her to Riverside was out of the question. Miss Bryce would have no sympathy with the plight of a mill child; her comments on hearing of Ravendale's rescue of this one from the machines proved that. Mr Bryce could not possibly be appealed to after the morning's confrontation. Lord Ravendale, she knew, was away from home that day, for she had heard Miss Bryce say so. Furthermore, there were laws related to the disappearance of apprentices, and she knew that she could not risk breaking such laws, and thus drawing attention to her brother at the very time when he most wanted her to be discreet.

'Please?' the child said again.

'I'll tell you what I'll do,' Freya said after another pause. 'I believe that you must go back to the mill, for I think that a paper has been signed that says you must work there.'

Beth began to back away, shaking her head. 'No, wait Beth! Listen to me. Because of that paper, they will be able to force you to go back, whether you want to or not. I will go with you and tell them that you agreed to come back with me. That will mean that they will be much less angry with you. And meantime, I will go and find Lord Ravendale and tell him of this, and I am sure that he will help you if he can. How would that be?'

The child shook her head again, and the expression of fear came back over her features. 'You said you'd help me,' she said. 'I won't go back!'

'You must,' insisted Freya. 'Mr Bryce will not let you escape. Last night he was talking about sending the dogs out. You will certainly be caught. But if you go with me now, everyone will see that you want to do what's right.' The child continued to look at her stubbornly. 'I *promise* that I will go with you and put your case to them.' She thought of kindly Mr Smithson. Surely he would be reasonable. Beth looked at her for a moment or two, then dropped her head; and when Freya put out her hand, the child put hers into it.

Together, they walked back down the path that Freya had taken only lately, passing the apprentices' house, but then taking the path that curved down to the right and led to the mill. As they drew nearer to it, Freya felt Beth's hand tightening its grip on hers, and she squeezed it in return.

As they turned into the mill courtyard, Freya was astonished and horrified to see Mr Bryce there, talking to Mr Smithson. Had it been possible, she would have withdrawn there and then, and waited in the shelter of the wood until Bryce had gone. As ill luck would have it, however, Bryce happened to turn and see them, and an expression of satisfaction came over his face.

'Ah! Our runaway, I presume,' he exclaimed. 'Miss Pascoe, I am indebted to you. You did well to find her. And as for you, you disgusting brat, you're going to get the punishment you deserve!' The child shrank away from him, tightening her hold on Freya's hand.

'Mr Bryce, the child is frightened,' Freya protested.

'And well she might be,' he answered. 'She's been disobedient and must be punished for it.' By now a group of those who happened to be in the vicinity had gathered to witness the scene. Bryce turned to two of the men amongst the group, 'Take the brat and lock her up in the apprentices' house.'

'Nooooo!' screamed the child, clinging to

Freya. 'You promised!'

'Mr Bryce,' urged Freya. 'I promised Beth that I would speak for her.'

'Beth?' he queried.

'It is the child's name,' she answered with dignity.

'You had no business to promise the brat anything,' he said; and as she looked into his eyes, she became quite certain that he was exacting a most unfair revenge for her rejection of him earlier that day. He turned to the two men. 'Take her, you cretins.'

Seeing that she could never win the struggle, and that Beth would almost certainly be the one who would be hurt if she persisted, Freya said to her, 'Go with them! I will do what I can.' She watched helplessly whilst one of the men picked Beth up and carried her, kicking and screaming, whilst the other man walked beside. Then she turned to Bryce. 'There was no need for that,' she said.

'Of course there was a need,' replied Bryce. 'She wouldn't have gone without a struggle. You saw that.'

'She was frightened. She hates the mill,' pursued Freya.

'If she didn't want to be frightened, she shouldn't have run away,' he said dispassionately. 'She may hate the mill, but it puts food in her belly and a roof over her head.'

'But Mr Bryce . . . '

'Enough,' he shouted. 'You forget yourself and your position; but I suppose that should not surprise me, for I have already noticed that you have unreliable instincts and a strange sense of values. Upon my soul, I see no reason why I should be at pains to oblige you today. The brat has done wrong. She shall be punished, and then she'll go back to the mill. And you, Miss Pascoe, will be present this evening in order to witness that punishment administered. It might teach you to be less busy in future about other people's affairs!' So saying, he strode off in the direction of the mill office without a backward glance.

# 14

Freya took a step after him, then stopped. It was unlikely that he would be prepared to listen to any representations of hers, least of all today. Slowly, she walked back to the house, trying desperately to think of some way of helping Beth. As she neared Riverside, she turned to look at the bridge that crossed the stream, and the road that wound up to Ravendale. At once, she remembered her promise that she would tell Lord Ravendale of what had happened. She glanced at the Bryces' house, then resolutely crossed the bridge. She and Ravendale had exchanged bitter words, and their encounter at the ball had not resolved the situation between them. But he was the man who had saved Beth at great risk to himself, and he was the one to whom Beth herself had wanted to turn.

Somewhat to her surprise, she realized that she too was convinced that Ravendale was the only one who would be prepared to concern himself with the welfare of a mill child. Given his other weaknesses, it seemed strange; but so it was.

She had so steeled herself to face him, that

she had forgotten that he would not be there; so on her arrival, she was rather nonplussed to find that he was away. Lady Ravendale was within, however, and the butler conducted her to the drawing-room, where her ladyship was sitting, enjoying a cup of tea.

'My dear Miss Pascoe!' she exclaimed. 'This is a most agreeable surprise. Do come in and join me. The tea has only just arrived. Hobbs, bring another cup for Miss Pascoe.'

'Thank you, ma'am,' replied Freya distract-edly. 'But I need to communicate with . . . that is, I knew Lord Ravendale was away, but was hoping against hope . . . '

Lady Ravendale's expression changed to one of concern. 'Miss Pascoe! You are agitated! Come and sit down at once, and compose yourself.'

'Thank you,' replied Freya. She sat down, suddenly realizing that all the excitement had quite drained her. When the butler returned with a cup for her, the countess poured her some tea, and she drank it gratefully.

'I am sorry for descending upon you in such a way,' said Freya.

'Think nothing of it,' said her ladyship. 'I'm sorry that Daniel is not here. He went out this morning on a matter of business, and I am not at all sure when he will return. He is rather unpredictable these days. Is it anything

I can help you with?'

So sympathetic was her tone that Freya found herself telling her about the escape of the child, her discovery in the woods, and Mr Bryce's brutal attitude (although needless to say, she said nothing about the mill-owner's dishonourable proposal.)

'And so you came to find Daniel,' said Lady Ravendale, as soon as Freya had finished her account of events. 'I have to say that you have done very right; but it surprises me that you should be so sure that he would be the one to help you.'

'But ma'am, that's because of what happened when we all went round the mill,' explained Freya. 'Lord Ravendale saved the very same child from a horrible death beneath one of the machines, at some risk to himself. I could not help but believe that he is a man of great humanity, despite his faults.' She could have bitten her tongue out, so vexed was she with herself at having said those last few words out loud.

'His faults, my dear?' said the countess, wrinkling her brow.

Thinking that this betokened annoyance at the personal nature of her comment, Freya said quickly, 'Forgive me. I should not have said such a thing. It is none of my business. I had no wish to offend you.'

Her ladyship smiled faintly. 'You haven't offended me; but I must confess to being a little puzzled. Oh, don't mistake me! Daniel has his share of faults, as much as any mortal man, I suppose. But none that are worth commenting upon, really.'

'But surely . . . his gambling,' ventured Freya.

'You are mistaken. Daniel does not gamble; at least, not to excess. It is a matter of principle with him.'

Freya stared at her for a long moment. 'But you said . . . you told me . . . '

'Yes?'

'His mother's necklace . . . ' murmured Freya.

'His mother's necklace?' echoed Lady Ravendale, frowning. 'Oh, I see!' she exclaimed, her brow clearing. 'No, it was his *father* who did that. Daniel would never, ever do such a thing. How on earth could you have supposed that he did?'

Freya stared at her, her expression one of complete bewilderment. 'But ma'am, you yourself told me so. You said that the earl . . . ' Her voice faded away. 'You didn't mean the present earl, did you?' she concluded hollowly.

Her ladyship sighed. 'I can see that I shall have to tell you the whole sordid story,' she said resignedly. 'The damage began with Daniel's grandfather. He had a great weakness for the card table and reduced the family fortune considerably. When he inherited, there was a London house, a hunting box in Leicestershire, a small estate in Hertfordshire and lands in Suffolk, in addition to this place. By the time he died, only this property, the London house and the Hertfordshire estate were left.

'My husband, Gervase, was the older son, and was cut from a very different cloth. When my father-in-law died, Gervase did all he could to mend matters, and indeed, the land that was left became profitable in his hands. But we were never blessed with children, and when Gervase died, far too young, his brother Roger, Daniel's father, inherited.

'Roger's weakness was horse racing, rather than the tables, but he completed the damage that his father had done, and undid all of Gervase's good work. And all that time, Daniel was in the army. He should really have been here at home, learning to run the estate, but his father did all he could to persuade him to remain where he was. I'm sure, now, that this was because Roger knew that his son would have exerted all his influence to put a stop to it; and Daniel has a very strong will.' She paused for a moment.

'I blame myself to some degree,' she went on in a low tone. 'I had some influence over Daniel's mother and it may be that I could have done something if I had only tried. But I had no idea that matters had become so serious. Roger was very cunning, you see; very good at hiding his weakness. Otherwise, I think that I might have written to Daniel informing him of his father's dealings, improper though it would have been.

'By the time Daniel inherited, this estate was all that was left, and it was grossly encumbered. Daniel works so hard, and I believe that we shall come about; but it seems so unfair that he should have to pay for the weaknesses of two previous generations.'

'Oh, good God,' breathed Freya, turning rather white.

'It is a dreadful story,' agreed Lady Ravendale. 'I'm not surprised that you are shocked.'

Freya said nothing. She *was* shocked; but not so much at this news as at the recollection of the accusations which she had thrown at him, when in fact he was completely innocent of wrongdoing.

After this, she found it very difficult to sustain any kind of normal conversation and would indeed have been at a loss to tell anyone afterwards what had been said. When it was finally time for her to leave, Lady Ravendale said, 'I shall tell Daniel what you have told me when he arrives home. Try not to worry. I'm sure that he will return in time. And if he does not,' she went on resolutely, 'I shall come myself.'

Freya thanked her and left. She took the route that she had followed on her way there, but if questioned afterwards, she would have found it quite impossible to describe any part of her journey, for her mind was completely taken up with what she had just learned.

Part of what she was feeling was relief. Even whilst all the evidence had seemed to point to the fact that the earl was a gambler, she had always been convinced that there must be good in him, or that at any rate he could change. To discover that he was in fact honourable could not but be gratifying. But coupled with that was the shame that she now felt at accusing him. She had not even given him an opportunity to explain himself. So convinced had she been of her own rightness, that she had not been prepared to hear any other arguments.

And yet, in justice to herself, she had to remember that there were those who had gone out of their way to encourage her to believe the worst about him. It was only as she was walking over the bridge and back to

Riverside that she began to wonder why both Mr and Miss Bryce should have been at such pains to convince her of Ravendale's ruinous habits. The only answer that occurred to her was that Miss Bryce, in her determination to keep away any female from the man she had chosen for herself, was even prepared to damage his character in order to keep him at her side. Perhaps she had persuaded her brother to support her in this enterprise. If this was the truth of the matter, then such slanderous behaviour could only arouse contempt. Suddenly, Freya understood something of what it would mean for the earl to be married to someone who cared so little for the honour of his name; and the thought felt like a physical blow.

As she reached the house, she remembered that the punishment of the child Beth was to be administered that evening, and that she was to witness it. Not that she could have stayed away. Having promised Beth that she would see that all would be made right, and having humiliatingly failed to protect her, the very least that she could do would be to be present, even if Bryce had not insisted upon it. She might be powerless to plead for the child or in any way deflect Bryce from his purpose, but at least her presence might in some way strengthen the child for the ordeal to come, whatever it might be; for Bryce had not disclosed the nature of the punishment.

It was at this point that the sound of a carriage arriving informed her that Miss Bryce and her friends had returned from their day out; and at the same moment, Bryce emerged from the doorway.

'In a good hour!' he exclaimed, when the carriage had drawn to a halt. 'My dear sister! Mrs Baxter! Mrs Siddall; Siddall; I trust you've had a pleasant visit.'

'Motht agweeable,' said Mrs Siddall, in a rather distracted tone, 'exthept that poor mama ith not well!' Mr Siddall assisted his mother-in-law down from the carriage and into the house, whilst Mrs Siddall twittered along behind, carrying her mother's shawl and reticule.

'Our day was pleasant, but fatiguing,' said Claudia in response to her brother. 'Unfortunately, on top of everything, Mrs Baxter decided to be ill so we had to come away early,' she went on, her tone implying that Mrs Baxter had done it deliberately, just to be annoying, and could be perfectly well if only she tried.

'I trust you are not too fatigued to congratulate Miss Pascoe,' said Mr Bryce after the rest of the party had gone inside. There was a malicious gleam in his eye.

'Congratulate her?' queried his sister. 'Upon what matter could Miss Pascoe possibly need congratulation? Surely Mr Simpkins has not proposed?'

'Not to my knowledge. No, she has discovered our runaway from the mill,' he replied. 'She recaptured the brat this afternoon; and I am this very moment ready to escort her to the mill so that she might witness its punishment.'

' 'It' is 'she',' said Freya indignantly. 'And her name is Beth.'

'Well, what is that to the purpose?' asked Miss Bryce. Freya took a step closer to her. It seemed impossible that Claudia would exert herself to help, but she had to try.

'Miss Bryce, she is only a child and she has suffered enough,' she said urgently. 'Please, use your influence.'

'Oh, for goodness sake!' exclaimed Miss Bryce, cutting her off. 'Have the brat beaten, or locked away, or fined, or hanged or whatever, but let us get the wretched business over and done with so that we can have dinner.'

'That is exactly what I intend to do,' said her brother. 'Do you wish to attend?'

His sister made a moue of distaste. 'Attend the punishment of a mill brat? Please, Piers, develop a proper sense of priority! I have to

271

dress for dinner,' she replied.

Freya looked at both of them aghast. It was clearly impossible to expect any help or sense of decency from anyone present. She would just have to see what form the punishment took, and try to temper it as best she could.

As she and Bryce walked towards the mill, she decided to try one last time. She had no hope of success; but she felt that she could not possibly meet Beth's eyes if she had not done all that she could.

'Mr Bryce,' she began.

'Miss Pascoe, I do hope that you are not about to berate me again on the treatment of mill fodder,' he interrupted.

'It is not a question of 'mill fodder' as you call it,' she said scornfully. 'It is a question of common humanity.' She could have bitten her tongue out the moment she had spoken. Taking a high hand at this time would not achieve her anything, she knew, but the phrase he had used had angered her so greatly that she had not thought before speaking.

'Common is the right word,' he agreed. 'I believe I have already had cause to remark today that your instincts do not appear to be those of a well-bred lady, and your sentimental attitude towards this brat proves it. These people are toughened against the difficulties of life. They lack sensibility. They do not feel things in the way that refined persons do. They are also, for the most part, extremely stupid. They cannot observe for themselves the wisdom of a certain course of action. But witness the foolishness of that child's flight, when the meanest intelligence would have informed her that recapture would be inevitable.'

'Mr Bryce, she is *seven years old!*' exclaimed Freya incredulously.

'And what if she is?' he replied. 'Whatever may be their age, brutality is the only thing that they understand, and the only way of motivating them. Let one child run off and escape punishment, and they'll all start doing it. Then where would our industry be? Believe me, if you punish one child severely it will save a lot of trouble later with the others; and *this* one won't do it again in a hurry.' He paused, then added smoothly, 'Of course, if you really want to save her, you know what to do. In those circumstances, my dear, no doubt I should be delighted to oblige you.' He stopped walking, took hold of her hand and raised it to his lips. She snatched it away angrily.

'You disgust me!' she said venomously.

His eyes narrowed. 'Then the punishment takes place,' he replied. 'And you watch.'

When they arrived at the mill yard, it was full of working people. They were talking quietly together, and the atmosphere, though not hostile, was not cordial either. They all looked tired, and they certainly did not look ready to leap to the child's aid.

Beth had already been lifted and made to stand in a low-sided cart so that everyone could see her. A short, thickset man with no neck held on to her arm; but in all honesty, she looked far too shocked to attempt to run away.

On their arrival, Bryce nodded to the manager who had conducted them around the mill, and he, too, climbed up on to the cart. He did not look as if this part of his work gave him any satisfaction. The crowd fell silent. Smithson cleared his throat a little nervously and began to speak.

'As you know, the wench Beth Brown ran away from her employment, thus defrauding her master and putting extra work on to her workmates,' he said.

Freya glanced around, wondering whether Lord Ravendale would come in time, and indeed whether he would come at all. He was under no obligation to intervene here. He might, quite understandably, resist coming at her bidding when she had spoken to him so dismissively. His resistance might be all the greater because her accusation of him had been so unjust; and at the remembrance of this, a feeling of mortification flooded her once more.

Suddenly conscious that her attention had strayed from what was happening, she began to listen again, just as Smithson was finishing his speech. ' . . . and so the child will be subject to the usual punishment for runaways.' He nodded to a stout woman, then climbed down, allowing her to get up on to the cart. In her hand was a large pair of scissors.

'What is she going to do?' asked Freya, unwilling to speak one word more to Bryce, but desperately anxious about what might be going to happen.

'Cut off all the wench's hair, as close to her head as she can, then shave off the rest.'

'No!' exclaimed Freya, horrified. 'That is barbaric!'

'She won't run away again, at all events,' was the dispassionate reply. Freya looked at his face, and could not see a shred of pity for the child. If anything, he was rather enjoying the spectacle; or, perhaps, enjoying the sensation of being the great man. 'I'll make sure you have a lock of it as a memento, if you like. It might remind you not to meddle in what don't concern you.'

Freya looked up at the cart, and the three figures forming a tableau there. The woman holding the scissors had not begun her work, but was looking at something behind them. Freya turned to see what it was, and beheld Lord Ravendale coming towards them, mounted on a splendid grey horse with a white mane. Her heart missed a beat, perhaps owing to the relief that she felt at his arrival. He was dressed for riding, in a dark blue coat with buckskin breeches and boots that shone like glass. Never had he looked more magnificent, not even on the night of the ball in his dress uniform. He was riding easily, the reins of his horse held in one hand, the other resting lightly on his hip.

'What is happening here?' he asked, speaking to Bryce. His tone expressed no more than casual interest.

'It's the runaway, caught very obligingly by Miss Pascoe,' replied Bryce. 'She's about to learn a valuable lesson in obedience and loyalty.'

'By having her hair cut off?' asked Ravendale. He coaxed his horse towards the cart, and circled it slowly. Those who were closer to it, instinctively cleared a way for him. When he had completed the circuit, he said, 'I've a fancy for that hair. It's a good colour. Who gets the money if I choose to buy it?' No one answered for a moment. But there was now a buzz of excitement running through the crowd that had been quite absent at the beginning of the proceedings. This was not at all how anyone had expected things to go. 'Well? Who gets the money? Or can't I buy the child's hair?'

Freya's heart sank into her sturdy shoes. From relief at his arrival, her feelings had turned to disgust that he should be contemplating such a sordid bargain. Had she really gone to ask for his help only for this?

'It's me, m'lord,' said the woman with the scissors. 'I get the money for the hair. But I usually sells it after.'

'Do you object to my buying it now?' the earl asked. He was still circling the cart, and every eye was upon him. 'It'll save you time later.' The woman hesitated. 'I'll pay you a good price for it.'

'That's agreeable to me,' said the woman.

Bryce stirred restlessly. 'Oh, let's get on with it,' he said eventually. 'Is the brat to be punished or not?' No one took any notice of him. Ravendale in particular seemed not to hear.

'Will five guineas be sufficient?' he asked. The woman's eyes gleamed, and she nodded. This was far more than she could ever hope to gain in Buxton. Ravendale took a purse from his pocket and tossed it to the woman. Then, after a moment's hesitation, he took another coin out, and threw that to her as well. 'I've a fancy for the scissors too,' he said with a smile.

'The scissors?' said the woman, puzzled; but Freya's heart leaped with hope.

'Yes,' replied Ravendale. 'Nothing so useful as a good pair of scissors.' The money and scissors exchanged hands. Then Ravendale added, 'Now the hair's mine, I've decided to have it remain on her head.' He turned to Bryce and smiled. 'It really looks so much better there, you know.'

There was a stunned silence. It was broken by the laughter of the woman in the cart. A few people joined in; and eventually, the entire crowd was laughing. Beth was looking bewildered, as if she could not understand what to make of it. The thickset man who had been holding her arm scratched his head, then slowly began to laugh as well. Soon, the only person in the yard who was not laughing was Mr Bryce. He strode over to Ravendale and seized hold of his horse's bridle.

'You want the wench's hair — take her as well,' he hissed. 'I've no use for a brat who can't work when she's supposed to.' With that, he strode off in the direction of Riverside House.

Freya had joined in with the laughter, her amusement mingled with relief at the outcome of the affair. Now, she looked up at the earl, but he had turned away to ride back to the cart. She watched as he bent to speak to Beth, and a few moments later, she saw the little girl wrap her skinny arms around his neck, whilst he lifted her up in front of him. It occurred to her that she would not mind having Beth's place. She smiled at the absurdity of the picture, and as she did so, she realized that Ravendale was looking at her. Their eyes met; their gaze locked and he returned her smile. He began to move towards her, and there was something in his expression which made her heart beat faster. Then, as if realizing that this was not the moment to speak, he inclined his head, turned his horse and rode through the mill yard and out of sight.

# 15

After Ravendale had ridden off with Beth, the crowd swiftly dispersed, good humoured and talkative, for the events had given them much to discuss. Bryce, with an exclamation of disgust had turned back towards the house, quite forgetting the social niceties. Freya followed on slowly.

Had she not allowed herself to be so easily convinced of the earl's shortcomings, she must have acknowledged her feelings for him much earlier, she thought. True, they had made a bad beginning with that encounter on Mam Tor. And yet, she conceded reluctantly, on that occasion it was she who had behaved the worse of the two. She should not have been hill-climbing alone in the first place. More than one person had warned her of that; and but for Ravendale's timely intervention, she might easily have become injured, or lost, or even fallen to her death. But for his assistance — however arrogantly given — she might have become just one more person who had disappeared on Mam Tor, never to be seen again. She shuddered at the thought.

The next time she had seen him had been

at Peveril Castle. He had been the more badly behaved on that occasion. She thought of how he had kissed her, and blushed. Briefly, she was conscious once again of the indignation she had felt at the time. No gentleman should have done such a thing! And yet, her own behaviour had not been faultless. She had hurled accusations at him until it would have been very wonderful if he had not retaliated.

Then of course there was the journey through the caverns, and those few moments when, understanding her fears, he had calmed them by holding her close. Even now, she could remember the warmth of his embrace.

Then he had officially become engaged to be married to Claudia Bryce. That thought effectively put an end to all her romantic musings. It was no good to think about him, useless to discover that she loved him. She wrinkled her brow as she recalled how Ravendale had driven her back from his house to the Bryces' one day, and about how she had told him that a man must do his duty. She had thought, then, that he was considering abandoning his gambling habits. She now realized, with distressing clarity, that he had been talking about rescuing his estate by marrying a woman of property.

His father and his grandfather had wasted what should have been regarded as a trust to hand on to future generations. His uncle had done what he could, but now, clearly, the situation was beyond mending, except with the help of a large capital sum. Ravendale was ready to make the sacrifice of a loveless marriage, in order to save his estate for those who came after him.

Freya smiled bitterly. It seemed that the worst that she could find to say of him now was that he was prepared to marry a woman for her money. He himself had admitted it at the ball. What would he say, what would any of them say, if they knew that her fortune was enough to buy those of Ravendale and the Bryces put together, twice over? She, who had regarded fortune-hunters with the greatest contempt, felt in that moment that given the opportunity, she would gladly change places with Claudia Bryce.

She began to walk slowly back to the house, but she had not got very far from the mill when she realized that Bryce was waiting for her.

'I wondered at the time why you rejected my offer so vehemently,' he said as she drew near. 'I thought that you might have been trying to increase my offer; but now I see that you have hopes . . . elsewhere, shall we say?'

'Mr Bryce, I have no idea what you are talking about, and as I have no desire to have speech with you at present, I suggest that we return separately to the house,' she said coldly.

He seized hold of her arm. 'Don't pretend that you don't understand me,' he said, 'You're in love with Ravendale; and don't bother to deny it! I suspected as much at the ball, but when you watched him come riding up on that white charger of his, it was written all over your face!'

Angrily, she pulled her arm out of his grasp. 'You're despicable,' she spat at him. 'How dare you make such an accusation?' She was conscious that her face was flaming, and she hoped that he might think that this was induced by anger. She turned to go, but Bryce moved to stand in her way.

'Do you imagine that Ravendale would set you up as his mistress?' he asked her. 'He'd never do it. He's far too honourable; and even if he weren't, Claudia would never let him go.'

Freya looked straight at him, her attention suddenly caught by something that he had said. 'You say now that he is honourable, but you cannot deny that you went out of your way to give the impression that he was a wastrel,' she accused him

He smiled unpleasantly. 'Claudia wants him, and life is much easier for me if Claudia gets what she wants,' he said simply. 'It does no harm to warn off the opposition.'

Words failed her. She could only look at him in disgust.

'My offer still stands,' he said at last. 'Even more so, now that I've seen who you really want. Think about it. Claudia will certainly not keep you for another day, let alone another hour, when she discovers you want Ravendale. What else is there for you?'

She turned her back on him, and after a moment or two, she heard him walk away.

Her one desire now was to escape. Her love for Ravendale had been painful enough when she had thought that it was a secret known only to herself. She now realized with some surprise that its detection gave rise to even more pain.

For the first time, she thought about what life would be like once she had left Derbyshire behind. Although she had been half-joking when she had talked to Lady Terrington about retiring eccentrically to the country and breeding dogs, she had certainly had it in mind to withdraw from the social scene, where she had always felt so out of place. Spinsterhood had held no fears for her, and she had felt for some time that she would enjoy being an aunt to John's children. Now, however, such an existence did not seem so appealing, and Freya did not have to think very hard to find the reason for this change of heart.

Before she left, however, there was something that she must put right; she must apologize to Lord Ravendale. She had accused him of being a liar, a gambler, a thief, a libertine, and goodness knew what else as well. He would probably not want to listen to her, but she must make the attempt. She could not bear to walk out of his life, allowing him to believe that she thought of him in such a way.

But when could she do this? The obvious thing to do was to go now. If, as Piers threatened, he told his sister of her feelings for Ravendale, then she would be sent away with no opportunity of speaking to him. At least she knew that the earl was at home, unless he had gone out very quickly after taking Beth to his house; and that was not likely, given that he had been out all day.

Quickly, before she could lose her courage, she set off up the lane which led to Ravendale Manor. It was not until she was approaching the house that it occurred to her that Lady Ravendale might think it strange that she was coming to see the earl twice in one day. In the event, however, no explanations to the countess proved to be necessary; for as Freya drew near to the front of the house, the earl himself came round from the stables with Princess at his heels.

'Miss Pascoe!' he exclaimed; and if she had had any doubt about whether her feelings were returned, then the unguarded expression on his face when he saw her unprepared would have laid them to rest. He walked towards her. 'May I be of assistance in some way?'

Princess came up to her, sniffing and wagging her tail, and she bent down to stroke her. Freya had been rehearsing what she might say to him all the way up the hill. Now, meeting him face to face, every sentence that she had gone over so carefully went completely out of her mind, and all she could think of to say was, 'How is Beth?'

Immediately she berated herself inwardly for enquiring about the well-being of a child whom she had last seen less than an hour ago. It did not appear to occur to Ravendale that her enquiry was at all strange, however, for he merely said: 'She is well, although I suspect that she does not yet fully realize what has happened to her. I discovered that both her parents are dead, and since she is only seven, I have decided to pay one of my tenants to take her in. Extraordinary, isn't it, that we consider these new mills so advanced, but we put children to work in them when they wouldn't be considered for employment in my kitchens until almost twice that age?'

'She certainly looked delighted to be carried off on your horse,' said Freya impulsively. Then she wished she had not spoken, for she now recalled the look that they had exchanged just before he had ridden off with Beth.

'You sound as if you envied her,' he remarked. Freya coloured deeply.

'Of course I did not!' she said nervously, turning her back on him. 'Don't be absurd!'

'Forgive me!' he said quickly. There fell a silence between them that seemed charged with emotion.

Quickly, Freya said, 'To be honest, my lord, much though I am concerned about Beth, it was not concerning her that I wanted to speak with you.' She took a deep breath. 'I have something very important which I must say to you, and I must say it now, before I lose my courage.'

'In that case, Miss Pascoe, perhaps we had better go somewhere a little more private.' He gestured towards a little summer house which was situated a short distance away from the Hall. They walked towards it in silence, each one privately reflecting how well their paces matched each other's. When they were seated inside on the wooden bench, and Princess had flopped down on to the floor with a deep sigh, Ravendale said, 'Now, Miss Pascoe, what did you want to say to me?'

Deciding that there was no easy way to begin, she simply said, 'I wanted to apologize for misjudging you.'

'For misjudging me?' he queried, raising his brows. His tone was not particularly encouraging, but Freya could not allow herself to be put off. This would be her one and only chance to speak.

'I heard reports about . . . about . . . ' She was going to say *about your father*, but suddenly realizing that this might be less than tactful, she said instead, 'My Lord, I accused you of many things and I was wrong. I should not have been so ready to listen to false reports, or so hasty in my judgements, and I ask for your forgiveness.'

He was silent for a few moments. 'You called me a thief ma'am, and a liar,' he said eventually, in an even tone.

'Yes, I know, I know, and I am sorry,' she said wretchedly, avoiding his eyes.

'Also a gambler, and a cheat.'

'For that also, I apologize,' she replied, still looking down.

'*And*,' he pursued, 'a libertine and a scoundrel!'

She looked up then. 'Those were my own judgements, and I think that you partly deserve them, so I shall only apologize in part.'

He smiled at her. 'I am far from contradicting you ma'am,' he said. 'Nor shall I torment you further by asking you for which part you are apologizing.'

She could not help smiling back at him then.

'But,' he went on, 'you told me that your first judgements of me had been based on false reports, and I should be very much obliged to you if you would tell me who was responsible for traducing my character.'

Freya recounted how she had seen him entering the card room in London, and then told him of what his aunt had said. Of Piers's and Claudia's comments she said nothing.

He listened patiently, and when she had finished, he said, 'Is that all, or is there something else?'

She stared at him, colouring. Little though she cared for Claudia, she found it quite impossible to tell him how his future wife and brother-in-law to be were willing to blacken his character.

He looked at her steadily in silence for a

few moments, then said 'I see. I understand you, I believe.' There was another silence.

'What will you do?' she said eventually. He looked at her for a long moment, then stood up and turned abruptly away.

'What can I do?' he replied in subdued tones. 'I'm a man of honour, and my word is given.' He turned to face her then. 'Ironic, isn't it, that the whole thing would be so simple, if only I were the scoundrel that you had believed me to be. And what of you?'

She got to her feet as well. 'What of me?' she repeated, not comprehending his meaning.

'You will scarcely want to stay with Claudia now. What will you do?'

She stared at him, not knowing what to say.

He took hold of her hands, and looked down at them. 'God knows I have no right to ask this, but I beg of you . . . ' his voice faltered, 'don't marry Simpkins, Freya. I don't think I could bear it.'

Freya's look of horror was utterly unfeigned.

'No, of course not!' she exclaimed.

'You have the right to marry; of course you do! But . . . '

'I shall never marry,' she declared.

He squeezed her hands tightly. 'Maybe one day you will,' he said in a subdued tone. 'I have to pray that it may be so. In the meantime, I cannot provide for you as I would wish, nor can I recommend you to another situation. The reference of a single man would hardly do you any good, I'm afraid. But perhaps Aunt Rosie — '

She had to interrupt him, then. 'No, no my lord, I beg you,' she exclaimed distressfully.

He squeezed her hands more tightly.

'Freya, you must allow me to do *something* for you,' he begged, his voice not quite steady. 'I cannot bear that you should be in want.'

'I'm sorry,' she said. And whether she meant that she was sorry for misjudging him, or for her deceit, or for the whole wretched situation, she would have found it impossible to say. She was on the point of explaining everything to him, despite her word to John, when the thought came into her mind: *Just a few more hours, then I shall he gone from here and I shall never see him again.* Suddenly, the implication of this came home to her with a painful intensity, and she felt her eyes filling with tears that she was powerless to hold back.

'Oh God!' he exclaimed; and by his tone, she knew that the pain that she felt was not hers alone. Then she was in his arms, held against his heart, where she had longed to be almost from the very first time that they had met, although it had taken her long enough to realize it. For a few brief moments, time seemed to stand still as they occupied that world which has been the property of lovers since time immemorial. At last, he slackened his grip, and only then did Freya realize how tightly they had been holding on to each other.

'I shouldn't be doing this,' he sighed at last. 'I shouldn't allow myself to be anywhere near you. Have you any idea what it did to me to see you in that gown? You had captivated me already, but that night, you were the most beautiful woman that I had ever seen.'

'You can't mean that,' she protested in a low tone.

'I wouldn't say it if I didn't mean it,' he replied.

'But no one thinks that about me,' she said. 'I'm too tall. My hair is the wrong colour. I'm plain. As for that gown, fine feathers make fine birds. Why, you yourself said . . . '

He coloured. 'My aunt said that Claudia wouldn't be able to resist repeating that,' he said ruefully. 'I wouldn't have said such a thing if I hadn't been furiously angry with you. What I said wasn't true. You are exactly the right height, and your hair is beautiful. You are entirely desirable, and I've always thought so. Even to see you is only to torture myself with hopeless dreams of what might have been, had I only met you first.'

She reached up and laid her hand on his lips. 'Don't say anything,' she said. 'I understand.'

He took hold of her hand, but only to guide it once more to his lips and press a fervent kiss within its palm.

'One more thing I must say, then I must let you go,' he said. 'I told you that I was marrying Claudia for her money — and that's true. God knows, it seemed like the only way out at the time, and the only honourable course. Now, it feels as if I am dishonouring you both, and myself. But I want you to know this, my love — and this is the first and the only time that I can permit myself to call you that — had I only met you first, then nothing — *nothing* — would have kept me from you: not your circumstances, nor my circumstances, nor anything. Do you believe me?'

She nodded mutely, tears coming again.

'Then that is enough for me. Indeed, it must be enough. I do not have the right to ask for more.' He stepped back, took her hand, pressed it fervently to his lips, never taking his eyes from her face the while, and then he was gone, with Princess trotting at his heels.

He walked back to the house, not turning once or hesitating in his stride, his back ramrod straight. He looked every inch the soldier that he had been, his shoulders squared, ready to do his duty. And she must do hers. She had done what she had come to do, which was to apologize for having misunderstood him. Now, she must help him by leaving at once. Perhaps, when she had gone, he might be able to make something of his marriage.

She stood watching until long after he had disappeared into the house. Eventually, she never knew how much later, she left the summer house herself, and was about to walk back to Riverside when Lady Ravendale emerged from the house and hurried across to her.

'My dear!' she exclaimed. 'Daniel has just come into the house. He said nothing to me, but on his face was an expression that was bleaker than any I have ever seen on his features; and now, I come out here to find you wearing just the same expression!'

Freya opened her mouth to speak, found that there was nothing that she could think of to say which seemed to be worth saying, closed it again, and simply shook her head.

Lady Ravendale's face was full of compassion. 'Is there nothing that can be done?' she said sorrowfully.

'I'm afraid not,' answered Freya, tears not

far away. 'My foolish suppositions about Lord Ravendale were all wrong. Of course, he is a man of honour; and being such, only one course is open to him, whatever may be our . . . our feelings for each other.'

The countess laid a hand on her arm. 'I am more sorry than I can say,' she said. 'If there is anything I can do . . . '

'There is nothing,' said Freya quickly. 'Except this. I must tell you something of myself, ma'am, and trust that you will forgive my deception.' So saying, she told Lady Ravendale the story of her bet with Lady Terrington.

The countess's eyes sparkled.

'So Claudia doesn't know that you are Miss Pascoe of Pascoe's bank? What I should give to be present when she finds out!'

Encouraged by this reaction, Freya told her ladyship about Mr Bryce's dishonourable proposal, and the countess was much shocked.

'How dared he!' she exclaimed.

'He did not know who I was, of course,' put in Freya.

'But that makes it even worse,' replied the other. 'You at least have somewhere else to go; but he did not know that. The scoundrel!' They were both silent for a moment, then

Lady Ravendale said, 'Does Daniel know who you are?'

Freya shook her head. 'No, and I don't want him to,' she said firmly. 'Do you think it would help for him to know that I could buy and sell the Bryces several times over? Better for him that I should simply fade out of his life for good.' She looked suspiciously at Lady Ravendale. 'Promise me you won't tell him,' she urged.

Lady Ravendale sighed. 'Very well,' she said. 'You have my word that I will not tell him of your true identity.'

'Then I shall go.' The two women looked at each other for a moment, then exchanged a fond embrace.

'Safe travelling, my dear,' said the countess. 'and please let me know of your arrival. Are you sure that you will be all right now?'

Freya smiled. 'I have some very good friends, and a splendid brother,' she answered. 'And I have one pleasure to come which I have been promising myself for a long time.'

'Which is . . . ?' enquired the countess.

'The satisfaction of giving Claudia a piece of my mind.'

# 16

Freya had told herself that she would not remain under the Bryces' roof for another minute. As she walked back to the house, however, she reflected that it would be as well to remain until the following morning, when the full two weeks for which she had engaged herself to Miss Bryce would be complete.

It was now almost dinner time. Indeed she had barely left herself enough time to change, and even though there was a moon, the nature of the roads would make it difficult for any kind of equipage to make its way to Castleton by night. On the other hand, if Mr Bryce had been so angry with her that he had spoken of his displeasure to his sister, then she might not have any choice. It all depended on what account, if any, Bryce had given his sister of the afternoon's events. She was also a little uneasy about facing him, so it was with great relief when she arrived at the dinner table to discover that Bryce and Siddall had gone to witness a cock fight in one of the nearby villages.

'I have no idea why they should want to go,' Miss Bryce said languidly. 'I cannot imagine a more revolting sight than watching two wretched birds tear each other to pieces.' For the first, and probably the last time, Freya found herself in complete agreement with her employer.

'Yeth indeed,' said Mrs Siddall predictably. 'In any cathe, I thought that they had dethided not to attend.'

'Yes, so did I,' agreed Claudia 'But Piers came in very excited and quite determined to go.'

Freya could not help wondering if part of the reason why Piers had chosen to be absent was a reluctance to face her after his dishonourable proposal. As for the events of the day, they were not referred to at all. She could only conclude that as Miss Bryce loathed the mill and everything to do with it, she had not the slightest interest in what had taken place there.

Mr Bryce had obviously said nothing. He could easily have urged her dismissal on the grounds of insolence, but there would always be the risk that Freya herself might repeat what he had suggested. This would mean that others would know about her rejection of him, and this would be damaging to his vanity. No doubt he reckoned that as she would be leaving soon anyway, nothing more would be said.

Almost as if she had read her thoughts, Miss Bryce spoke again. 'Miss Pascoe, as you well know I only employed you for a limited term, to give assistance at my betrothal ball and to help stave off my boredom until my friends came. Now that my friend Mrs Siddall is here I don't need you. In any case, I shall be far too busy to be bothered with you once I am preparing for my bride clothes, so you might as well go in the morning.'

Even knowing her employer as she did, Freya could not help being astounded at her insensitivity. She said nothing, but merely held Miss Bryce's eyes with a steady gaze, until the other looked away, colouring faintly. 'Of course, you will be paid for the time you have worked,' she added. 'Transport will be provided for you to Castleton, and from there you should be able to obtain a place on the stage to get back to London, or to go wherever you wish.'

'I have often wanted to twavel on the thtage,' lisped Mrs Siddall. 'Tho quaint!'

'Do you really think so?' murmured Miss Bryce disbelievingly. 'And mix with a lot of common people? What a dreadful idea! I had rather die.'

The subject then changed to that of Miss Bryce's bride clothes, and it seemed that there was no more to be said about Freya's travelling arrangements. Freya bore no further part in the conversation, and excused herself as soon as she could. She cherished no illusions; no one would be sent to help her with her packing, but she was glad to have something to do, so that she could occupy her mind.

As she put her personal bits and pieces into her trunk on top of her clothes, she paused to look at the last letter that she had received from Lady Terrington. What a long time ago it seemed since they had conspired together to make their wager. Now, her bet was won, and she could claim her prize. Her prize! A holiday in Derbyshire! She could not help smiling derisively. Taking into consideration the way that she was feeling at present, she could not imagine anything she wanted less.

She did not expect to sleep very well, and her expectations were fully justified. She heard the clock in the hall chime two, three and four before she drifted off into a fitful sleep in which Ravendale and Claudia were getting married inside a church whose walls seemed to be entirely transparent, and Reverend Tobias Simpkins was performing the ceremony. In her dream, Freya had something vitally important to tell Lord Ravendale, but there appeared to be no way into the building. Although she hammered on the glass walls with all her strength, no one saw her except for Mr Bryce, who was laughing and waving a great swathe of red hair in one hand and a pair of scissors in the other.

She woke from this dream soaked with perspiration, and shortly afterwards, she heard the clock downstairs chime six. She had had only two hours of sleep, but she knew that she would not sleep any more, so she got out of bed, and poured water from the ewer into the basin. The water was cold, but it refreshed her, and once dressed, she put the last of her belongings into her trunk.

The day was fine and bright, so she decided to take a last early-morning stroll in the gardens before breakfast. As she descended the stairs, she paused on the step where she had been standing on the evening when she had seen Lord Ravendale in the hall. She blushed at the recollection of the accusations that she had flung at him so unjustly. At least, she reflected, she had had the opportunity of putting that right before they said goodbye. The implications of that thought struck her afresh, and feeling tears come to her eyes, she hurried out into the garden, where she knew she would be alone, so that she could weep unobserved.

In the dark watches of the night, she had

toyed briefly with the idea of what it would be like if Claudia could magically disappear. But things like that did not happen in real life. Ravendale could not in honour withdraw from this engagement. All she could do for him now would be to pray for him and for his future happiness, and she vowed that she would do so every day, for the rest of her life.

She had hoped that she would be spared the company of any of the inhabitants of the house at the breakfast table, and mercifully this hope was realized. On enquiry, the butler disclosed that the two gentlemen had returned very late from the cock fight and, Freya deduced, rather the worse for wear.

'I understand that you are to leave us today, miss,' he said as he poured her more coffee.

'Yes,' she replied, smiling at him. He had always treated her well, never making her feel that she was of an inferior status to the others whom he served. 'I am to return to London as Miss Bryce does not need me any more.'

'May I venture to say that the staff will be sorry to see you go?' he said. 'A lady like you is a pleasure to serve.'

Freya was very much touched by this, and she said gratefully, 'Why thank you, Jones. How kind of you to say so. I wonder, can you tell me at what hour Miss Bryce has asked for the carriage to be ready to take me?'

'She didn't give a time, miss. I think she expected you to say when you wanted it.'

'Then in that case, I should like to wait until she comes downstairs,' she answered, finishing her coffee then standing up. 'I want to say goodbye to her, and I should hate to be negligent in any attention.'

'Very well miss,' said Jones holding the door open for her. 'I am sure that Miss Bryce will appreciate your courtesy.' They exchanged a brief look of complete comprehension before Freya went back up to her room.

She came back downstairs shortly after midday, dressed for travelling, and she was fortunate enough to find Miss Bryce in the saloon, with her brother in attendance. Miss Bryce raised her brows at her appearance.

'Why, Miss Pascoe!' she exclaimed. 'I told you that you might go today, and had thought that you would be long gone by now.'

'Certainly not,' replied Freya. 'I would not dream of leaving here without making my farewells.'

'Oh,' said Miss Bryce. 'I thought that we had already said everything last night.'

'By no means,' said Freya decisively. 'Pray sit down, Miss Bryce. There is a great deal that I would like to say to you.' Miss Bryce looked at her indignantly, and opened her mouth to speak, but what she was going to say was destined to remain unspoken.

At that moment, the butler came in and announced, 'Mr Pascoe, ma'am.' Freya turned to the new arrival, an expression of delight on her face.

'John!' she exclaimed. 'You come very opportunely, as I was about to leave. But first, let me present to you my host and hostess. Miss Bryce, Mr Bryce, this is my brother, Mr John Pascoe of Pascoe's bank.'

Into the silence intruded the sound of Mr Bryce's glass smashing as it broke on the floor, having slipped from his grasp. Miss Bryce did sit down then, looking almost as surprised as if one of the cushions had spoken.

Freya went on. 'I have endured — is that too strong a word? No, I think not — endured two weeks of your company, and without any shadow of doubt it has been two weeks too much. You, ma'am, are probably the rudest woman of my acquaintance. Even the fact that you have been paying me does not justify your appalling lack of manners, and your lack of consideration towards those whom you consider to be your inferiors beggars belief. And as for you,' she went on, turning to Mr Bryce, 'the way that you have behaved towards me has been nothing short of scandalous. You show no feeling towards your workers, no sense of duty with regard to your responsibilities, and your conversation proves you to be as stupid as you are insensitive. I leave this place without the slightest twinge of regret, and if I never see either of you again, I shall be exceedingly glad of it.'

For a moment, silence reigned in the saloon, and both the Bryces gazed at her open-mouthed. Bryce was the first to recover.

'Miss Pascoe, you have been pleased to criticize our hospitality, but I think you have some explaining to do,' he said. 'If this gentleman is indeed your brother, and Mr Pascoe of Pascoe's bank, then I would very much like to know why you have come here as my sister's companion.'

Miss Bryce had turned rather white. Now she rose to her feet, two spots of colour flaming in her cheeks. 'Yes indeed, why this masquerade? Or, in fact, can I guess?' Her eyes narrowed. 'You saw Ravendale in London, didn't you? You came here with the express intention of taking him away from me, didn't you?'

'No, certainly not,' exclaimed Freya; but because she was taken unawares by the mention of his name, she coloured, and

Claudia immediately noticed it.

'Do you deny that you saw him in London'?' she demanded.

'No, I do not. I did see him,' Freya admitted. 'But . . . '

'You found a way of coming here so that you could meet him,' declared Bryce. 'Can you deny that you are in love with him?'

Freya put her chin up. This scene was not going at all as she had expected, but she could at least protect herself from this final hurt.

'I certainly can,' she said firmly. 'The only reason I came here was to win a small wager that I had with . . . with a friend as to whether I could endure a fortnight as companion here. I shall be just as glad to see the back of Lord Ravendale as to see the back of any of you.' She turned to go and then halted in her tracks as she saw Lord Ravendale standing in the doorway, staring at her.

'Ah, Daniel!' exclaimed Miss Bryce. 'Miss Pascoe has just been telling us about her little joke at our expense. Apparently — '

'Yes, I heard,' he interrupted, his voice cold. He turned to Freya. 'I presume that that is your brother.'

'Yes — that is my brother John,' said Freya uncertainly.

'Your brother the banker and not your brother the tutor about whom you told me so affectingly?'

Freya coloured.

'Yes. Lord Ravendale, I want you to know that — '

Ravendale interrupted her. 'In fact, your brother the tutor does not exist.'

'No, but . . . '

The earl stepped back and bowed. 'I think you were about to leave,' he said in the same icy tone. 'Pray do not allow me to detain you.'

Freya desperately wanted to explain to him how she had come to act as she did; but it occurred to her that if she and the earl parted on bad terms, then it might help his future relationship with Claudia. Despite every consideration, however, she might have spoken then, but that she felt a hand lightly touch her arm, and turning, she saw that John was standing at her elbow.

'Shall we leave now, my dear?' he asked. 'I do not think that there is anything remaining for you here.'

She looked up at Ravendale's rigid face for one last long moment.

'No, John,' she replied at last. 'There is nothing for me to stay for.'

Without a word, they left the house and climbed into John's carriage, which was waiting for them at the door. As they drove off, Freya turned to see the Bryces standing at the door to watch them go, and Ravendale was beside them. None of them waved goodbye.

# 17

After their journey had begun, they both sat in silence for some time, while the carriage crossed the bridge and began the uneven climb up the lane that led past Ravendale Hall. As they passed the house, Freya resolutely turned her face away. She did not want to see anything that might remind her of the earl, for fear her fragile composure would give way.

Eventually, John said, 'Freya, my dear, it's quite obvious to me that since we last met, you have had enough experiences to last you a lifetime. I have no desire to pry — after all you're a grown woman — but I want you to know that I am prepared to listen to anything that you want to tell me.'

Freya smiled gratefully at him. Touched by his kindness, she felt the tears prickling at the back of her eyes, but she managed to hold them back. The relationship between her and John, although always affectionate, had never been an emotional one; but she knew that his concern was real.

'A lot *has* happened,' she admitted, 'and it seems very unfair of me not to be prepared to share it with you after you have come all this way to fetch me, but I cannot say anything just at present. Perhaps I will, quite soon, but just now . . . ' Her voice faded away, and her hands moved in a helpless gesture.

John caught hold of them.

'It's all right, sis,' he said, giving them a squeeze. 'Haven't I said I won't pry? Tell you what, shall I tell you about some of the things that I have been doing instead?'

Freya nodded, but John had barely opened his mouth before the carriage came to an abrupt halt.

'What is it?' he wondered.

'Perhaps they want us to get out and walk,' suggested Freya. A moment later, the door was flung open, and Ravendale stood looking at them.

'Madam, a word with you,' he said coldly. 'Sir, by your leave?' he added to John.

'Freya?' questioned John, his brows raised.

'It's all right, I'll get down,' she said, suiting her actions to her words. 'He won't hurt me.' Her voice was steady, but her colour was high, and her heart was beating like a drum.

'You sound very sure of yourself,' said Ravendale, as soon as they were out of earshot. 'Let us hope your confidence is not misplaced.'

'Ravendale, why have you come after me?'

she asked him with a voice that was not quite steady. 'Surely, there is no more to be said?'

'Yesterday, I would have agreed with you, madam,' he answered. 'But today, I find that when I spoke to you before, I was labouring under a misapprehension. As for why I have come after you; well, to tell you the truth I wanted to see you again.'

'To . . . see me?' she faltered. The words might have been what she would have hoped to hear; but the tone was not encouraging.

'Why certainly,' he replied. 'I wanted to see what a liar looks like.'

Freya whitened, but said nothing.

'Dear God, to think you berated *me* on *my* reputation,' he went on, 'when all the time, you were playing us for fools, all for the sake of your bet. Was it part of the bet to entrap me too? Was it?' He seized hold of her shoulders and shook her while he spoke.

'No! No, it wasn't! It . . . '

'Because if it was, you've won hands down, my lovely. When I looked into your eyes, I thought that I could see everything that was pure and honourable and true. But I was wrong, wasn't I? You even stood there listening to my fears about your future. Your future! My God, that's rich! And as for my begging you not to marry Simpkins! What a lucky escape for the poor fellow!'

'Daniel! Please, listen!' she begged him.

'I don't believe I gave you the right to use my Christian name,' he said coldly. 'And pray don't trouble to explain yourself. You are under no obligation to me that I know of. Not even the ordinary obligations of society such as truthfulness and respect, it seems.' He turned away then, but she took a step after him.

'Daniel . . . my lord . . . ' she ventured.

He turned round, then, in a fury.

'Get out of my sight!' he demanded. 'Go back to your bank and your gold! I wish you joy of it!' Swiftly, he took his horse back from the servant who had been holding it, and galloped back down the lane, leaving Freya standing at the side of the lane, weeping bitterly.

★ ★ ★

After Ravendale had departed, John's first concern was to get her back into the carriage away from prying eyes. Once inside, however, he was all for calling the earl to account for his treatment of his sister.

'I'm not having you upset in this way,' he declared.

'No, no, John, you don't understand what has happened!' she pleaded as she dried her tears with the handkerchief that he had handed to her, her own proving to be sadly inadequate. 'You don't realize . . . '

'I don't care what has gone before,' he said decidedly. 'He has no right to distress you like this.'

Seeing that there was nothing else for it, she said, 'John, I'll explain; then perhaps you'll understand. Only please, let us get on our way.'

He looked at her for a long moment then said, before signalling to the coachman to drive on, 'Very well, but only if you tell me the whole story.'

In the end, there was a certain relief to Freya in finally being able to speak openly, when over the past weeks she had had to keep all kinds of things to herself. John was a good listener, not interrupting except to ask for clarification on one or two points; and he did exclaim with disgust when he heard about Bryce's dishonourable proposal.

'The scoundrel!' he declared. 'I've a good mind to call him out!' Freya had to smile. This kind of reaction was quite unusual for one of his phlegmatic temperament, and it heartened her to think that this display showed how much she meant to him.

'You can't possibly call both of them out,'

she replied. 'Just listen to the rest of the story.'

He frowned. 'Very well,' he said at last. 'But I still maintain that the fellow's a scoundrel.'

To divert him, Freya moved swiftly on to the story of Beth and the scissors, and John smiled as she had hoped that he would.

'I like the manner of that, and I see that you did too,' he said.

She had smiled as well at the memory of the incident, but now her smile faded. 'Yes I did; but now everything has gone wrong and I don't know how to put things right.'

After she had completed her account, John said, 'However things may have fallen out, it seems to me that you have been placed in an intolerable situation because of your promise to me; and for that I am more sorry than I can say.'

Freya shook her head.

'You didn't want me to take part in this bet with Eunice, and now I am justly served,' she said wearily. 'All that I want now is to go home.'

John thought of Lady Terrington, who was at that moment waiting in Castleton to take Freya on the holiday which by the terms of the bet should take place immediately, and prudently held his peace.

Freya's initial reaction when seeing her

friend was to burst into tears on her shoulder. John had led his sister into the private parlour which he had reserved for their use. Lady Terrington signalled to him over Freya's shoulder and, correctly interpreting her meaning, he withdrew.

The countess was very surprised to see her normally self-possessed friend so moved, and once the first rush of tears had ceased — which was quite soon, Freya having cried herself out earlier, and only succumbing again at the surprise of seeing Lady Terrington so unexpectedly — she rang for a very welcome cup of tea.

'My dear Freya,' she said eventually. 'Why all this distress? You wrote me such amusing letters that I made sure that you would greet me in high spirits!'

Eventually, after a little gentle coaxing, Freya found herself able to speak about her feelings for Ravendale, something which she had not been able to do with John.

'So is there *really* no hope?' the countess asked.

Freya shook her head. 'Even if he were not engaged to Claudia, he despises me thoroughly,' she replied sadly. Then making a valiant attempt to pull herself together, she said brightly, 'But what happy chance brings you here, my dear friend? I cannot think of

315

anyone whom I would rather see, but I am at a loss as to explain it.'

Lady Terrington looked at her with a puzzled expression. 'You surely cannot have forgotten the terms of our bet?' she said cautiously. 'You did insist that your Derbyshire holiday should take place immediately.'

Freya stared at her, an appalled expression on her face.

'No! No, I can't! Eunice, I must get away as soon as possible. Can you not understand?'

'I'm sorry,' replied Lady Terrington remorsefully. 'When I came with John I had no idea . . . '

Freya's expression softened.

'No, of course you didn't,' she said. 'I didn't mean to criticize.'

'Well, perhaps we could agree to a compromise,' suggested the countess after a short silence. 'What do you say to the lakes? We could go straight there, if you like.'

Freya agreed to consider the suggestion, but inside, all she wanted was to go home and lick her wounds in private.

That evening after dinner, John said, 'Do you mind if we stay at 'The Castle' just for a day or two? We have had a long journey, and besides, there are one or two people in the neighbourhood whom I need to see.'

Freya very much wanted to insist that they

left immediately, but she accepted the justice of John's request. She was very anxious not to meet any of the inhabitants of Cressbrook; but upon reflection she decided that they would probably avoid Castleton for a day or two, being undoubtedly just as reluctant to see her as she was to see them.

She did not sleep well that night. For some considerable time, she tossed and turned, going over and over in her mind the scene that had taken place between her and Ravendale the previous day, and trying to imagine how it might have had a better outcome. *We might at least have parted as friends*, she thought to herself; but deep down inside, she knew that it was not as a friend that she wanted him.

The new day dawned bright and sunny, and the top of Mam Tor stood out clearly against the blue sky. Freya could see it from her bedroom window, and as she looked at it, a desire was born within her to climb it again. To attempt the hill when there was no mist would make a welcome change; and perhaps there, on its summit, where she had first met Lord Ravendale, she might be able to lay the ghosts of her previous visit to rest and say goodbye to him in her heart.

Like both the Pascoes, Lady Terrington was an early riser, and the three of them sat at

317

breakfast together, enjoying the fragrant coffee, and the crisp bacon and warm, fresh bread.

'Since we are staying for a few days, I should like to climb Mam Tor,' said Freya eventually. As soon as she had spoken the words, she was filled with a sudden dread that one of them would want to come with her, and she very much wanted to go alone.

'Do you wish me to accompany you?' John asked her. 'I have another errand to accomplish; but if you would like me to come with you, then I can go later.'

'No, not at all,' replied Freya, too relieved at his response to ask what this errand might be. 'I am very happy to go by myself.'

'I think that I will be quite content with something more sedate,' said Lady Terrington. 'If you want to go on a long walk, then do so by all means. I shall be quite happy wandering about the town. All I ask is that you take some provisions with you, and tell someone the way that you are going in case of emergency.'

'That's easily done,' answered Freya cheerfully, pouring her friend another cup of coffee. 'The kitchens here packed an excellent lunch for me before, and no doubt they will do so again. And as for my route, I shall walk up by Winnats Pass, and come back down the same way.'

'Winnats Pass! Is that not the place with the grisly legend attached to it?' asked Lady Terrington eagerly.

'Yes, indeed,' agreed Freya, getting up from the table. 'You must ask the landlord to tell you it. I am sure that he will be able to make it far grislier than I ever could!' She smiled fondly down at her friend. On every other occasion, Eunice would have scolded her for walking alone. Today, she clearly had the sensitivity to realize that that was what Freya needed to do, and in response to that unspoken sensitivity, Freya bent down and hugged her friend warmly. 'It's a long walk, so don't expect me back early.'

The landlord had recognized Freya and welcomed her with pleasure, and he did not show any surprise at the fact that she was now accompanying Lady Terrington rather than Miss Bryce.

'You've picked a better week for walking in the hills, ma'am,' he told her as she left 'The Castle' with her lunch securely packed into her canvas bag. 'It'll be fine and clear for the next few days, I'll reckon.'

Shortly afterwards, she was walking up the main street of Castleton at a swinging pace in the direction of Mam Tor. As she went, she tried not to think about Lord Ravendale, but it was no use. A picture came into her mind of him on the top of Mam Tor, the breeze stirring his golden hair. One day, maybe, if she kept herself busy doing other things, she would be able to think of him without pain; but now, the agony that she felt at his loss seemed to be almost more than she could bear. Perhaps the love that she had for him was something from which she would never fully recover.

After breakfast was over, and before Freya had left 'The Castle', John set out on an errand of his own. A just man, he had realized by the end of Freya's tale that although he might deplore the distress caused to his sister, Lord Ravendale had been justified in being angry. The conduct of Piers Bryce was another matter, however. His deplorable behaviour could not in any way be excused by his ignorance of Freya's circumstances, so John had decided to call him to book. He had never fought a duel, and did not intend to do so now. What he had in mind was to administer a good thrashing, which would at once relieve his feelings, and hopefully teach Mr Bryce to treat others with more respect. He set off on horseback, choosing to go in the direction of Hope. He did not want to risk being seen by his sister, for he was not at all sure how much he would disclose to her concerning his day's errand.

He had only just reached Hope when he saw a horseman riding towards him, and as the man drew closer, he saw that it was Lord Ravendale. The two men eyed one another warily.

'A fine day, my lord,' said John cautiously.

'Exactly so,' replied Ravendale in much the same manner. 'Just the day to take a ride for pleasure.'

'If one had no other pressing tasks to perform,' said John.

'Then I must not detain you,' murmured the earl, 'Unless your business is with me, of course.'

John shook his head. 'My business is with Bryce.'

Ravendale smiled grimly. 'Then I trust you will not be too discommoded,' he said politely. 'I am afraid that Mr Bryce is not receiving visitors at present.'

'He'll damn . . . dashed well see me,' retorted John fiercely.

'You sound very angry,' remarked Ravendale. 'May I ask whether you intend to call him to account?'

John nodded. 'For the insult to my sister; but I don't suppose you will be concerned about that. Now, if you will excuse me . . . '

The earl coaxed his horse to block John's way.

'Wait,' he said. 'Believe me, I have no desire to prevent you from carrying out your plan; but before you go, I think you should hear what I have to say.'

John said nothing, but gestured for the earl to continue. 'I suspect that you intend to knock Bryce down; but I don't think you should do so today.'

'Why not?' asked John suspiciously.

'Because I've already done it,' said his lordship with a rueful smile.

John looked completely nonplussed, so the earl went on, 'There is a tolerable hostelry in Hope. What say we adjourn there, and I will tell you what I have done and why, and what by your leave, I plan to do?'

★ ★ ★

It was such a short time since she had made this climb, Freya reflected, and yet so much had happened since then. The last time she had set out to climb Mam Tor, she had not met Lord Ravendale, and she had been heart-whole. Yet she found that even if she could have blotted out the whole experience, she would not have done so. Those of a poetic turn of mind would doubtless say that it was better to have loved and lost than never to have loved at all, she reflected. Certainly, she would not have missed knowing him for anything. But oh, how she wished that she had not lost him!

Her final ascent was unhampered by the mist that had descended on her previous visit; and soon, she was at the summit, looking down at Castleton. The hill topped by Peveril Castle, which looked so high to those walking in the town, now seemed very tiny from the top of Mam Tor. The view was so splendid, and the climb had been so exhilarating, that she wished she had someone with whom she could share the experience. Then, as soon as the thought had popped into her mind, she heard a step behind her and turning, she found herself face to face with Lord Ravendale, standing just a couple of yards away.

'I believe I have warned you before, ma'am, about the dangers of walking in these hills alone.' The last time she had seen him, he had hurled accusations at her, and her instinct was to flee. She turned to run in the opposite direction, but before she could take more than two steps, he had caught hold of her by the arm. 'No, Freya, wait! Listen to me!'

She turned to look at him, then.

'Why should I?' she demanded. 'You wouldn't listen to me yesterday! Why have you come after me now? Let go of me at once!' He released her. 'I deserved that,' he admitted. 'Why have I come after you? To beg your pardon for misjudging you so harshly and for not allowing you to explain yourself.' He took a deep breath. 'Most of all, I want to tell you again that I love you; and to ask you to be my wife.'

She looked up at him, and saw on his face an expression that was full of tenderness.

'I beg your pardon?' she murmured faintly, unable to believe that this was really happening.

'I said I want you to be my wife,' he repeated, taking hold of her hand.

'But Claudia . . . '

'Claudia has given me back my ring,' he said. 'Freya, I'm a free man, but not for long, I hope. What do you say'?'

She was silent, still half expecting to wake up at any moment.

'Don't say that I've destroyed any chance of winning you,' he said anxiously. 'I have to warn you that I am very tenacious, Miss Pascoe. If you refuse me, I intend to dog your footsteps until you change your mind.'

'Did you follow me up here?' she asked him, smiling tremulously at his words.

He took a step closer and pulled her into his arms.

'I certainly did,' he replied. 'And I intend to go on doing so.' Slowly, he lowered his head and their lips met. His touch sent a sensation of tingling awareness coursing through her body and almost involuntarily, her arms wrapped themselves around his neck.

When at last they drew apart, she said, 'You were right to warn me before, sir. Dreadful things can happen on these hills. Marauding Norman knights — '

But she was not allowed to finish her sentence, for once more the earl covered her mouth with his own. They kissed until they were breathless, and when eventually they stopped, they were holding one another in a close embrace.

'Do you realize for how long I've been wanting to do that?' Ravendale asked her, with a tender note in his voice that caught at her heart-strings. Freya shook her head.

'Tell me,' she replied, her eyes shining.

'Ever since I did it last, of course,' he replied, smiling at her.

'How do you come to be released from your engagement to Claudia?' Freya asked him.

He smiled ruefully.

'Let me go back a little further than that,'

he said. 'When you told Aunt Rosie not to reveal your identity, you said nothing to her about not disclosing Bryce's dishonourable proposal. When she told me about what he had suggested, I went to Riverside breathing fire. That was when I came into the room in time to hear you say that you would be glad to see the back of me, and that you had only come to Derbyshire to win a bet.'

'I'm sorry,' she said remorsefully. 'It is quite true that Eunice and I had a bet, and looking back, I can see that it was improper, but I swear that you were never the subject of it. And I was also to blame for leaping to conclusions about you, and then for being less than frank about myself. It was not surprising that you felt betrayed.'

He took her hand. 'I should have listened to my heart,' he replied. 'When I looked into your eyes, I knew that you were honest and true, but I was angry that you had not taken me into your confidence, when the Bryces clearly knew who you were.'

'The Bryces had only just learned with John's arrival,' answered Freya. 'I wanted to tell you *and* your aunt about my true circumstances, but I was bound by my promise to John. And in spite of everything, I nearly did tell you in the summer house that day; but then I suddenly realized that we were

326

about to part for ever, and everything else went out of my mind.'

He kissed the top of her head.

'Yes, I can understand that,' he said, smiling ruefully. 'In fact, my aunt told me of your promise, and so did your brother.'

'My brother? You have seen John?' she exclaimed, surprised.

'Yes, and we had a fascinating conversation which enlightened us both. But let me finish my story. After what I had overheard, I was so incensed that I forgot about what had brought me to Riverside in the first place, and thought only about giving you a piece of my mind.'

Freya tucked her hand in his arm, and by mutual consent, they began the descent to Castleton. 'After that, I had no wish to speak to anybody, so I went for a very long ride, only arriving home during the early evening. Encountering Aunt Rosie as I came in from the stables, I spilled the whole story out to her, and she told me the remainder of your tale.' He stopped briefly, and looked down at her, covering her hand resting on his arm with his own. 'You must not think that she betrayed you,' he assured her. 'She only revealed what she knew after she had discovered that I had hold of a very one-sided version of events.'

'It's all right,' she told him. 'Go on.'

'When I had heard her out, it occurred to me that I still had unfinished business at Riverside, namely, the need to call Bryce to book. So I went there at once. The last time the Bryces had seen me, I had seemed to be ranged upon their side, so they decided to tear your reputation to pieces. Suddenly, I saw more than ever before what petty people they were, and I began to see red. The next minute, Bryce was sprawled on the floor, I was standing over him, and Claudia was handing me back my ring. I think that one or two things that had happened recently had made her regret accepting me in any case, but she is very attached to her brother, and my punishment of him sealed my fate — thank God.'

'I must say that I wish I could have seen you knock him down,' admitted Freya. 'I have been wanting to do that very thing myself.'

'His conduct was unpardonable,' said the earl decisively. 'Indeed, I think I should tell you that had I not knocked him down, your brother would have done so.'

'John?' exclaimed Freya incredulously. 'But he is not at all violent.'

'The slight to you obviously aroused the demon in him. As indeed it did in me, my sweet.' He stopped, took hold of her face gently between his hands, and kissed her tenderly. 'You will not be troubled by Bryce again,' he said. 'I made it quite clear to him that he was to keep well away from me and from my family. I think you'll find that when he is in Derbyshire, he will, however reluctantly, keep to his own property.'

Freya looked up at him, her mischievous expression belying the fast beating of her heart.

'But how will his keeping away from your family affect me, my lord?'

His lordship looked into the middle distance.

'As my wife, you will naturally be part of my family,' he said, his casual tone a little too studied to be natural.

Freya looked a little puzzled. 'Perhaps something has somehow escaped me, but I do not seem to remember accepting your proposal,' she said mischievously. He seized hold of her swiftly, then, and pulled her against him.

'Freya, you know I love you,' he said urgently. 'And, scoundrel though I am, I know that you love me too.'

'My lord?' Freya questioned, trying to sound indignant; but her eyes told a different story, and immediately she relented. 'I do love you Daniel,' she admitted, 'and I think I began to love you even when you were being so arrogant and domineering on the top of this very hill.'

He laughed. 'It was just the same for me,' he said. 'You captivated me from the moment you stood there defying me with the wind catching at your hair the way it's doing now, and blowing your gown about you in the most disturbing way. I told you when I thought that we must part that your circumstances would never have prevented me from claiming you. I said those words when I thought you were poor; but they still hold true. I don't care whether you're the richest woman in England, or whether you don't have a penny to your name. I want you for my own, Freya Pascoe. Will you have me?'

Once more, she put her arms around his neck, and as she drew his head down and their lips met, he knew that he had his answer.

## THE END

We do hope that you have enjoyed reading this large print book.

Did you know that all of our titles are available for purchase?

We publish a wide range of high quality large print books including:
**Romances, Mysteries, Classics**
**General Fiction**
**Non Fiction and Westerns**

Special interest titles available in large print are:
**The Little Oxford Dictionary**
**Music Book**
**Song Book**
**Hymn Book**
**Service Book**

Also available from us courtesy of Oxford University Press:
**Young Readers' Dictionary**
**(large print edition)**
**Young Readers' Thesaurus**
**(large print edition)**

For further information or a free brochure, please contact us at:
**Ulverscroft Large Print Books Ltd.,**
**The Green, Bradgate Road, Anstey,**
**Leicester, LE7 7FU, England.**
**Tel:** (00 44) 0116 236 4325
**Fax:** (00 44) 0116 234 0205

# THE GRAND TOUR

## Ann Barker

When Lord Craythorne dismisses his niece's governess, Flora Chayter, for immoral behaviour he makes two assumptions: that she is a woman of low character, and that he will never come across her again. He is indignant, therefore, when he discovers that Flora is to be the travelling companion of Mrs Wylde, whom he has agreed to escort to Venice. On the journey, Flora attracts the attention of a number of men, but steadfastly rejects every advance. It is not until the travellers reach Venice, where tragedy threatens, that Craythorne is forced to confront his true feelings for Flora.

# HIS LORDSHIP'S GARDENER

## Ann Barker

Arriving home after three years' absence, Lord Lyddington discovers that his sister is having his garden remodelled. The Earl is pleased to discover a roistering companion in his gardener's nephew, 'Master' Sutcliffe. However, young Sutcliffe is not all he seems, and soon the Earl is obliged to reassess his previous ideas concerning appropriate female behaviour and attire. Meanwhile, someone seeks to sabotage the garden alterations, viciously attacks Sutcliffe senior and even assaults the Earl himself. Who could be responsible? The Earl's happiness depends on a swift resolution of this matter.

# THE WAYS OF LOVE

## June Barraclough

Without a mother since she was a baby, Mary Settle of Cliff House adores her nursemaid, Jemima Green. The girl leaves Mary when she gets married and it is up to Aunt Clara Demaine to bring up the child in France. When she is eighteen, Mary is attracted to a young Englishman in Biarritz. Eventually she marries, but is it to the wrong man? What happens then is strangely connected to Mary's earliest days.

# EARL FOR A SEASON

## Brenda Dow

When Roderick Anhurst returns to England after a diplomatic posting in British North America, he finds himself heir to an unwelcome earldom. Not only that, an old flame is determined to reclaim her old beau — by fair means or foul! Unfortunately, the Earl of Selchurch is falling in love with lively, independent Julia, a lady as lacking in respect for wealth and high estate as he is himself. Meanwhile, the Dowager Countess of Selchurch is nursing a secret — a secret she calls a miracle. Will this miracle be the means by which Roderick will escape from his quandary?

# ARROWS OF LONGING

## Virginia Moriconi

When Gretchen decides to spend a year on the south-west coast of Ireland she knows that she is entering a world quite different from that of her strict Pennsylvania childhood. To her parents, Ireland is teeming with alcoholics and slipshod Catholics. To Gretchen, it is the native home of mystery and rapture. It does not take her long, however, in the dilapidated grandeur of Dufresne Hall — where squalor rules and nothing works — to change her views. But she finds a new direction for her feelings in a personal involvement that surprises and overwhelms her.